CAST IN DOUBT

DOUBT

LYNNE TILLMAN

LONDON

NEW YORK

First published 1992 in the United States by Poseidon Press

This edition published 1993 by
Serpent's Tail, 4 Blackstock Mews, London N4 2BT
and 401 West Broadway, New York, NY 10012

ISBN 1-85242-340-4

British Library Cataloguing-in-Publication Data
Tillman, Lynne,
Cast in Doubt.
I. Title   II. Series

This is a work of fiction. Any similarity of persons, places,
or events depicted herein to actual persons, places, or events
is entirely coincidental.

Book design by Liney Li

Printed in the United States of America

Portions of this book have appeared in *The Village Voice Literary
Supplement*, *Bomb*, and *Fiction South/Fiction North*.

For Heather Wilson

in appreciation

"Behind our thoughts, true and false, there is always to be found a dark background, which we are only able to bring into the light and express as a thought."

LUDWIG WITTGENSTEIN

"Then what is the question?"

GERTRUDE STEIN

PART · I

A DARK

BACKGROUND

CHAPTER

1

Early in the morning, in this part of the world, in the summer, the sun is so strong and direct, I believe that all the spirits must be holding that fiery globe in its heavenly place and shining it down on us. This early in the morning, and before the first news of murder or robbery, of war or famine, the sunlight casts miracles across the dark, blue water and life itself seems to emanate from its movement. I'm not a religious man, but at this time of day, when it is not yet hot, the sky is so brilliant as if to mean that something, some great secret of the world, might be revealed. Later, it is too hot even to appear on one's porch.

The summer's heat may have been just what her doctor ordered. Though her doctor may not actually have said anything of the sort, maybe heat, perhaps warmth, and when he said it there may have been a paternal look in his penetrating eyes. She had printed "analyst" in block letters on the cover of a book, a diary meant for thoughts and dreams.

I saw the word the first time we met. That is, technically speaking, the first time we met she showed the diary to me. A friend had given it to her, she said. I imagined it was presented to her just before she sailed away from home, before she flew away from America and then sailed overnight from Athens to Crete. It was, she suggested, with a look or just so many words, an old-fashioned gift and gesture, one that might have no relationship to their lives. It represented instead a poignant moment others might have shared. It was a kind of wistful parody. She did say parody, I think.

The hotel where I have rooms is weather-beaten, but well-kept and clean. The small whitewashed building is stark. There's usually a bright sky overhead, and it is hard to feel dark or gloomy, except during the winter months. Generally this island life is not the right background for depression; the sky here is not for secret thoughts or mean-spirited reflection. Yet murders are committed, vile acts reported. Though I've lived here for quite some time, I find this unnerving, in spite of the fact that, or perhaps this is why, I write crime stories. My fascination with the gory details of life that hurtle toward us unblinkered and appalling is unabated even here. Right now I am working on a mystery based on a real-life crime that was never solved. In my book I solve it, of course. Though some things will remain open to question.

People here are open. Nectaria, the concierge, told the American girl almost immediately that there was a house left by an English painter, left standing, barely standing, in terrible shape, nearly uninhabitable and with no hot water, but she could rent it for very little money. The young woman took out her traveler's checks and offered six months' rent. Nectaria pushed her hand away, to indicate that she needn't give so much in advance, but the younger woman persisted and Nectaria took the checks somewhat reluctantly, placing them in a drawer in the reception desk.

I could have had the house years ago but I had not wanted it, preferring the ministrations of Nectaria, the concierge, and her husband, Christos, who manages the restaurant down the street. The American intended to stay. She would teach English, she told me. She would live abstemiously, I thought, like a nun or a recluse. If she had the talent for it, she might draw fast, uninteresting portraits of tourists for money, though the cliché might depress her, were she to turn out to be a sensitive soul. Nectaria called her Helen, which wasn't her name but was close enough to it, and that's how she became known on the island.

I met Helen then, some days before she moved into Peter

Bliss' broken-down house overlooking the harbor. It had just three small rooms on as many stories—a rickety structure, but still a charming antiquity, with romantic dilapidated walls and ruined floors. Across the lane lived Chrissoula, who was caretaking Bliss' house in his habitual absence. Nectaria handed over Helen's traveler's checks to Chrissoula, I believe. Chrissoula and I alone took immediately to Helen, and in fact Chrissoula loved her from the moment they met. It was an unconditional love of a kind I'd not seen before, I think, and I use unconditional advisedly as Helen was an unusual girl, one an elderly Greek woman might well be wary of. Chrissoula wasn't, unlike some of the others of my acquaintance. In any case, Helen happily settled into Bliss' place, which had a terrace that looked out to the harbor and the sea. It was usual to find Helen there.

To myself I sometimes called her Smith or Smitty, because of an expression that came over her face as we talked, as if she were placing a hard metal object into a blazing fire and bending it to her will. I thought she was a tough modern type but then I am one of those old, older men who find young people, young women, in particular, incomprehensible. I've never slept with a woman, young or old, but Smitty, if I were younger, I might have wanted to. Perhaps she is androgynous enough for me or a little dangerous. I usually find women soft or vulnerable, and that frightens me. I have a horror of hurting people. It's pathological, I suppose. But I am never afraid to stick the knife in when I'm writing.

It wasn't that Helen let me drop in whenever I wanted. Even when she was with me, she kept to herself, held herself in check, which is strange, I think, for a girl or young woman who's only twenty. She liked to go for car rides, and some trace of girlishness brightened her face when she entered my little VW. I like to drive around the island; it's my escape from the book I'm meant to be writing.

My real work is based on my family; my great-grandfather was a man of some importance. The family are figures in a novel I have been struggling with for years now. When Helen entered my life I was stuck at the Civil War or rather that period just before it. My maternal line was feminist and abolitionist, and my paternal line was neither. Certainly not feminist, and some held slaves, probably using Mr. Jefferson as justification, though that's nowhere in any of the letters or diaries in my possession. Helen doesn't yet know about the mysteries I toss off, as if I were wanking not writing. Still I must admit I enjoy writing them very much. The other, purely literary venture is speculative and nonremunerative, but as I tell my young friend, if nothing else, it fills the time. I know Helen finds this notion abhorrent or worse. Young people don't fill time.

I can see her from my small terrace. She is on her larger terrace wearing a romantic broad-brimmed straw hat; it is tilted back on her head. She is reading. She seems to be consuming all the books in Bliss' library. I know he has everything Matthew Arnold, Flaubert, and Walter Pater ever wrote, and I'm sure some of these are curiosities to Helen, though she's diligently plowing through each, I believe. It's reassuring since one hears so much about how young people these days don't read. When I awaken in the morning she's always already there on her terrace. She's adopted a kitten which the Cretans might have killed since they have scant affection for pets.

I awaken much later than my young friend and my mornings are groggy. I drink too much, particularly in the summer months, but I never drink before five, and then, if I do, I always dilute my wine with water. Some in my line were alcoholic but none died in the gutter. Some even died in bed. I imagine I'll go quietly. That is how I envision it, my end. I will be content, happy to go, surrounded by angels that I've hallucinated, Caravaggesque ones that will dance around me, supple fleshy bodies cavorting as the light grows dimmer and dimmer. Wait, don't leave, I'll cry. I think about death rather a lot since having turned sixty-five.

Helen does too. She is eccentric in her young way. I suppose she's been suicidal as she alludes to dark incidents that might make me shudder were she to reveal them. I try to put myself in her frame of mind but I cannot realize or fully imagine the murky deposits of memory to which she refers. Nor can I mentally fit my frame inside her frame. Helen is slender and terribly sweet-looking. It seems to me she should be happy as she is lovely and bright and, most important, has many years in front of her. She says this is why she is unhappy. What is she going to do? she asks. Life is overwhelmingly empty. Sometimes I think we are isomorphs.

Young women oughtn't be so unhappy. I've read *Madame Bovary* but Helen's unhappiness is not of that sort. Or maybe it is, in a revamped version. Perhaps she is an Anna Karenina in love with one of those long-haired and unpleasant rock musicians. Tragic love or bourgeois life may be pressing down on the girl. One day, I tell her, you will fall in love and marry, bear a child or find some good work to do. Helen laughs at me and tells me I am way off base; that her distress—angst, I say—is different. It quite escapes me. Much escapes me and I escape some of it. Living here, time just passes, and people come and go; it's possible to fool oneself about what one is missing or misunderstanding.

When I first arrived, I kept to myself, the way Helen does now. I was suspicious of others like me. That is, those more like me than the natives. I avoided their company and posed as a self-sufficient litterateur who had come for reasons different from anyone else's. This went on for months. Months and months. Gradually I was drawn in, perhaps first by Alicia, Alicia of the beautiful voice. Yes, I think so. It was Alicia's inviting me to tea at her plain but sumptuous apartment, where she almost undressed me, figuratively speaking, of course. And once my clothes were off I found I couldn't quite force them back on again. And then she had me to dinner with Roger and some of the others. Alicia was the queen of the scene then, the Queen Bee. She'd been an opera singer and had abandoned her career for reasons that were never spelled out, and that may have involved a man or men, or not; it may have been that her voice was giving out. Alicia never said. There are photographs of her in costume around her apartment, and occasionally I've commented on the beauty of her appearance, but that was years ago, and here she still is, still the Queen Bee. After almost twenty years the scene has become a bit frayed at the edges. Thinner, balder, less bright, more brittle. Like me.

Stephen was at that first dinner, and Roger, and Duncan, I think. Stephen fascinated me, as does Helen now. He and I necked one night; it was pleasant but not passionate and so we immediately became friends, never lovers. It is awful what happened to him. I hope Helen isn't actually anything like him. He's a cranky hermit and never bathes, and yet he was such a beautiful young man. His breath smelled of spring onions—is that what Auden wrote? I can't remember. Helen probably isn't anything like him, though at my first sight of her, he, Stephen—my Stephen Dedalus—came to mind. Helen might be Molly. She says yes from her bed, but of course leaves it too, which poor Molly never did. This is an argument I've had with Roger, about Molly's ecstasy on the bed, from her small bedroom. He says my point of view is jaundiced by the ghosts of my feminist ancestors. I do practice, as Alicia has succinctly put it, a form of ancestor worship.

Helen doesn't live abstemiously or like a nun, I've discovered. I take care of a young Greek named Yannis; he is my companion and lover, whom I help and will send to college should he want that and if he is bright enough. He has a terrible temper, and we fight when I've drunk too much. Before me, but very briefly, he was with Roger, another American. Yannis was considerably calmer then, Roger likes to claim. I do not believe this. Roger is from the South and is a braggart with the temper of a disturbed snake. My temper is not the best, either. My charge Yannis and I forgive each other, though. I never talk about him to Helen but he is with me at meals at the restaurant Christos manages. I don't need to talk about him.

I have dinner at the same restaurant every night. I adore their lamb and fish, and their salads are always fresh. When I go to the movies I take Yannis, if he wants. Helen and Yannis appear to tolerate each other. She knows a little Greek and they transact whatever is necessary in a simple tongue. The foreign movies have Greek subtitles, are never dubbed, and apart from the noise of the worry beads that are swung wildly during action movies, it is perfectly easy for any English-speaking foreigner to follow them. We go often, Helen and I, at 6 P.M. generally.

It was Yannis who told me that Helen sleeps with sailors from the naval base. So it wasn't precisely my discovery; it was Yannis', and he is much more in the position than I to find out such material. When he told me he clasped his hands together and rubbed his palms in what amounts to a lewd gesture. He is a simple boy, after all, and simple peasant boys, even those who sleep with rich foreigners—foreigners here are thought to be rich and are, relatively so—these boys are terribly self-righteous and bigoted. My first thought was, when does she do it? because she seems always to be at home, on her terrace. Of course they may visit her in that decrepit house and leave stealthily in the early morning, when the sun is just nudging up over the harbor. Nectaria as well as Chrissoula must know what is going on, but neither has let on to me. Nectaria is terribly open-minded for one raised in such a seemingly rigid society. But then we are foreigners, and their rules don't apply to us. No one can be as good as they are. I think I am slightly disappointed in Helen, my vision of Helen, though I hesitate to admit this even to myself and never would to the others.

I rub my hands, the way Yannis did but without the lewdness. Lately there's been a numbness in my hands and feet. Luckily I'm not a painter like Bliss, wherever he is, with wife number-whatever-it-is, because my hands, when numb, are useless and couldn't hold a brush or even a rag. They tingle annoyingly. Were my eyes to become numb so that they froze in their sockets, I'd be morbidly worried. I wouldn't be able to read. And life would be over for me.

As if to forestall such a terrible fate, I vigorously shake my legs and arms. Yannis must think me mad. I leap up and down, stamping my feet and jerking my hands. Then I pull my short white terry around me and recline in my favorite chair. The blood must have shot to the colder points of my body. I'm not in good health, and in the States I'd receive better medical attention or be compelled to by high-minded friends. Still, I'm quite happy to be outside of Massachusetts and out of the reach of my brother and his Puritan wife, who would probably love to place me in a hospital.

Perhaps my eyes are already numb and stuck in their sockets. They are large and protruding, colored a limpid blue, which, after much wine, turns milky and pale, while the whites go pink. My eyes might be a suitable flag for the spanking-new gay republic in the States. Though I believe there may already be one. If I stare into the mirror for any length of time and fix my eyes upon myself, I realize again what I did when I was only seven. I am quite repulsive, like a frog.

Helen doesn't seem to care or notice how strange-looking I am. My head, for instance, is too big for my body. I always had the largest hat size in any class at school, and when measured, the hatmaker would invariably remark on it. I was called alternately Big Head or Egg Head, and fortunately my other extremities were of normal size so I didn't suffer much from that, when I was young. Here the boys don't seem so focused on size as we are in the States. From what I can tell, before puberty they all play with each other's genitals and at puberty some boys are the girls, and some the boys. There is now a young pretty blond who is much fussed over by the others, even courted by them. When they walk along the harbor, he is positioned in the center. The other boys keep their arms around him, or at times one of the boys might hold the favorite more possessively, to claim his rights in the moment. It swiftly changes, but the blond boy always remains the girl. And if his future is like that of the others I've seen, he will probably wind up a homosexual, despised by his present mates and sexual partners, and exiled to Athens where he will find others of his kind.

Helen is friendly with these boys and may not be aware of their arrangements. Their contact is limited by language, although one of them has told me that he will take her English class as soon as he finishes high school. He says his mother might pay for it. Helen goes with them to the beach. She does not like going there alone. It is a novelty for Cretan men to see young women on their own, as well as lying half-naked on the beach; to them it is always an invitation. Sometimes they just stand and look at her, from a distance. Sometimes they take out their penises to show her. She is frightened by this.

I haven't the heart to tell her that I probably would be delighted if they did that with me. It would not frighten me. But then I am different from Helen. In many important ways. She may be as promiscuous as I, or more, but that would be in her own feminine manner. This manner seems not to include cooking. We had one lamentable meal which she cooked and we ate on my terrace. Smitty had the good grace not to apologize for it. I don't believe people should apologize for what they can't help. Helen professes to having no artistic ability. In any case, she can't render life as it is or even close to what it is. I am not sure what she is good at, though I am sure she is good at something. I have always been good with words, and wrote terribly smart compositions about military heroes when I was a lad, pleasing my mother but not impressing my father, who would have, in true American fashion, preferred brawn to brain, especially in a boy that age. My brother, older by four years, was his favorite. Instinctively I knew fairly early that I would never please my father and gave up before beginning, really. I realized he wouldn't ever love me, and I clung to my mother beyond reason—though I don't know why I put it quite like that—and she adored me, even when I came to despise her a little. As I grew older and I outgrew her, I was less in need of her protection, such as it was. Nevertheless, when I was at home, I always took her side; my brother, my father's. I don't know how Helen feels about her paterfamilias or materfamilias.

Helen has reminded me there is no word in English for man-hating, no equivalent to the Greek misogyny. This bothers her but she is careful not to seem as if it really matters to her. I appreciate her sangfroid, because I would hate to have to minister to her. She never makes this necessary, however, although from what I hear from Yannis, much occurs in her life, as if she were a contemporary Colette. I wonder what that woman was truly like. I'd rather know Jean Genet, but I don't think he'd be interested in me.

I walk to the restaurant where my usual table awaits me. Christos brings a bottle of wine and opens it with a flourish. *Kali spera*, Horace, he exclaims. We exchange pleasantries. I look up and see Helen on her terrace. It's just after five. The fishermen are doing what they do with their boats and talking among themselves. Their faces are brown and their skin, even from this distance, seems thick as hide. I'd like to pinch one of their cheeks, to see if he feels it. To me these men are impervious. I pour myself a glass of wine. The wine is cold and dry, much needed after a frustrating afternoon of work on Household Gods. It is so difficult to understand the mind of a woman of that time, perhaps a woman of any time. Like Helen. Though my Helen is, in so many ways, sympathetic and, of course, present. But trying to conceive and fashion the sense and sensibility of a nineteenth-century feminist abolitionist temperance reformer, and fold her character into a modern novel—it's Great-Aunt Martha who drives me to drink.

That misery Roger has taken a table near me, not with me; we are cautious about possible presumptions. Yannis hardly glances at him, the other American with whom he once lived, very briefly. Roger sucks on his cigarette, looks toward Helen's house, and through his small teeth hisses a distasteful remark about her. I declare him a Nelly, and he waves me off with his hand, as if it were possible to banish me. He is not alone in his contempt for Helen. Of the expatriates I am the only one who spends time with her. She doesn't seem to mind and has indicated that she finds the others very uncool, which is how she put it. When someone speaks like that, uses words such as cool and so forth, I think of the forties and fifties and clubs in New York and Boston where I heard jazz played by excellent musicians, Negro musicians, who seemed indifferent to their white audiences. Black musicians. When it came into existence not so long ago, the phrase "Black is Beautiful" delighted me. It still does. Black is beautiful.

Roger shifts in his chair and pretends to write in his journal. We are, unfortunately, almost all of us here, writers. This is a curse at times though relatively amusing at others, especially after I've had a few glasses of wine. Roger had a minor success with his first novel, set in the South, a coming-of-age drama that elided his homosexuality, masking it through other characters that the cognoscenti recognized. Then he received a good advance for his next, which is what he's still working on, and left the States. Years ago. Even in this place he lives somewhat in the closet. I don't know why he is here. The Greeks don't care, not about us. I've even seen him flirting with Helen as if he might actually want her.

It was late one night in Christos' restaurant and one of the waiters had taken out his guitar and was playing bouzoúki music. There were very few people about. Bouzoúki music has an insistent, demanding sound, and its nervous rhythm set the tone that night. Roger bowed to Helen and fairly lifted her out of her chair, waltzing her around the room while gazing ardently into her eyes as he moved her this way and that. It was quite a performance. That was in the first month she was here.

I don't know if Helen was taken in. He can be charming and has the foulest mouth. Again Roger says something about Our Miss Helen and The Sailors. Roger gets so Tennessee Williams, more Tenn than Tenn. He's not from the Deep South, but from North Carolina only, yet he taunts me with his Southern drawl. When he feels he's scored a point—Roger surely keeps score—his bright blue eyes flash triumphantly. His eyes are much more beautiful than my own, which pale by comparison. So bright shines our Roger. Oh, shut up, I hiss back. Tsk, tsk, Roger responds. I close my eyes, like a turtle in the sun, and turn away to show my disdain. But now Alicia arrives and walks our way. Her presence has an immediate salutary effect. Around Alicia, we keep our gloves on, so to speak.

Alicia has had affairs with a few important literary men, who have deigned to write about her, one salaciously, in fact, and though well past fifty, I'd say, Alicia moves like a much younger woman. She is subtly sensual. Her operatic past surrounds her, and she's dramatic without being oppressive. A tall, athletic woman, Alicia nevertheless gives the impression of fragility, a fragility that is generally contradicted by her tough-minded, though gently spoken, discourse. Alicia nearly escapes the categories I ordinarily place people in. Her conversation is often elliptical, and like Roger, she can be sharp-tongued; but she is never as vulgar as he. Alicia is suspicious of Helen, whom she's had for tea and to whom she has offered piano lessons, should Helen want them.

I'd like to find out why Alicia suspects Helen and what she suspects her of. But not in front of Roger. And why has Alicia offered Helen music lessons? What happened at that tea?

The Maori love, Roger is saying, just as we do. The aborigines love as we do. Love, Roger is saying, is universal, whatever form it may take. Alicia interjects liltingly, Yes, dear, but who are we and what do we love? Roger's cunning eyes take her in joyfully, as if they are, and he is, eating her up. Then he clasps one of her pearlescent hands in his and kisses it. Why, Alicia, we love each other, he says. I love you, dear. Alicia taps the filtered end of her Greek cigarette. She taps it incisively, as if to signal that she is about to make her point. Ever so distinctly she whispers, Roger, I haven't a clue what love is. Do you want to teach me? Alicia calls his bluff every time, but so gracefully, Roger cannot figure out how best to respond. He has never reviled her with his wicked tongue. I am sure he would like to. Alicia's mouth asserts her intelligence, curving into a calculated smile that sets Roger back a drink or two.

Tonight I am annoyed by this charade and bored. Sometimes I don't mind repetitions, but I always prefer originality. I look toward Helen's terrace, and this time her head bobs up. She waves her tan arms above her head energetically, calling to me. There's your Psyche, Alicia says. Perhaps you'd better go to the sweet girl, all alone. Roger howls. Alicia exhales a mouthful of smoke. You two, I say waspishly, are unkind, despicable.

I am shaky on my feet. The water slaps against the harbor and the blue sky is under my feet as well as above my head. My legs have gone numb again. Yannis helps me walk away from the table. I believe I'm leaning on him coquettishly, like some Southern belle, or perhaps I'm merely an old drunk, a silly aging queer. I don't care what they think. Sometimes I hate everyone but Nectaria, Helen and Yannis. Yannis is quite solicitous this evening. I wonder what he wants. Or how much. I rest my head on his broad shoulder—he is short but muscular. I thank the gods for my family's ingenuity which has provided what I have, such as it is. I can keep Yannis and myself. Alicia and Roger are laughing in the background. I simply don't care.

CHAPTER

2

Bring me my slippers. Give me my robe. Coffee. Yannis hands these to me sulkily, and as it is early, and as I am barely awake, barely alive, and cannot face an argument with a boy a good deal less than one third my age, not at this hour, I do not complain, do not comment on his surly manner. The coffee is lukewarm. I pull myself together, like a shanty thrown up against a storm, and look instead toward Helen's terrace.

There she is. She glances up as if I had in some magical way contacted her. She waves her hand above her head and points toward the sea. I suppose this means she is going to go to the beach. And now—at this I lean forward against the rusty railing—she thrusts her arms out in front of her as if gripping a wheel, a steering wheel. She'd like to go for a drive with me. I nod yes and indicate with a flourish of the hands—not this minute, later. She looks down at her book.

She is a trusting soul. Of course that is the way to get hurt. Presumably she has been. Even a girl that age—twenty or twenty-one—could be indelibly marked by painful events and circumstances, blown by misfortune and regret this way and that. Or bounced this way and that. I don't know which I prefer. The coffee is cold and my hands are numb. I don't feel the cup between them. A bad sign. Not like chicken entrails spilled on one's front door, or whatever, but a bad sign nonetheless.

I don't know why everything seems so funny to me this morning. I suppose I dreamed something that delighted me, some absurdity, some revenge. Perhaps I murdered Roger and got away with it. The perfect crime. He will figure in my next crime story—the unsuspecting victim. He won't be Roger completely—Roger is not unsuspecting—but a writer on an island who finds out something he isn't supposed to know, and before he does, is embroiled in The Situation, from which he can't extract himself except by spilling the beans. I will model him on Humphrey Bogart as he was in *Beat the Devil*, a favorite movie of mine, in which Bogart's character is something of a joke but still knowledgeable, savvy. Death by garroting, I think, Roger with a rope around his neck. Old-fashioned but mean. I prefer it to knives and certainly to guns. The sky is so blue today I can scarcely bear it.

The post has fallen with a thud at the front door and Yannis, penitentially, leaves the room to run downstairs and fetch it. Probably he will gossip with Nectaria. From the force of the drop, I'd say magazines and newspapers have arrived as well as a book or two. Now I have time to look at my face in the mirror. I am embarrassed to engage my narcissism in front of Yannis, for he must know I find myself ugly or he must find me so, even though he is, by no stretch of the imagination, a Greek god. Not at all. His nose was broken in a fight, one of his eyes crosses and seems to seek his nose, and he walks oddly because he is so bowlegged; but it doesn't matter at all. He is better-looking than I ever was at his age, though I'm not sure why. Perhaps it is just that he is not me, and that is enough. I drink all the coffee even though it's cold and leaves a flat, repellent coating on my tongue. I'd like to spit it out but I'm too lazy to leave my chair. Helen hasn't left hers. What taste is on her tongue?

The post brings a pleasant surprise, a droll événement. Alicia has invited me to tea. She must not have minded my mood of the other evening, last week. Was it that long ago? Time races so. I too am repetitive, my little habits and eccentricities, even my bitchiness, are so well known to Alicia and Roger that they may even be appreciated. I don't really feel judged by them. That would be intolerable. Alicia's invitation is clever and charming.

She says we will be alone. She must have something up her sleeve, prosaic as that sounds. I will pen a note, a charming response, and give it to Yannis to deliver by hand. She'll appreciate that and invite him to tea, and he'll be flattered to have small cakes served to him by a lady. He'll be there an hour or so during which time I can collect myself, shower and wake enough to take Helen and him, if he wants, for a drive. I'd like to show Helen a small village where I know one of the peasants. He fought the Turks and is, as Yannis would put it, "strong like bull." Of course, I write to Alicia in my best hand, I'll be there. I wouldn't miss it for the world. I can see her fluff her hair, her long fingers coiling rapturously around her thick curls—no gray yet. I see her smile to herself, containing the secret within her until she has me alone in her lair.

Generally I like women. Roger says that is because I am part woman, whereas he, he implies, is not, since he doesn't enjoy their company as I do. I think that is pure foolishness. And besides, we are all part male and part female. I don't like all women, naturally. For a time I loitered on the fringes of a group— in college and after, around Cambridge—which was united not just by its love of literature and each other, but also by its contempt—even hatred—for women. I didn't and don't feel this, not at all. I like women but I am glad to be a man. I identified strongly with my mother when I was very young, and even as I grew away from her, I maintained an atavistic sympathy for her, oppressed as she was by my father, who was the classic cold and distant patriarch, absorbed in his business—trains.

In company with them, Roger pretends to like women, to flirt with them, to seek their approval and admiration, and I'm sure that the wiser ones see through him as if he were a flimsy curtain. I could have Roger murdered, in the book I'm planning next, when he is living in a dreary, rented room decorated with cheap curtains. The curtains could be a filmy nylon, reminiscent of the lingerie Lana Turner might have worn, in the movies, when she beckoned to her gangster lover. In a sordid hotel room. In the forties. The forties. A wonderful, terrible time, but a time of right and wrong. We all knew where we stood, even if we were all a bit anti-semitic. Roger, I believe, is half-Jewish, and

Harvey is not his real surname, but his stepfather's name, and for the life of me, or his, he won't tell me with what name he entered the world.

The fishermen are calling to each other. They're sailing into the harbor with their catch, and they'll disgorge the octopus and squid they trapped pitilessly. The creatures are flung onto the concrete and lie there grotesquely, like bulbous sacks of wet clay no one wants. The octopuses' slimy gray pockmarked tentacles are disgusting to me as they cook under the hot sun. They'll lie like that, the fishermen passing the time, smoking and talking, until the restaurants have taken their pick of the catch. I vomit at the merest taste of octopus, almost at the sight. But I perversely enjoy looking at them as they die. I am fascinated after all this time. Watching the octopus is a habit of the day. And sometimes, much as I hate them, the sight of them lying there, those ugly beasts, makes me want to cry.

I open a *New York Times* that Gwen, my best friend in Manhattan, mailed months ago by boat, along with other magazines and clippings, news items culled from diverse sources. Watergate is dragging on even now; Nixon is supposedly anguished about the men who were sentenced. President Ford, who pardoned him, has formed a commission to investigate the CIA's spying on citizens, domestically, under Nixon's administration. It is vile. I find Ford's naming Nelson Rockefeller as the commission's chairman entirely dubious, even though he is Vice President. I've always disliked Rockefeller. The story goes—Alicia told me this—that years ago he was at a meeting with some of his employees, and one of them mentioned "take-home pay." Rockefeller asked, What is take-home pay? And this man became governor of the state of New York. And then there was Attica. A horrible man. A small item catches my attention. A man has been found strangled in his Upper East Side apartment—no sign of struggle, no forced entry, no robbery. There is a story there. I clip the article and put it into my story file.

Tea with Alicia tomorrow. A drive with Helen today. It's all right that I'm not working. I can take the weekend off, and if I don't drink much at dinner, I might get something done tonight. What does Alicia want to chat about? Wouldn't it be strange if Helen were Alicia's given-up-for-adoption child? There was one, years and years back, I am almost certain of that. Perhaps this is why Alicia dislikes Helen. She might be her child, the child that represents a rebuke to Alicia, and Alicia may be more like a mother cat than a human being who, finished with the child/ kitten, wants nothing more to do with her. Helen has never mentioned her mother. Never her family, not really, now that I think of it, maybe something about her parents once, the source of many of her problems. Of course. I am so glad not to have children and not to be a father. Except to Yannis but that is different. I don't even know if Helen has siblings. I'll try to ask her this afternoon.

Helen is wearing leather flats, with slippery soles, and the shoes are entirely unsuitable for climbing. In some ways she has no sense. But I say nothing to her when she gets into my car. Yannis has stayed home. So be it. He's in a bad mood. Helen is less than talkative, and to draw her out, I ramble on about Roger. He is, I tell her, no bon vivant. He's not rich enough. His Greek is better than passable and he lords that over the passersby, the tourists, to make himself a bigger Roger. She asks if I like him at all. I love Roger, I say, surprised. He is like a brother to me. This is not precisely the truth, and as I don't particularly like my own brother, nor have I actually ever felt that any other man was one, in the spiritual sense, I am dissembling. Or, as they say, lying through my teeth. But why do I? I want Helen to think I am a good person, I suppose. I don't want her to know that I can be mean, even monstrous. I'd like her to think I am above all manner of pettiness. But obviously, since she thinks I hate Roger, she has already discovered the truth, or part of it. I sense she has already known bad people, evil ones. Why else would she have such an enigmatic smile and be so uneasy with her laugh, clapping her hand over her mouth just as she begins to chortle. Not chortle. I don't know what to call it.

She's looking out the window now. The donkeys dot the rough landscape. The women who walk on the side of the dirt road and whom we pass rapidly, though I drive slowly, are wearing black and carrying bundles, faggots, on their backs, as if they too were donkeys. Beasts of burden. They are solid women, of the earth, whom young Helen must view with as much sense of mystery as I. I ask her, Do you have anything in common with these women? She tells me that she has made contact with a Gypsy, a woman who recently came into our town. Contact? I wonder aloud. Daily, they pass each other near the baker's shop. And they stare at, Helen says, look at each other. The Gypsy knows something about her, Helen thinks, and she knows something about the Gypsy. That sounds mystical, Helen, I didn't suspect you went in for that sort of thing. She smiles and claims that she doesn't.

How Helen's young skin glows! It is so clear and clean, unsullied, without a sign of adolescent disruption. A smooth, cool surface. I had terrible skin as a boy and always thought it had to do with evil thoughts or how I reached for my secret part much too often, to stroke it and comfort myself and bring myself to what pleasure I could. My dog, I called it, because I wasn't allowed to have one. Will you lick my dog? I once asked Yannis. I was drunk, of course. Nowadays people are much more liberal about masturbation, but all of us then were in desperate conflict about its odious consequences.

Helen is clear and clean. Her dark-brown, nearly black, hair stops just short of her chin and is thick and straight, and her hazel eyes are sometimes more green than brown, even yellow, like her cat Maybelline's. Her sunglasses—black frames, dark-green lens—perch on the middle of her nose and just now she reminds me of Jean Seberg, as visited by Monica Vitti. I must keep my eyes on the road. I don't need to look at Helen, she is my tabula rasa. There is absolutely no reason in the world for my feelings for her, but somehow I identify with her completely and feel her as if she lived inside me. It is so odd. My fascination with her is deeper than for the octopus lying, dying, on the wharf. I shoot a glance at her from the corner of my eye, as if she knew how I was comparing her—let me count the ways! Were she to hear my thoughts, would she laugh or be insulted? Would she care at all?

Perhaps she is something like the girls I went to school with who terrified me with their self-possession and indifference, but in those days they did not hang out in discos or nightclubs or spend nights with men in bars or take men back to their apartments and make love with them. I guess some did but I didn't know them. Helen makes casual remarks, now and then, about such events, as if they were only in the past and did not enter her life here, as I know they do, as I know men enter her life, enter her door, enter her. Have you any siblings? I ask. Yes, she answers, but then states that she doesn't really like to talk about her family. I'm sorry, I say.

There's a boring silence and she looks out the window again. I feel I have done something terribly wrong. Or she has done something terribly wrong. But what could that be? Finally she insists that we should just forget it, or drop it, as she puts it, because it doesn't matter. She doesn't want to think about the past. It's bad for her. "Bad for me, Horace." She pronounces my name in two distinct syllables, for emphasis. I love it when she uses my name. From her lips it sounds like an interesting one.

To mollify me, she tells me that she dropped out of college in her second semester, which is indeed precocious, I remark, but she continues as if I hadn't said that. Then, in New York, she worked as an artist's model, posing nude four times a week, three hours each sitting, for students from an art school and also for some private classes. Helen frequented clubs and bars all during that time—Max's especially. She dyed her hair orange, wore flat white powder on her face, and painted dark red lipstick on her naturally blush pink lips. She acquired a series of musician boyfriends who had apartments; she lived with each for about a month, until it wasn't cool anymore, as she puts it. But, she states definitively, she'd never do it for money. I am slightly shocked, to hear that she might even consider doing it for money. She's not romantic, she admits, which I can almost grasp, though it's difficult to accept from one so young and, in a way, delicate. She is in another league altogether. I think of that—other leagues and other clubs. Twenty thousand leagues under the sea dwell those fascinating and grotesque octopuses. Why do they disgust me so? Has she read Jules Verne? I think not.

When she and I walk together in town, men watch her move—women too—and I can't tell if she's doing something with her surprisingly round bottom or if it's just the shape of it and her general demeanor. She's not classically beautiful, but pretty and appealing, I think, and sexy in an awkward, almost androgynous way. She is also knowing, but then that's an appropriately cool pose. As we get out of the car, having reached the village, which is just a few cottages, she rushes to explain that I don't have to tell her anything I don't want to, ever, that that ought to be our rule—no rules but that—our friendship must be different, unique. She says this so earnestly I want to embrace her, but feel that would be more common than unique and not at all hip. I respond pensively and formally, given the gravity of her statements: One should never have to say anything if one doesn't want to do so. Helen tells me that she knows I want to be a mystery. With her, she asserts, I don't have to try. I am one. I think quite the same thing about her, but would probably never tell her.

The sun must be directly overhead. Twelve-thirty or one in the afternoon, and still the women labor in the rocky fields—what is this always called? stubborn earth. Their tanned faces are streaked with sweat and dirt. Kostas, the peasant who fought the Turks, is sitting under the shade of his arbor, the green grapes weighing down the slight structure. I don't know how old he is but his age has afforded him a respected position in the village, that and his having fought the hated Turks. His BMW motor-cycle, a remnant of World War II and the presence of the Germans, is parked next to a small barn where several donkeys bray, annoyed by flies. It is a wonderful, pastoral scene, a scene from the past one thought evanescent. Yet it exists and is untouched, by something. Innocent, isn't it? Is Helen affected as I am by the beauty of such simplicity?

Kostas offers us brandy—*raki*—in small glasses, and though it is too early for liquor and against my rules, I swallow my drink in one gulp. Helen sips hers slowly. Kostas and I converse in Greek and he pats Helen's knee which, I can tell, doesn't bother her. She appears to accept everything, almost neutrally. The youngest of the village children gather around us, having heard that foreigners have arrived. We are watched by dark-haired boys and girls who stand mutely by the side of the road. They stare at us guilelessly and as if we were noteworthy. Helen waves to them. Kostas eyes her and tells me, in Greek, that I am lucky to have her. I explain that we are friends, but he does not accept this and wants to know if I will marry her. It is lucky that there are many words for love in Greek, but I think he allows only one, in this case. Helen won't have understood any of this, but I'm certain she knows we are talking about her. To change the subject I ask Kostas to show us the ruins at the top of the hill or small mountain that is the background to this scene, the backyard to his house.

He pours us another shot and disperses the children with a shake of his walking stick, perhaps a bull's penis or some such thing. They scamper away. Helen waves good-bye, something like a queen or more likely a fairy princess, and sips a little more of her raki. I down another. To hell with rules, to hell with noon. It's a high noon. Kostas takes her hand, which is little in his rough, big one, more like a baseball mitt—a catcher's mitt—than a hand, and she follows him up the hill, slipping and sliding in his wake. He wears those black leather boots that reach to the knee and that, even though he's probably worn them for decades, are stiff, very stiff. Most uncomfortable, I should think. But masculine, I suppose, in their stiffness. I've never thought of that before. Helen carries on up the hill, struggling but undaunted, Kostas pulling her after him. I trudge behind them silently, and the odd thing is that once we get to the top, nothing memorable occurs. I can't, now, remember what Kostas showed us. A ruin, of course, which I'd wanted to see, and probably had already viewed, years ago, but we looked around briefly and Helen seemed uninterested, and I'm embarrassed to admit that it all escapes me. I have to admit also that I am a terrible sightseer, for when in the site I have set out to visit I usually experience disappointment, not unlike that which one has after sex. I don't want to make too much of this.

But one sight I will always remember has nothing to do with what we ought to have seen. Perhaps the ruin was so ruined it was almost invisible. Perhaps we looked at hallowed, sacred and flat earth. Walking down the hill, Helen slipped and fell. Those stupid shoes of hers. Kostas swooped over to her, lifted her up and placed her on his back, and this ancient man carried her in that manner, on his back like a sack of potatoes, all the way down the mountain. Helen's legs stuck out from his sides. I wouldn't tell her so, but in the heat of the day, with her skirt riding up and her bare, tanned legs exposed, it was as if, indeed, Kostas were having her, as if they were making the beast with two backs. At the bottom of the hill, when he bent down to let her slide off his back, he kissed her cheek. It was very odd, and I don't know what she made of it. Or what he made of it, that peculiar intimacy. She was silent all the way home but kissed me on the cheek when we returned to town, a kiss that seemed to me a bond. That's what I thought at the time.

It's not yet 6 P.M. The sun has already begun its descent, relinquishing its place at the top of the heavens. I watch Helen walk away, her round bottom swaying or shifting with each determined step. What is she thinking about? I have time to go to a movie, though my head feels dull and my eyes hurt from having looked continuously at the road. Those winding, horrible roads on the sides of mountains. I would leave civilization at the bottom of a hill rather than carry it on my back to the top, the way Kostas carried Helen. Helen is a kind of civilization. I must be tipsy to think that Helen is civilization, for if she is, she is of a different order from any I know. I'm certain she's a new type, and I am somewhat proud to have discovered her while the others haven't. This is probably why I want to know her, she who is scarcely more than a child.

I pass the cafés. The men are playing *tavoli*, backgammon, at the tables. A few tourists have come into town. I notice their cars first and then I see them, excited and expectant. They depress me, always. I wonder if the Gypsy woman will make further contact with Helen. I pass the theater. The movie's a Western which I've already seen three times so that makes up my mind. No movie tonight. Work. I love decisions being made for me, like the wonderful blizzards that closed school and kept one at home for the day. Sadly this is not unique to me, even here on Crete, and I am not alone in remembering those wintry New

England days, remembering them on hot sunny ones and reliving them, even feeling them, with a poignant pleasure.

My mother never entirely believed me when I announced I was sick; and I never believed her when she took to her bed, saying she was ill. Like all children I certainly didn't think she'd ever leave me and die—she did, of breast cancer. Poor Mother. Father died years before her, in an airplane crash. He was with his secretary, and she perished too. I suspect she was his mistress. It was an abiding suspicion—the devoted employee is the patrician boss's lover—but if my mother suspected as well, I never found out. She was circumspect. Father's office, at his death, was filled with copies of *Time* magazine. He had subscribed to it from its beginning, from issue number one, and never threw a single copy away. Not one. He was that kind of man, economical and deliberate. He kept all the issues neatly piled and they were in mint condition at his death. *Time* was the only thing he collected, and in his will he left his collection to me, his younger son, his black sheep, his prodigal and wastrel. To my brother, Father willed his set of the *Encyclopaedia Britannica*, not that my brother was in any way bookish. Mother was to live out her days in the family house, which would one day pass on to me and my brother. According to the terms of Father's will, after Mother died my brother and I would divide up the estate, and whatever was left would be shared jointly. In the meantime, and until her death, everything was in Mother's name. I'm happy to say she spent her remaining days in comfort and peace. Generous to a fault, Mother scrupled to leave us as much as she could. Fortunately, I'd already received a reasonable inheritance from my paternal grandfather. I'm not certain what *Time* magazine meant to my father, why he collected it, or why he left all those issues to me. I got rid of them, of course. Even from his grave, Father may still have been hoping to make, as he would have said, a man of me. He may have thought Henry Luce the right kind to emulate. Indeed! I myself try to make men of boys and to have them make something of me.

Perhaps my fascination with Smitty is another type of atavism. It may simply be boredom. It's odd. I don't consciously worry about men loving or accepting me. I know one did deeply and assume two or three others probably have. Of course I always hope there will be another one or two on the horizon. I have always had male friends, in any case. Yet I am, I think, more comfortable with women; I seek out their company and friend-ship. Occasionally I fear they won't love me. Gwen does, I know. And Alicia. I know my mother did. But I rejected her when I was young. Perhaps I am punishing myself, even now. I didn't visit her when she was in the hospital. I don't know what pos-sessed me not to fly home right away. I kept saying to myself it wasn't time yet. Then one day I received a telephone call from my brother, who told me, rather self-righteously, that she had died. I suppose he wanted me to express my guilt to him, in that very moment, but I didn't. Nor have I. Not at the funeral, not ever.

Famished and dry as a bone, I enter the restaurant. Some of the excited new tourists are also here. I ignore them, take my regular table in the rear of the terrace, and order white wine and light a cigarette. The wine is just cold enough; it sits dryly on my tongue, prolonging those vapors and bubbles of memory, cham-pagne bubbles of memory.

Night is now falling, and the moon begins its ascent. The lights glow across the harbor, and one of the fishing boats is making ready to set sail. A slight wind lifts the pink tablecloths, and the water slaps more vigorously against the seawalls. What a strange idea, that night falls. Perhaps not. I muse and sip the cold wine. The moon does go down, the sun does rise. Christos brings me broiled fish—sardines caught this morning, I like small fish—and a salad, some bread and more wine, though I see Nec-taria trying to stop him from offering me another bottle. The day has been shot to hell anyway, lost when earlier I broke my drinking rule.

Roger ambles over to the table, complaining about how the plumber didn't come again today. It's Saturday, I remind him. Roger also complains that he couldn't get any writing done. He heard from his publisher yesterday. I don't care, I want to say, but don't, even though the wine has loosened me up. I stiffen instead, smile cryptically and hold myself more erect than usual, to fight the dreadful desire to blurt out something awful. He goes on jabbering. I ought to poke him in the eye or tell him what I think of his petty problems. His conservatism drives me mad. He would be terribly shocked were I to articulate what I really thought. We've had so many arguments over the years, the truth is, he must have an inkling, and not care a jot.

Roger and I have often argued about the terrible imbalance of wealth in our country, with Roger taking the position finally that the poor can shift. I think it is a good thing he is not in the States, though his views are as obnoxious here as they would be there. Poverty is all around us here too. Rich people, I once told him, become lawyers because they know how to defend themselves. He called me a class traitor. Very amusing really, as he is not from my class but wishes he were.

A privileged lad, I used to cavort on the streets of Manhattan and Boston at 4 A.M. when the police didn't care what a crazy white boy from Harvard did as long as he didn't get himself killed. He would never kill someone. That's what they thought. But rich people do murder, they murder each other the way the poor do—perhaps not in such great numbers—and they make killings on the market that certainly cause great societal distress. Roger hates the flamboyant in me; he likes to imagine he is always in control—of himself, of the conversation and so on.

Roger suggests that we play chess later. I announce that I'm going home to work. He arches one eyebrow, as if to say, Oh, Horace, poof, you aren't going to write anything, nothing of value in your current state or, for that matter, ever. He glances at Yannis, who's sitting nearby, chewing his fingernails, which I've told him not to do. Roger is figuring, I can see it in his transparent blue eyes, how to steal Yannis away from me, because though he let Yannis go, or rather though Yannis quickly left him, Roger likes to steal my lovers. He's done it before. My book, my Household Gods, I insist unsteadily, will be an important work. Roger stands up and flutters his eyelashes at me. Then he most ungraciously laughs and says, while patting me patronizingly on the back, Blow it out your asshole, Horace! Can you imagine?

CHAPTER

3

The walk to Alicia's apartment is sublime. It's cool this afternoon and perhaps this means that fall is coming sooner rather than later. I hate thoughts like that. Let fall come when it will. Her house is perched atop a hill, is covered in purple flowers and has a few stone gargoyles shooting out from the roof. Little stones lodge between my toes as I walk up her path, making my entrance less elegant than I had wanted it to be. This is when I feel old, when in bending down to shake out my shoes, I tremble and need to hold on to the side of the front door. Alicia watches this without contempt, I think, and I quickly recover my balance, in all senses.

Paintings and drawings hang on most of the walls, though the room we sit in, a screened porch, is underdecorated, bare but for the two chairs and small round table on which is set a blue teapot, white cups and saucers, and pastries. Honeyed Greek dainties that eat into the enamel of one's teeth. The view down the hill to the harbor is magnificent and Alicia gazes at it with the look of someone who has seen this, and it, all before. She owns the view, not because it's hers—one doesn't own views— but because she has incorporated it into her being. Today, because of something she's done with her hair, I think, she reminds me of Maria Callas, were Callas an American of German and Polish descent, not Greek. Alicia's mother was born and raised in the Polish countryside; and part of Alicia's inheritance is a broad jaw, prominent nose, and square shoulders. She has always been a good friend to me, though there is a way in which she seems not to need anyone.

Perhaps this is because there is a Supreme Being for Alicia. She believes in God, but I'm not sure what kind of God, and all around her apartment are religious symbols from the major faiths, and probably from some of the minor ones, too. I can only think, because I think in terms of family and tradition, that Alicia must have had an early religious education from which she turned away—it is hard for me to believe her faith wouldn't have been shaken at some time—and to which she returned with renewed fervor after a terrible event. The loss of the child I've already fantasized for her, the acceptance of great failure on her part, the death of a lover, the loss of her singing voice—something must have made her turn again to God. God is a repellent idea to me, and were Alicia not so spiritually ambiguous in effect, whatever her beliefs, I would not be so fond of her. I would not even take tea with her. But she is and I do, with pleasure.

She pours us tea, while asking the usual questions. How's the work going? She loves my title, Household Gods, for reasons already given. But I'm sure she'd be disappointed or confused by the project were she to read it. No one ever has. The crime books I write go out under another name, and no one here reads them, I'm fairly certain. Alicia and Roger don't consider it to be real writing, which bothers me but not very much since I too depreciate it. I am more than ambivalent about what I produce under the name Norman East. Now I'm not even sure why I chose that name. It may have had something to do with *East Lynne* or summers at Northeast Harbor, in Maine. In truth, I've forgotten.

Alicia is all in white—white Indian shirt, white duck trousers, which billow about her, and white espadrilles. There's a white cotton scarf around her throat and probably she is hiding her neck, which may be crepey, showing more years than her face, which is remarkable for its taut skin. But the scarf is tied loosely so that she may be wearing it solely for decoration, not to disguise her age. Alicia doesn't strike one as a woman who would hide anything in an obvious way, simply not to be a cliché, simply not to appear bourgeois, not to seem to care about what ideally oughtn't be a concern to an intelligent, rational person. But I always think it is the irrational that tells us much more than the rational; and I am eager to have her get to the point of our meeting. She does so more quickly than is usual.

"Don't you think it is terrible what young Helen did to poor John?" My first impulse is to say, Who is John? But then I vaguely recall having seen in the distance a lanky, long-haired, nondescript guy—I can't think of him as a man—wandering in town about the time Helen arrived; then I saw him no more. Or did I? Dear, what did she do to him? I ask. I really have no idea.

Alicia won't believe this as I have intentionally laid into my voice a qualified archness, and so she will believe that I know what I don't. I hate not knowing what everyone else knows. She continues and divulges, more or less in this fashion, that John followed Helen here after she refused to marry him. Helen led him on. She allowed him to follow her here and now she refuses even to see him. She abandoned him and the poor boy has tried to kill himself. Ah, I retort, you mean that boy. Alicia, he's not a child, after all, and if she doesn't love him . . .

I'm playing for time. Alicia goes on: John is in the hospital and even now Helen refuses to go to him. And he nearly died. Helen was horrible to him. It's bad enough that she didn't want his child and had an abortion when he didn't want her to.

At this revelation I open my eyes very wide, surely they are popping out. Alicia, dear, are you really in a position to blame a young girl just setting out in life for not wanting to be hampered with a child from a man, a boy, who's wet behind the ears, one she doesn't love? Alicia says nothing and looks toward the harbor. And giving up a child for adoption is better? I continue.

Now Alicia's eyes widen and perhaps it will be this very moment when she can no longer contain within her that horrible secret—the abandoned child, the reckless life she led—but no, she just closes her eyes, takes a breath, during which time she collects herself so as to be able to dissemble, and says, I wouldn't know. I suppose I don't really approve of abortion. Then I say something to the effect that it is a good thing she is living here rather than in the States because she would surely be out of touch with the women who have recently won the battle for reproductive rights. I feel foolish putting it that way, as if I were making a speech. Perhaps my feminist ancestors are speaking through me, though probably they wouldn't have approved of abortion, either. Come to think of it, in the first half of the nineteenth century it was not illegal. Still it is strange to argue what I assume to be the woman's side, with a woman. I would not call myself a feminist, as I am uncomfortable with almost any label, and also, as I am a man, and rather uncomfortable generally with professing to understand completely the woman's point of view, I hesitate to make the assertion. Yet I don't really believe my being a man ought to prevent me from supporting or voicing support for the cause.

Alicia and I agree to disagree with some regularity—she maintains eclectic and inconsistent positions and has erratic views, some more obsolete than my own, some more advanced. In this case, her position demonstrates her stubbornness and a sort of prissy old-fashionedness that may be evidence, or the cause, of her enduring secretiveness. Actually I don't believe Alicia fully subscribes to what she is saying. I'm sure she's had abortions, as most free-thinking women who have sex lives usually have had. She is being irrational. Perhaps this is serious.

John visited me days before he—Alicia pauses—before he slit his throat. Slit his throat, I repeat after her, how ghastly. I love the word ghastly. Now I am thinking, there may be more to John, whoever he is, than I imagined. He is a sweet, sweet young man, she goes on, and I can't see why he clings so to Helen.

Alicia is calling on me, she has summoned me to defend Helen, about whom I know not enough, not that much at all. Helen is brilliant, I respond quickly. She is honest and good-natured. She is independent, a different kind of young woman, Alicia, very different. Rising to the occasion, I continue rhapsodically: Helen is to me like new poetry, a kind of writing I don't quite fathom; her rhythm and style will be discerned in time. I say this with a flourish and then sip some tea.

Alicia doesn't know what to do with my exaggerated view, my way of describing Helen, and neither do I. It just came to me in a flash, but I think it's true, or rather, I am prepared to defend its truth. Especially if Helen is my tabula rasa. But then that means I am writing her, and I am not, since I couldn't possibly make her up. I do try in my modest way to make it new, as Pound exhorted. It is also important to be able to recognize what is new, as I do in Helen. I attempt, in my real work, to follow that adage. On the surface, and to the world, the world of appearances, I seem not terribly underground in my manner and thinking. Burroughs, for example, is not to my taste. I live my life and exist, in a certain sense, underground, but even that is underground. I am guarded. I don't flaunt anything, except when I'm drunk. There's nothing novel about that. Maybe bohemian or vulgar but not new.

Alicia asks me what I'm smiling about. I tell her, as winningly as I can, that I'd once fantasized that Helen was her daughter, that it seemed to me they should like one another. Why don't you? I ask her. What happened when she came here for tea? Nothing, Alicia answers, nothing at all. Then, with some hesitation, as if biting back more damaging words, Alicia complains that Helen sleeps with too many men and reveals that she, Alicia, can't bear it, that it upsets her. I feel humiliated for her, she admits, because Helen hasn't the sense to feel shame. The way she walks, Alicia adds.

Alicia pauses and pours us more tea. That doesn't, I say finally and primly, sound like nothing. Perhaps Helen is guileless, I expand, rather than shameless. But why then have you offered her piano lessons? I ask. Alicia explains that it is because she is older than Helen and ought to set an example, especially as she hasn't had children, nor did she ever want them. I suppose I feel guilty, Alicia offers with reluctance. Ah, guilt, I repeat, I am no stranger to that. I smile at her fondly. I do wonder with whom she's involved now, if she is. She's more secretive than I, surely.

Alicia walks down the hill with me. She intends to visit John in the hospital. Just before we left her house, she applied a peachy lipstick to her full lips and now she looks rather peachy herself,

as if she were a Renoir still life of that fruit. There's some excitement in her gait. She may be in love with John. Why not? I
like young men too. Perhaps, she says to me as we go our separate
ways—quaint but true—perhaps I am being harsh about Helen.
But suicide, Horace, and John's a darling, very special. We cluck
each other on the cheeks like aging hens.

Alicia disappears in white down the dusty road. I am both
full and weightless. It's mad but I enjoy the melodrama enormously and suddenly feel that I am privy to Helen's life, the one
she hides from me. Perhaps she doesn't hide it. Simply doesn't
mention it. After all, that was the vow I took with her—not to
ask, not to pry, to be free of all that.

The hotel is divided, cast equally in sun and shade, appropriately
enough, I reflect. Nectaria greets me—Yá sou, Horace—and I
greet her and take the mail.

Where is Yannis? There Helen is, on her sun deck—she says
Greece is like southern California. I've never been. Her head is
down; she is reading a book, and just now she glances behind
her, and I see a form in the doorway to the terrace, a male form.
It looks like Yannis from here, but that's mad. Besides, the figure
is taller, more like John, though that too is mad as John is in the
hospital. When Yannis appears here moments later, I am assured
that I am crazy, driven by paranoia, the fate of homosexuals,
wrote Freud, driven to bizarre conjurings and hallucinations, to
flee the face of the true loved one. Alicia could be right about
Helen, of course; it is within the realm of possibility. Helen might
be cruel, sadistic in the extreme. Amoral. But it is not probable.
I am not paranoid about her. In any case I don't subscribe to
Freud's theory about paranoia. Doubt is doubt, as a cigar is just
a good smoke. Helen waves to me suddenly; I'd forgotten I was
staring in her direction. She draws circles around her eyes with
her fingers. A movie tonight? Why not.

Why not? Because I ought to be working, getting on with the
crime novel. A simple story: a rich boy murders his mother and
father. It is based on a case that occurred not far from where I
grew up. I knew boys like him. I might have been a boy like

him, if we'd been even richer and I'd been more aggressive, even more perverse than I am. The rich boy evades the law—he has an alibi—until the canny, sarcastic detective, Stan Green, discovers evidence that the boy thought he'd destroyed. But he hadn't, otherwise there'd be no story for me to tell.

Much of it is written, and some parts I am rewriting, but lately I am filled with such ennui, I wonder why go on, why bother—and my novel, Household Gods, awaits, petulantly, in a special box, one I've had since college, with a drawing of a rat in the style of Michelangelo on its cover. A cloud shoots across the sun and covers it; the sky darkens and with it my mood. Just like that, just as if I were a Manichaean or some such dualist. Why does one have to do anything, especially if one is, as I am, relatively well off, especially here. Might I not just while away my short time on this mundane stage rather than engage in the drama of creation? Blow it out your asshole! Roger's crude phrase echoes heartlessly. I laugh aloud anyway. Yannis glances at me quizzically. Roger's right occasionally, right on the money, as they say, even if he doesn't have any money, another one of those things that makes our friendship tense.

It's 5:30 P.M., and where has time gone; the day is gone. I must have been with Alicia for over an hour and have been sitting here for an hour or more, staring into space and toward the harbor and then gazing inward, inward staring, navel gazing, my father called it. There is a word for that, Greek, of course, which has come into English: omphaloskepsis, or meditating while staring at one's navel. Marvelous, isn't it. I love words. I shuffle across the floor, slap after-shave on my puffy face, ask Yannis whether he wants to join us, and leave without him, running, not exactly, to the spot where Helen and I always meet.

She is punctual, which I find disarming in a young person. She is even waiting for me, sitting on the curb and reading a book. As I approach she closes it and pats it, as if saying good-bye or, more likely, adieu. She takes my arm and without a word, except Hello, we walk toward the outdoor cinema to see an old Clint Eastwood movie, *The Good, the Bad and the Ugly*— it's been here many times before, but it's always such a pleasure.

I'm very glad the Italians took up the Western when we'd let it drop, which was as it should be, given the history it covered over or distorted. But still, and I hate to admit it, I love those early Westerns, with their picturing of the bold and brave crossing the old frontier. I can feel my breath nearly stop when all the wagons line up next to each other, or behind each other, ready for the shout—Westward Ho!—that starts the dangerous journey. And I know all of this is wrong to feel—there is such juvenile pride in these feelings—and the West couldn't possibly have looked the way it did in the movies; and Turner's frontier thesis was incorrect anyway. But for a movie, it's breathtaking—the screen filled with women in bonnets and men in rawhide. I suppose rawhide gives off a horrible odor. The Italians don't go in much for wagons in circles. But those close-ups! Clint Eastwood is not my type at all, though I like his squinting in the sun and chewing on a stogie. The lines at the corners of his eyes are deep as burrows in the ground and I think of Alicia and the thin, scratchy lines about her eyes, her dark, penetrating eyes.

Helen's knees are clasped to her chest; she's like a human ball, curled up into herself. Of course mental patients do that too, and rock back and forth. Perhaps her uterus hurts her. Oh hush, Horace, I say to myself. Shut up. The movie's so exaggerated, the actors, their gestures and expressions, the divide between the good and the bad, the music so grand and wonderful, that after a while I do forget the lines around Alicia's eyes and my questions about Helen and John. It's a long movie, and time will stretch and stretch here. I feel happy. I take Helen's hand and squeeze it. She looks at me furtively; I realize she's crying. Tears are most definitely in her eyes, but could they be there for any of the characters on the screen? It seems unlikely. I hand her my handkerchief and she takes it with a small laugh, so she must be all right. Nevertheless she does wipe her eyes and, I might add, blow her nose. It's possible she's allergic to the weeds here, to something in the air.

The Greeks are swinging their worry beads full force now. I tried them when I was first here but discovered that I am in no way the sort to be able to go native. I felt completely ridiculous. Helen is not the type, either, which relieves me.

As we walk out of the theater, several men make quite a show of watching her bottom—her ass—and I pretend not to notice them. But Helen turns on her heel and in Greek tells them to fuck off. They are as astonished as I am. My Smitty, my Helen, is full of surprises. She has yet to disappoint me in any important way and if she's now being crude, it is her right, for, I ask myself, why should she let those men devour her with their greedy eyes and make rude comments? Yet the speed and harshness of her attack is a shock. Helen takes my arm and we walk back to the harbor.

These are the only Westerns she likes, she tells me, she can't sit through the others; they're too straight. Instantly I feel a twinge of sadness, even futility, at this blatant expression of the gap between us; the sadness settles just below my breastbone or in my solar plexus where anguish resides, I think. Certainly I can't adequately explain to her my nostalgia for the older American ones, mendacious as they are. She'd be mystified and out of sympathy with me, though I'm sure she'd listen attentively and without malice. Helen doesn't make fun of me. Were I to express myself, she'd respect my opinion and be very interested, intrigued at how differently I thought from her. Still, I'm embarrassed, as if mentally enfeebled, hobbled for a moment by age; I am determined not to let that show. Jovially, I invite her to dinner. But no, she won't join me. And no, I can't find the words to ask her about John, and besides I'm not supposed to. She expects she will encounter the Gypsy and intends to speak to her soon, maybe tomorrow. But will she visit John, I wonder, but I don't dare ask. Helen says she may travel, take a short trip, for a few days perhaps. Each of us—Alicia, Roger, Helen—comes and goes. We often do not see each other for days; but we do not monitor each other's movements. There is a way in which time is not of the essence here. It is a luxury each of us cherishes.

4

I might visit John. I just might. Later, that came into my mind—
rather than having to ask Helen anything. She might not like my
doing it, but I'm free, as is she. I could pay him a call in the
hospital—do a good deed, be a good Samaritan. Tell him Alicia
said he needed company. She didn't say he didn't. Alicia never
mentioned the idea of his needing company at all. John could be
entirely harmless, a blessed event, or a malevolent soul, and it
would be perfectly within reason for me to want to see if what
Alicia thinks of him is true or has any relation to reality. Even
a trace. Since Helen is my good friend.

The water dashes against the harbor, excited by something stirring beneath it. A beast, a hideous octopus is moving down below,
a war is being waged between monsters of the deep, that kind
of thing. I have been working steadily for some hours. Helen is
not on her terrace.

The restaurant beckons, and I take my usual table. The wine is
cold and tingles in my gullet and on my tongue. Alicia is not
here again, which is good, as I might feel compelled to reveal
something I oughtn't, but that awful Wallace is. Is he out of jail
so soon? Do I have to talk with him? He's not really one of our
crowd, such as it is, but an interloper on the scene, a madman,
different from Stephen, whom I haven't seen in months. Perhaps

Wallace will tell me again his idea for irrigating the Sahara—planting a gigantic rubber tube in a fertile source, from which it will suck water, carry it miles and miles, then expel it into the parched desert. He talks about his invention with such unwarranted excitement he means it to be taken seriously.

Wallace plops down at my table, uninvited, pulling along his Dutch girlfriend, who understands his Afrikaans. I ought to feel pity for Wallace, in and out of mental asylums and jails, this last time for indecent exposure, which could have gotten him thrown out of the country, but someone—probably Roger, he plays chess with one of the judges—interceded. Wallace's parents own one of the major newspapers in South Africa, and all of this must have been trotted out—Wallace's respected books of poetry along with his mother and father, whom Wallace despises for their politics and so on. On the basis of this, no doubt, he was set free. And here he is. I wish I'd been on the beach last week when he ran into the water wearing a red net bikini bathing suit. Not the thing to do here, even if men expose themselves, and certainly touch themselves, regularly. They do it furtively—but not Wallace, he's a flaunter. I ought to have sympathy for him—committed to a mental institution when he was just a boy of sixteen, deemed insane for opposing apartheid. He was sane then but has over the years lost whatever marbles he had, I think, though occasionally he's lucid and amusing. I find it hard to tolerate him. He talks so much, in that annoying accent.

I cut my fish, lifting the flesh away from the bone. My hand is steady and as usual I wonder if I oughtn't to have become a surgeon, since I enjoy doing this so much. I always think this when I cut flesh, exactly the same thought, and always wonder, in precisely the same way, if others have the same thought when they do simple tasks over and again, and then what would it be like, if that were so, to be working in a factory, on the line, doing the same job daily, repetitively? I do a good job with my fish and feel satisfied. Little things please me. My mother could never serve fish that was not riven with bones. I hated fish, the way most children do, and it took me years to develop a taste for it, and if I hadn't I couldn't have made my home in Greece.

At the moment I seem to be invisible at my own table, which is to my liking. Wallace and his friend chatter away in Afrikaans. I'm sure his Dutch girlfriend is kind but I have an antipathy to the Dutch and may be the only non-Belgian or non-German so inclined, or disinclined. Years ago I visited Amsterdam and had a most dreadful time. I stayed a few months, it rained constantly, and I met no one and found the Dutch barely civil. Everyone says they're so nice, so I never interject that I think they are dull. Actually I don't know if they are, but I nurse my secret dislike, my prejudice, and allow it to develop unhindered by scrutiny. The Dutch, I want to tell Wallace, have given tolerance a bad name.

I don't know how Wallace held up in court, if he did, or whether he had to face the judge at all. What does his girlfriend find appealing about him? This is a man who is never at a loss for the ladies, to be euphemistic about it. He's had more lovers than one would ever guess from looking at him; only a distorted notion of sexual freedom could have allowed this outrage, this flourishing of a lunatic Don Juan. Wallace professes to adore the female sex and has set many poems in bedrooms where his beloved lies *déshabillée* on a bed, which allows him to describe in fanatic detail the beauty of the female body, the pearl he nuzzles with his nose and licks with his tongue, that sort of thing. Of course the French have a word for poems celebrating the woman's body—*blasons*. But what do women see in him? Perhaps when he was young he had a certain *je ne sais quoi* . . . .

But now? He has a paunch and is disheveled. He has the worst set of caps I've ever seen. He whistles through them when he speaks. His eyes protrude like mine. And he tends to leer when he looks, projecting a mad intensity; I suppose someone else might say it signalled genius but to me it is most hilarious, signifying nothing like intelligence. His girlfriend's not laughing. Oh dear, Wallace is reading his poetry aloud, in English, something about a dog. I'm barely listening. Where the hell is Roger? Roger might relieve me of the burden of seeming to listen to Wallace. I know Roger plans to relieve Wallace of some of his money, to pluck it from him for some scheme or other, to buy property here through a Greek lawyer, to open a café. Roger always has something on the boil; he's one of those kinds of people who keep things moving by concocting ideas—for money, usually—which other people ought to invest in or become involved with. A magazine he'd edit or a property he'd administer. Sometimes they do give him money, but I never have. It's a point of pride with me.

Wallace has stopped reciting his poem. Now he's defending Pound to the Dutchwoman. She must be completely uninterested. He's whistling on about T. S. Eliot, being fierce as usual about Pound, about whom he's ambivalent. Whatever sympathy he has for Pound was aroused because he—Wallace—and Pound are both considered traitors by some of their countrymen. I think Pound's support of Fascism was a type of temporary psychosis, to which Wallace is no stranger either, I might add. Wallace is more paranoid than I could ever be; and he is rabidly heterosexual. Though, again, I can't see why any woman would want to sleep with him.

I've often noticed that even the most unpleasant men attract reasonable and kind women; these women put up with and serve these men for ages. They cook and clean for them, tidy up their social messes. And what for? The love of genius. It's not likely that genius could be attached to so many miscreants. Sometimes the women are masochistic, but then so am I, I should think, in some ways, and I'd never want a man like Wallace. He's unbearable.

He seems to think he saw Pound in St. Elizabeth's, insisting that he did visit him and even hid behind a tree to watch him after he was supposed to have left the hospital grounds. I hope Wallace was sane when he did so, although it doesn't sound as if he was. Imagine how Pound must have felt being incarcerated in a mental hospital, locked up with and surrounded by manic depressives and schizophrenics, and then to have an ambulatory lunatic like Wallace pop up, scot-free, raving as wildly as any in there with him! I don't believe Pound was truly insane. He was an arrogant and disagreeable man but an important poet, nonetheless. In this I agree with Wallace. T. S. Eliot was playing possum, Wallace now declares. Wallace has dropped to the ground to imitate a possum, and his girlfriend is urging him to stand up or sit down. This is tiresome.

I look away. Helen has returned and is now on her terrace. The sun has almost entirely set, leaving behind glorious slashes of red and purple in the darkening sky. She's turned one light on; it's hanging above her head but she's not reading. Drawn to the light as I am, Wallace looks in Helen's direction and says that he met "that young woman"—he knows her name—at the market and asked her if she ever intended to marry and would she consider him if she did. Wallace says that he dropped to one knee to ask her for her hand and that Helen laughed and told him to get up and relax. Wallace's girlfriend is not amused. What is her name? Something guttural—Brechje, I think. Wallace explains that he asked Helen to marry him only to make her feel better, for surely a woman on her own is lonely. The life of a spinster is barren, he warned Helen. I can just picture Wallace doing that and imagine Helen's disgust. He seems to have a penchant for dropping to the ground.

Once, when he was in Paris, Wallace trotted about the city wearing a pith helmet and dunked his head under the cascading waters of several stone fountains. He filled his pith helmet with water to throw over himself. It was a hot summer. He showered in the street and lay on the ground next to Notre Dame until the gendarmes removed him. That was the summer his mother came to Paris to see him, to rescue him from the Beats and so forth. But Wallace was not for rescuing. He enjoyed the bohemian life and also enjoyed throwing himself at his mother's feet, accusing her in a loud moan of driving him crazy. When he tells this story he always notes: My mother shook and so did her gold jewelry. Wallace loves making a scene.

Roger is approaching, affecting his usual manly gait, and I spy a peculiar little smirk on his lips that I'd like to rub off. Or rub out, rub him out. I must be drunk or Helen is right and I hate him. He kisses the Dutchwoman's hand elegantly and Wallace sits up, like a well-trained dog, to pay attention to him, as if to a teacher. To my eye Roger is in no way commanding. He can be pedantic, though. They all chatter together aimlessly for a bit and Roger asks how my book is going and if I didn't finish a big chunk the other night. My work is progressing, I lie, and yours, dear? I'm past the hurdle, he says. I act as if I believed him. Then he goes on to talk about his novel, its structure, as if all one wanted to hear about were his artistic trials and tribulations. It is one thing to discuss a literary subject, it is quite another to complain endlessly about the difficulty of writing. These things, I believe, ought never be the topic of discussion. Would a carpenter take up the dinner hour telling all assembled how hard it was to finish this or that job? No, he'd get on with it. If he were intelligent he might talk about an aspect of carpentry from which all assembled might learn something. Carpentry affords many metaphors.

You're airing your clean laundry again, I say to Roger. In this you and I have no meeting of the mind. Unhappy with my castoff, he responds and points to Yannis, who's dying of boredom, I assume, at another table. Oh Roger, I retort, in mock horror, you strain credulity. You are très transparent. And you, Horace, he answers, are in no position to talk. I am sure Yannis has heard Roger's remark; this bodes ill for the rest of the evening.

The evening ends as most do. It blurs into a watery mass of colors, amorphous moments and words, the night's palette. Helen's light is still on but she is no longer on her terrace. Her curtains are drawn. I wonder if she is making love. I want to make love, though that is not what Yannis and I often do. He sometimes permits me to love him and occasionally he responds to or services me. I content myself with the past. There was a love of my life, years and years ago. He and I shared a bed and a home for fifteen years, and it ended finally and suddenly, broken off mysteriously and mutually after a petty quarrel, and I've never understood it. That was many years ago, and he's been dead for ten, and I never again truly shared my life and lived with anyone that way, so profoundly, not after him. I was involved with a few, but none like him.

Yannis is no grand passion, not even a small one. He's a

comfort to me, and sometimes he is not, as when I am irritable from drink and he is sulking about some wound that is probably self-inflicted. I do have a sharp tongue and say things I don't mean, most of which I'm sure he doesn't understand, but the boy has a terrific capacity for dark moods, which sometimes frighten me. I try to cheer him up with gifts and small trips. I don't understand him and he certainly doesn't understand me. He thinks I putter about and just type, for example, and I think— I don't know what I think. I am too old to expect more. I am ridiculous. My body is decaying, the flesh literally weakens and drops from the bone, gravity is pulling at me. I grow old, I grow old. Alicia says it's the drink and perhaps she is right.

T. S. Eliot understood decay, I've often said that was his métier. But need and lust, in me they have not weakened and from me they have not fled, even though my body shrinks, grows tired, and my flesh loses its hold, its grip on life. It doesn't matter—matter's not the matter—and more's the pity, because my thoughts are the same, and if I allow myself these—primitive, primordial, and ageless—they make me young again, in my mind, and I feel a blast of lust, of full-bodied, young desire rising up from my darkest self. Furiously it rushes into my mouth and then to my genitals where it settles, only to become cold and solid and still. I can taste it, my desire and lust, like Proust's madeleine. I can become terribly sad, despondent. I want to rage against this inevitable fate, to rage like so many men before me. Sometimes I want to die.

I often picture my funeral, even when I'm happy, especially when I'm happy. I see the faces of friends, back in the States where I'll be buried, of course, in the family plot, just beneath— in the row below, that is—my father and mother. My parents visited their future gravesite once a year, to place flowers on their mothers' graves—their mothers knew each other well—and I was taken along, my spot pointed out to me with pride. At my funeral—I can see it very clearly—friends who haven't heard from me for years and years will remember me and my antics in prep school and college. Then my publisher will say a few words, and some of the New York crowd, whoever's alive, will make the trip, and say how charming I could be, and so forth. I will leave the world in relative anonymity. It's unbearable to me. I drink until I can drink no more.

The magnanimous black sky is bottomless, fathomless like death and life too, and it comforts me in a way Yannis can't, which is not the dear boy's fault. He's asleep on the bed, a body made tender by unconsciousness. I am looking out at the harbor, still as death at this time of night. Nothing is moving but the water and the clouds. Even the wind blows silently. The air is cold and startling. The night gods have chilly breath. Whatever paradise is, it must happen when everyone's asleep, when there can be no complaints, and that must be why night gets so dark, so that we cannot see any imperfections in our world, and there can be nothing to complain about. Pound wanted to write paradise at the end: "Let the wind speak, that is paradise." My enduring, stubborn passion must be written on the wind. And there it goes, there it goes, blown away by an indifferent blast of black and silent night air. Helen's light is finally out.

CHAPTER

5

It might be a policeman's flashlight shining on my puffy face. It could be the police. But it is not. It is sunlight. I'm groggy and Yannis has gone to make coffee, I suppose, though he may not have, depending on his mood. Each day is different and in some ways the same. What an awful truism with which to start this one. I feel oddly light-headed and well. The day, for no reason I can perceive, begins brightly, like a newborn babe, all pink and naked, and the sun is a marvel, amazing, burning so fiercely, lighting up this part of the world. Were I consistent, I would become a nudist, or some sort of nature lover, or at least a sun worshiper, and walk every morning to the end of the harbor to watch the sun rise, or go to the beach, with suntan lotion and blanket, and lie near the ocean and let the sun bake and warm me. Perhaps I ought to sing songs to it. I don't know why I don't. For no reason at all, except that I am alive, and awake, and can't remember my dreams, or my dreams have decided to let me forget them, I feel optimistic today. Hopeful as a clear blue sky, with no clouds at all, no signs of trouble. The coffee is terribly hot, brewed to my liking, and Yannis is not sullen. The small blessings of life make it bearable. I am a lucky man. I have never been arrested, and I ought to have been.

I hand Yannis some drachmas and tell him to go buy something for himself, for the house, and to have a good time. With each sip of coffee, traces of last night's debauch slide into view, as if my eyes were binoculars—no, not binoculars, what were those things that Mother had in which one put postcard slides? A stereopticon. Yes, it's as if I were seeing portions of last night through that optic antique. Indeed I may be that optic antique, but just now, lying here and looking out at the harbor, which I can see even from my bed, I don't mind. I remember more and more of the night's debates and ludicrous Wallace. Did I dance with him or was it the Dutchwoman? I believe Roger and I even kissed good night. Was it Roger? Well, no matter. This is a day to embroider upon, but why should it feel so? A wonderful smell wafts in the air, aromatic yet not too sweet, redolent of youth, my youth of course, and youth must be served. I will visit Helen's John today, I really think I will, after I have gotten some writing done. By meeting him I'll sort things out, see what's what.

I walk to the window and wave to Helen on her terrace; she waves back. She has no idea what I'm planning, of course, and I feel a bit like one of my furtive characters, a confidence man or a CIA agent investigating domestic matters, spying on oblivious American citizens.

My detective Stan Green always feels furtive, so keeping secrets comes naturally to him. Secrecy fits him like a glove. I make it fit him like that. Green's girlfriends know nothing of the real world he inhabits, and his wife suffers silently and plots her revenge. I haven't decided whether it will ever be enacted. In the book I'm writing now, the young, rich murderer, whom Green pursues, thinks, like Leopold and Loeb, that he has committed the perfect crime. This book is a thinly disguised attack on would-be geniuses like Roger, men who think they can get away with anything, murder included, because they're so damned superior. I am smarter than most of them and will receive no recognition whatsoever for my acuity, in part because I don't lord what I do know over lesser lights. How can one have a meeting of the minds with people whose minds are concocted more of ego than anything else? I thought I'd left that problem behind in Cambridge and New York, but it surfaces here often, even in this obscure part of the world.

When Roger first arrived, I thought, he's a good man, we can talk. We shared Faulkner, Forster, Joyce, Firbank, of course, and Plato, and even some obscure English writers he and I both knew and loved. He doesn't appreciate Gertrude Stein the way I do, and that was perhaps our first great disagreement. Her *Making of Americans*, I believe, is a masterpiece, and she is the godmother of Household Gods, so to speak. A vast subject. I can't bear to think about it just now.

As the years passed, Roger's peculiarities emerged. He has a strange expression these days, his face having set a bit—he's ten years younger than I, I think. He never troubles to look one straight in the eye. He has the disconcerting habit of peering at one through half-closed eyes, as if one were under suspicion of a great crime. There is something sinister in him, something that I cannot quite comprehend, but sense. It is as if his suspicions of others were only the reflections of his own dubious nature. I don't mean to dramatize, but one doesn't ever know what to expect from Roger, especially because he appears so pulled together and chipper, so in control.

One worsens with age; at the least our failings graduate with us, with age, and some become exaggerated. I'm sure I have gotten worse, although the truth is I'm not sure in just which ways. I'd never admit my failings to others. Obviously I drink too much and lose patience quickly and can be petulant. There's no one here I trust enough for the kind of dissection I ought to undergo. I almost trust Alicia enough, almost, but her secretiveness produces greater discretion on my part than I truly care to employ. I would like to reveal myself more fully to her. There's Gwen in Manhattan, though it's been ages since I've seen her. An extraordinary, singular person.

Gwen is from a lower-middle-class black family in Queens, New York. She attended Radcliffe on scholarship, which is where I met her, in Cambridge in the fifties, years after I was graduated from Harvard. Actually she is now close to the age I was when I met her. Gwen is never without something clever to say. It is, as she once said, her best defense, and then in the next breath she went on to dub herself Manhattan's double entendre. That indeed does suit her, as it begins to define her complex nature. To me she's the black Dorothy Parker, as she is a great wit, a talented writer of stories and screenplays, does editorial work for a living, and turns out the occasional review or essay when she can rouse herself to it. She drinks and is extremely critical and, even more, is a cynic like Parker and has, like her as well, a penchant for gay men, such as myself, not that she was ever in love with me. I do, did trust her, even though she can be an outrageous gossip, but it's true to say that, with her, minds do meet. It's been too long since we last were together. That must be remedied. I'll write her and invite her here. I'll offer to pay her way. Yes. I really need to see her.

I find it easier to arrive at my typewriter if first I plan a simple task, such as writing a long-overdue letter. Even paying a bill sometimes unlocks the door to creativity. It's odd what helps, because the activity is so odd in itself. Dearest Gwen, I write, and so on, and will you come, and so on, and be my guest, and so on, and then I use some of what I've written about the sky and the sea, and ask her to join my sunbathing club, and so on. I'm as excited as a pup. Gwen is not in any way doglike or puplike. She is an original, a rare bird, a tan, lithe creature. The color of coffee ice cream, she has said, not brown sugar, a locution that offended her in part because it derived from a song sung by wimpy English boys, as she put it in a letter. She's writing a screenplay called Dark Angels, whose title comes from a postcard Gwen found in the South. It shows three young black boys in a pastoral setting. At the bottom of the card, which she once showed me, there is a motto: Dark Angels. She hasn't yet let me see the script.

Gwen is canny as a con man, an art historian gifted with the touch of a grifter. Her postgraduate work was in art history. Will Gwen like Helen? Might they not fall in love, for one Greek moment? But Gwen isn't really drawn to women. I should probably hate their becoming lovers. I should hate it also if she got on with Roger, and so I immediately amend my letter to include a shovelful of dirt aimed his way. I believe Gwen knew Stephen the Hermit; but he's so rarely in sight these days, I needn't mention him. And Duncan is back in England, falling in love over and over, I suppose. God, what if she liked South African Wallace, and what if she went to bed with him, just to spite me; but I will not put one more negative comment in this letter, as I want her to visit me. I ought not put her off by portraying a scene filled with lunatics and failures. I give the letter to Yannis to mail immediately, express. It will reach her in no time. I will also telephone her. That will speed her to me.

The clippings Gwen mails me are like aspects of her, small pieces of her. André Malraux's book *Lazarus* sounds interesting. A meditation on death, the review says; I suppose Gwen has read it already. She keeps up with everything, and the subject of death fits her mordant humor, as it does mine. I see that a Dr. Christiaan Barnard has done a twin-heart operation. There's a CIA file on Eartha Kitt, of all people, because she yelled at LBJ's wife at a dinner party in 1968. She yelled about our boys' being sent to be murdered. Good for her. I would have liked to have been there.

They ought to hire Roger for the CIA, he'd be perfect, a perfect architect for intrigue. He was furious when we lost the war in Vietnam. We didn't lose it, he bleated, we gave it away! I lorded it over him that our Kissingers ultimately had to bow low to tiny Vietnam. I could just imagine all those beefy military men in their uniforms, with stars on their chests, stunned and helpless, like octopuses lying on the harbor, gasping their last breaths. So many discussions with Roger about the parallels with Great Britain, when it lost its empire, and how he foresaw the end of Western civilization! I answered, if the U.S. is the last outpost of the West, then good riddance to it. I don't entirely mean that. After all, I am of the West. But what will come next? Sometimes I am glad to be old.

I believe I am patriotic in my fashion. I certainly wouldn't dupe my government and the people the way Nixon did. Power to the People indeed. Perhaps now our masculine American men will develop the self-deprecating humor Englishmen display so effortlessly. It charmed me when Duncan used to say he was so hopeless he couldn't organize lunch. One couldn't imagine an American man professing to hopelessness, to helplessness. I miss Duncan. I may even seek out the hermit Stephen; he's somewhere not that far from here, I heard, in the mountains. Perhaps he is in Mátala, living the life of a hippie. I believe the hippies are still there, in those caves. I couldn't live in a cave. Why on earth would one want to?

Alone, unencumbered by Yannis' incredulous or contemptuous gaze, I raise my hand and clench it into a fist, making a Black Power salute, which I would never do in public. It's odd, these kinds of desires. And the things one does alone in a room that one would never do in company. My arthritis doesn't allow me to close my hand fully, the index finger won't flatten, the pinky pokes up, and my hand flops open again. I lie down on the bed, my bones creaking. I've had creaking bones all my life. I never had a middle age, I went from twenty to sixty. In a sense, I'm used to being old. I like to imagine I take it in stride, that it is my stride, in fact.

I had my moments—raving with Gwen around New York and Cambridge years ago—and still do from time to time. But deep inside me lives a prim, elderly man, and sometimes a woman, like my mother or one of my aunts, or a combination of both, who constantly shakes this head of mine from side to side, as if to say, Oh, no, not that, and oh no, you can't do that, and none of the family ever did, and so on.

At the time they were popular I couldn't have imagined a mini-dress on Nectaria; it was unthinkable. Helen is surely an offshoot of the sexual revolution. I think she may even be a punk. Her free-wheeling attitudes and containers of birth-control pills, these are indeed the accoutrements of a time Alicia wasn't part of. Another reason, or the reason, why Alicia takes such exception to Helen; she sees Helen as wild, a libertine, which is strange because I'm sure Alicia is seen or was seen in that way by her parents' generation. I know my parents saw me that way. Libertine or not, Helen isn't happy.

She has taken up painting. Doing watercolors, I think. She bought some colors the other day when she went to Iráklion. I don't know how she got there. It may even have been Roger who drove her. He desperately wants Helen's approval or at least my disapproval. While he continues to gossip behind her back, he's courting her, perhaps fascinated as I am, but I doubt it. I am sure Helen and I are soulmates, which I'd never tell her. Roger must think she's got deep pockets or her daddy does and if he plumbs the well well enough, there'll be something for him.

Helen's head is bent low, at an angle of extreme concentration. Now she scratches her leg. Now she places her hand on her breast and absentmindedly fondles herself, loving herself. She looks up, as if she's heard something, and leaves the terrace. The curtains are drawn. Is she entertaining one of the sailors? No wonder she is unhappy. The boys are inconsiderate lovers; they leave women unsatisfied and fall asleep after intercourse or jump from the bed, pulling at their flies to close them quickly and flee. She's not even afraid of disease. She's grown up with antibiotics. Syphilis means nothing to her. I told her syphilis was first mentioned in a poem in 1530, by Fracastoro. She asked if I chose to remember that or did I remember it without thinking. I talked with her then about the life of the mind and continuity—how ideas and knowledge pass from generation to generation, about the work of intellectuals, who are the keepers of the flame, and that the flame is ideas and art. She asked if I really believed this.

I'm unable to decipher what she believes. Are these quick spurts of sex or love what she wants? I ventured one time to comment upon her casual attitude toward men and she stared at me for a moment, about to say something rather severe, I thought, but then she said that she didn't think of herself as I did and sleeping with different guys was fun sometimes, especially when she was bored and especially since she didn't want to get involved. I suppose this is just now a very American attitude, a young American woman's attitude. But she is so young. I am certain she will feel different later, although she doesn't seem to be full of illusions as I was when I was her age. Helen's young as the country she was born in, and yet she's old too, without those ideals and illusions. What a strange girl. Maybe one has no middle period, no middle age, just a beginning and an end. Countries age fast these days. So did I, I aged fast. Yet I made youthful errors. *Peccati*. When the sins lift from one's shoulders, Dante wrote, one feels lighter, capable of being borne up to Heaven. I don't expect to go to Heaven. Heaven defies logic, and I am logical. A. J. Ayer, I heard, is so great a logician that when Somerset Maugham lay dying, Maugham called the philosopher to his bedside to have him reassure him that life would definitely end at death, that there was no afterlife. There's no sign of life behind Helen's curtains. And I cannot observe her.

I move away from the window and pick up a Greek newspaper. The failed coup against Makarios in Cyprus continues to backfire and reverberate; its dramatic and devastating effects play havoc with political life here, much like our Watergate, except graver. The coup must have been engineered by the CIA. This I have argued with Roger. It is rumored that the junta intended to invade Turkey, too. Madness, madness.

I read the newspaper every day. Reading the newspaper is addictive. But do I do more than observe and keep up, in an endless race with time. I am acquainted with the events of the day and try to stay involved, engaged, and attentive to the world. I rue injustice. But sometimes I fear that I merely repeat others' analyses, that their involvement and knowledge provide me with a semblance of comprehension, about which I am too often uncritical. This is part of my insecurity. Gwen wrote once that I was, in a way, too accepting, that that was a facet of my appeal. It is funny—appeal. Alicia appeals to me, as do Duncan, Yannis, and Gwen, of course—and Helen. She touches me. Of course she is masculine in her independence, androgynous, I suppose, yet quite female. In a disquieting and subtle way, there is something dangerous about her, something in her that I fear and something that I fear for her. I've never thought that before.

My detective Stan Green is not afraid of anything except snakes, which is why he refuses to work in Texas, where the three poisonous snakes of the United States meet, another demonstration of nature's nefarious design. Green revels in the barroom brawl. He's quick with his hands and dances on his feet, like Joe Louis, though he's not brazen like Muhammad Ali. I still want to call him Cassius Clay. Cassius is a fine Civil War name. But it is also a slave name, and I can see why a black man would want to be rid of it. Certainly the answer to the question, what's in a name, would fill a book, and does.

Stan Green is not a bigot but works with cops who are. These are the people he enjoys hitting, as I would, were I not so morbidly afraid of violence and blood. When I was a small child, I accompanied my mother on her visit to the doctor. The doctor allowed me in the room with her when he took her blood. I fainted dead away. I was never interested in experimenting with any drugs that required needles, and this was another reason the poets around the Beat Hotel in Paris disdained me. I first met Wallace there but I'm not sure he remembers. I hope not.

A letter from an old school chum, who, years ago, started to write me for reasons I cannot assay, lies nearby. He, like Gwen, wishes to keep me abreast, though, in his case, I am not sure why. He has enclosed some clippings, but without their dates. President Ford fell down on his arrival at Salzburg, where he had traveled to see Bruno Kreisky and to hold talks with Anwar Sadat. I've never been to Salzburg and have no desire to go. In fact I have almost no desire to travel anywhere. My friend has also sent me a picture of Nelson Rockefeller in a Mickey Mouse cap, with a caption noting that Rockefeller's bogus commission has cleared the CIA of domestic civilian surveillance. "There was no widespread pattern of illegality." Does anyone believe this?

What was it I meant to do? Have Stan Green investigate the murder at the scene of the crime. He must enter the town of Bedlam, where he will view the corpses, study the autopsy report, and, upon arriving at the home of the young alleged murderer, describe in detail the cruel and sadistic manner in which the young murderer stabbed to death his mother and father, after which he dragged their bodies, wrapped in blankets, to the backyard. There the son buried their mutilated corpses—near the grave of the family poodle, Fifi. Unfortunately I can't make reference to Edith Wharton who, at her summer home, The Mount, had a cemetery for her dogs. Stan Green wouldn't read Edith Wharton. Perhaps the murderer's mother would have. Still, it's improbable that the family buried their dog, complete with a tombstone, in imitation of Edith Wharton. In any case I can't for the life of me figure a way to work that into the plot.

From the records of that time, weather reports, and so on—the murder occurred on January 14, 1943—I have learned that it was a stormy night with no moonlight. This permits, indeed encourages, suspense and dread, as I can weave an alarming fabric of stealthy and dark elements against which to dramatize the evening's sinister activity. I must show Green as he follows the bloodstained carpet and the path the boy took as he walked down the attic stairs to his mother's bedroom. She may have turned slightly at the sound of him and probably was startled to see her son at home. Before she speaks even one word, a what-are-you-doing-home, son? he brandishes his knife and thrusts it into her back. A pathetic scream here. Then he slits her throat. He stabs her twenty-two times, plunging the knife in her again and again, until she emits no sounds at all. The son may have heard his father's footsteps. The boy drops to the floor, behind his mother's reading chair, a rocking chair—with pillows, a good effect always. There is blood on his hands and blood smears on the floral-patterned fabric. The father sees the slumped and bloodied body of his wife. In fear for his life, he runs downstairs to his rolltop desk where the telephone is. The son follows him and in a similar manner, with his father's back to him, he plunges the knife in, although he does not slit his father's throat. So much for the outline of this scene.

I type: Stan Green had a hunch. It was the father the crazy kid was after. Green thought he'd seen it all, but in the morgue, back then, looking at the father's corpse, he got sick to his stomach. He nearly lost his cookies. But Stan Green didn't want to think about that now. Green had a job to do.

I may include an act of sexual mutilation. It might add just the right touch and may be appropriate, although it was not part of the original newspaper report. But they wouldn't have included that anyway, at that time. We are much more open these days about such horror. As a knowledgeable detective, Green would surely be able to use his psychological acumen to provoke a response from a neurotic young man with a father fixation. Green could invoke through his own person the figure of the despised father. Green is sharp; he has a nose for crime and criminals. I've already established his nose as big and bulbous, something like a bloodhound's. Using cheap psychology, Green could slyly pry a confession loose; it would be easy as pie for Stan Green. But how to do that? Why do I make matters so complicated for myself? Simplify, Horace, simplify!

My fingers have gone numb. I shake them and hot points of pain pass through each digit as if my hands were an electrical circuit. I take another stab at it. But I'm not in a Stan Green mood at all. That passage, that chapter, will need a great deal of work and fleshing out, I think, to draw the reader's blood. I feel contemplative, not like a sleuthing man of action. Of course Green is, as I am, given to depression, which my publisher attempts to edit out as unmanly or undetective-like. We fight about this each time, then compromise. That is, I compromise. No doubt, out will go "big, bulbous nose," because it's humorous.

I ought really to work on Household Gods. Great-Aunt Martha argued incessantly, just like Gwen. But unlike me or Gwen, she led crusades and carried banners and was in fact one of the representatives at that first women's-rights convention in Seneca Falls. She was a temperance feminist; her husband was an alcoholic. I can't prove this but it seems to me that either her father drank or her husband did. The fury with which she engaged the battle against drink must have had some personal meaning to her, must not solely have been an abstraction. In some of her letters I can detect such discontent; that is, it seems to me, she is not just fighting the good fight.

She is a good woman, a very good woman, her goodness is her goodness alone. She lords her goodness over the brood. It is like a flower is her goodness, it buds and blooms, and it is her armor against him and all that is tainted by the material world.

I have given her a transcendental slant.

My fight is a different fight, if it is even a fight. I am not intemperate, but certainly not temperate, in Martha's sense of the word. My fight may not even be a skirmish. Is each life a struggle? Or does one have to be aware of struggle? I struggle with myself, my sense of futility, my desire to do good and to be original in my thinking, my need to find what is new and to hold on to what is good that is old. I'm actually somewhat less in thrall to and interested in my feminist forebears than in the abolitionist side of the family and the slavers.

I once was witness to a chain gang. A young child, I was traveling in the South with my parents. I couldn't have been more than twelve. I remember the trip as both astonishing and dreadful, the winding roads frightening for what one couldn't see behind the next bend. Gothic, truly. We came upon a chain gang, and I saw a man, a black man, a Negro. Actually he saw me. His eyes caught mine; the look was naked. His legs and hands were shackled. I was never more horrified. After that I began to imagine in the vivid way a child can the tortured life of a slave, the criminality of the white planters and their wives in regard to the treatment of these human beings. Since then, since that time, I have felt deeply that it was slavery that made my country the study in hypocrisy that it is. Reconstruction—! And what did Jefferson say to himself in the early enlightened days?

I've just learned—and how did I not know this?—that Liberia was settled in 1822 by freed slaves. Roger, a Southerner of all things, told me this recently, and I must admit, scoundrel that I am, that I pretended already to know it. But in fact I was stunned at my ignorance and thought immediately to research it further, perhaps to base a novel on the fearless black men. But I don't want to leave this island, and the truth is that some work I ought to be doing requires me to leave it, this glorious place. I cannot.

Instead I tangle with a jumble of family material, letters,

diaries, ledgers, all culled from brief homeside visits, all found in attics or seduced out of the houses of relatives whose guilt I fingered like the best pianist. It is my jungle, my undergrowth and overgrowth, and it cannot be clipped like a suburban lawn. It is uncontrollable, in a way. One's ancestors oughtn't to take one over, and yet they have me. I sit in my room, at my desk, in front of my typewriter, and see them. They are stern, foreboding figures. I don't visualize them, precisely, but will them, will them into being, into a great chain of being, the way I once willed, when I was a small boy, American Indians—Apaches—to stand in my doorway.

I have always been fascinated by my family's history. As a boy I learned that one of my ancestors had ridden with John Brown, and that another, from the Dutch side, traded in slaves. Since that time I have discovered that the Brown story was apocryphal, but on my father's side there were slave traders. Martha was definitely at Seneca Falls; her name is on a list. Martha noted in her journal that Seneca Falls was home to Elizabeth Cady Stanton, who, I think, was too radical for Martha. My father's family is nowhere as worthy as my mother's; Father's was loathsome and evil, I believe. Evil is always fascinating, to me at least, and that side did make the family's money.

I am considered the weak link, but I am a moral man. Many would say I am not because of my love of men, but just as they who would condemn me could not choose anything but heterosexuality—and is that truly a choice?—I could not choose anything but homosexuality.

I linger over lunch, a parsimonious affair. Closing my eyes I drift away for a bit, then focus on a few of the mementos from home that are displayed in my room. The letters and diaries I pirated away are enough; they do count as evidence. This is what I reiterate to myself sub rosa—or is it sotto voce? But I ought to have more material. Still, evidence of what? Lived lives. On bits of paper. Will I ever learn what Martha truly thought of Elizabeth Cady Stanton and why?

Forget rigorous research, Horace. This is how I often remonstrate with myself—just do what you do, what you can, and make it new. Besides, I am outside the academy, and I am engaged in writing fiction. Fiction is true, of course, its own truth, not Truth; yet I believe one must always seek Truth, that is the ultimate quest. Were I to do a conventional history, traveling to Athens for books, perusing its English-language shops, or mailing away for material from the States, as I have on occasion, all this would be insufficient. Asking Gwen to find books for me in New York, that too is inadequate. She is bemused by my interest in slavery, I think, and has refused, in her elusive but deliberate way, to talk earnestly to me about it.

I ought to be at Smith College, researching in its library among stacks of musty tomes and aging letters, sifting through diaries written by people like my ancestors. How far away a place like Smith seems. I knew an English professor there once, he was my lover. Then, after long service to the college, his homosexuality was discovered. He had lived quietly in Northampton for twenty-five years, teaching Milton, I believe, yet he was dishonorably dismissed. It was, it is a terrible thing, a hideous nightmare to live through, and for that I am glad to be here, in Greece, where I won't be bothered. Where do morals lie? That man hurt no one.

Whenever I begin to work and think that all this is inadequate and insufficient, and that I am not Gertrude Stein, or Virginia Woolf, or James Joyce, necessarily it makes it impossible for me to think, no less to write. I cycle like a rat in a maze. My mother thought me perfect and a perfectionist, but then I was her favorite child, for which my brother has never forgiven me. All seems futile—this frail, faded handwriting on a bit of yellow paper which may crumble at any moment and disappear. It might turn to dust, this fragment, this evidence of human life. It might disintegrate in my hot, puffy hands. My father thought me a dilettante, and perhaps I am, as I am one who's not quite sure what he is looking for, or why he looks, unlike Stan Green, who knows exactly what he needs to find. But I think I would know the right thing, were I to come upon it.

Stan Green wouldn't for a second hesitate if he wanted to

visit Helen's John, which makes him, John, sound tawdry, like a bad pun, and this observation rouses me to action, the pun and Stan Green, along with my need for escape. I put on my sandals and find my blue cotton cap that I used to wear when sailing in Boston Harbor. The cotton is very soft now and the blue has faded to a powdery hue from repeated washings. Helen has returned to her chair on the terrace. I wave to her but she doesn't see me, so engrossed is she in whatever she's doing or thinking.

Alas, alack, I am not Stan Green. When I think about that poor dear man, that lovely professor in Northampton, my will simply withers. I do intend to go to the hospital but not today. In a few days perhaps. I am tired just now. I sit down again and take out a novel, Mishima's *Confessions of a Mask*. Now, there is daring! I pour myself some Scotch even though it's early in the day. Yes, I'll go soon, in a few days. There is no rush. Tomorrow or the next day. Gwen may have already received my letter, and I'm sure she'll agree to come and will arrive here soon, bright and quirky. I will telephone her tonight. Who knows what the future has in store? Helen said the Gypsy woman was her age, just a girl, too. She read Helen's hand but Helen will not reveal her fortune. I wouldn't, either.

CHAPTER

6

The hospital is a small building, surrounded by flowering shrubs, in a quiet corner of town, a dusty corner, I might add, where the sun's insistent rays parch everything in sight, except for these colorful plants that bloom against all odds, I should think. I suppose they might grow in the desert. How anything grows here is astonishing. I don't want thoughts of Wallace and his idiotic irrigation idea to seep through just now, but they do, that nutty black rubber tube stretched across a vast expanse of desert, one end plugged into the sand, the other stuck in a huge pool. I can't keep from chortling as I walk into the nearly empty clinic. Yá sou, I exude, smiling broadly at the receptionist. I tell her whom I want to see and she leads me down the hall to a room that is much too bright for suffering and disease, though it may cheer up the sick. It wouldn't me were I sick.

The young man I take to be John is asleep, his head turned toward the window, and there is a gash, still prominent and red, on his neck. But it's not a very wide or long cut, so he must have given up rather quickly. Or perhaps he too becomes weak at the sight of blood and fainted straight away. Even thinking this produces dizziness; I feel as if I might throw up. I sit down and place my head between my knees to recover. I breathe deeply. It would be awful if I fainted. And just now, at this awkward moment, Alicia walks in with flowers in her arms, ruining everything and incriminating me in some way.

You? she inquires. Yes, I say, as if it were really necessary to affirm that it is I. I want to say, Who else do you think it is? Santa Claus? As usual I play for time and dissemble. What are you doing here, Horace? Alicia asks with some annoyance. She tucks John in. He stirs a bit. I am about to come face-to-face with Helen's lover, or whoever he is. Helen asked me to come, I answer. I promptly make the corners of my mouth turn down when they really want to sit up, clownishly like Emmett Kelly's. She did? Alicia asks. Usually, Alicia is not monosyllabic; and her cryptic questions give me hardly any time to concoct necessary lies, my cover story. Yes, Alicia, she did, I respond, giving as little as I am getting. Why do I have to explain myself anyway, I think, knowing full well I ought to. Yet I usually believe in my own fictions.

A relatively long silence is broken by John's opening his surprisingly violet eyes, eyes like Liz Taylor's or those of the teen idol Ricky Nelson, whom Gwen adored years ago, for reasons I couldn't fathom, except that he was, according to her, the perfect white boy, the kind of boy she'd love to spoil and ruin, who would have bored her to death, but she could have embraced him and imagined "Ozzie and Harriet." And like the television program, which Gwen told me about, based on the wholly wholesome American family, Ricky exuded a false but beguiling innocence. Gwen would have loved to mess him up, as she put it. I might want to adopt him rather than mess him up.

Horace, Horace, Alicia says, repeating my name several times, I believe, because I am absorbed in remembering Gwen and me at a Cambridge tea, where she announced to a frail, terribly white woman that she, Gwen, was the product of rape, of miscegenation—Gwen and I were drinking not tea but martinis, in teacups. Gwen hardly ever mentioned her race, so it was amusing and startling, and she was a mere slip of a girl then.

Horace, Alicia says, this is John.

John languidly waves to me and does so with such sweetness that I am instantly under his spell. His thick long lashes fairly sweep the soft skin under his violet eyes. I can see why Helen loved him, if she ever did. There's something wicked and win-

some about him. An Irish beauty, I should think, Catholic, un-
alterably opposed to abortion, I surmise, as if I were my detective
Stan Green. John's smile is akin to Vivien Leigh's. I am the frog
prince, I want to say, and you are Prince Charming. Instead I
say, Helen asked me to come see you, to see how you were doing.
At this he grins and Alicia stamps her foot, a short but vivid
thump. She did? John asks. I nod several times, my head rolling
on its base. I'm very tired, he says. Tell her to come herself,
man, okay? He adds, Tell her she can have my ax. John points
to the opposite side of the room where a long black case with
stickers on it is leaning against a not very antiseptic white wall.
Helen can have his ax; I make a mental note of this. From the
shape of the case and some of its stickers—New York Dolls; Live
Fast, Die Young—it appears that an ax is a guitar, and John must
be a rock and roller, perhaps a punk. All quite in keeping with
Helen. She may have met him at a bar, Max's perhaps, when he
was playing. She may even have been a groupie. Gwen once
wrote me a long letter about several she knew who were fascinated
with her. They were wild girls, she wrote, who thought she
could instruct them in mischief.

John stirs again. His startling eyes gaze on me with an intensity that might consume all of me. I return his look and wonder,
Why not take all of me? He marshals his strength and rests on
his elbows. Then he speaks quite deliberately. Tell her I'm okay.
Not like her sister, man.

After this rather compelling confession, he closes his eyes and
shakes his head from side to side. His eyes still closed, he is about
to speak again. Alicia and I are literally hanging, suspended, on
his every word. I watch his eyes, hoping they'll open again, as
a curtain might for the second act of a play. I'm not sure what
Alicia is watching, perhaps his soft wet mouth. He speaks: Nah,
it's not like that. Don't tell her anything. Just tell her I'm okay.
That's all. She can visit if she wants. It's cool.

Alicia fusses over him, making cooing noises. She smooths
John's hair, then turns to me and peremptorily commands,
Horace, you'd better leave now, which I do, as if being dismissed
by a disapproving teacher. I can see before me Mrs. Wheeler,

my fourth-grade teacher, who did disapprove of me. She is starched and bent over, the weight of her grand bosom too much for her body to hold; it seems to tip her toward the floor. Her pearl-handled cane taps the floor just next to my nine-year-old feet. It's a distinctly unpleasant and memorable sound. "Horace, you may go. Let us hope this never happens again." Will she tell my father? I wondered fearfully. What did I do, what was I, what am I, guilty of? I used to be able to see Mrs. Wheeler's face clearly, but now Alicia's fills that vague space. Alicia's bosom is of an average size, and she stands straight as a board, being, in addition to an opera singer and reasonably accomplished pianist, a practitioner of yoga.

I float away from the room, exiting a dream. I float out the hospital entranceway, past the clerk to whom I gaily, if not idiotically, call out Yá sou, then pass by once more the flowering shrubs, their pink blossoms an incitement to the heat that means to kill them. But to me they are a natural déjà vu.

Not like her sister, John said. He delivered a mixed message, and an extremely provocative one. Her sister, not like her sister. Helen has never mentioned a sister. And he is not like her, not like that. Does this mean that Helen's sister tried to kill herself? Or did she succeed?

Helen's sister may have been or was a suicide. Perhaps Helen's twin sister was a suicide. Helen doubled. There may have been two just like her, sharing a psyche. Two Helens and one John. How differently I am drawn to these young people, these children. They are children but children are not innocent. John, I could mother and father, could imagine stroking and petting, even kissing—yes, that soft mouth, Gwen's perfect boring white boy. But Helen—I love her at a distance, love her platonically. I dare not fondle even her abstraction. My interest is, how shall I put it, more scientific, perhaps. She is of a different tribe and immensely attractive, and it's true that once or twice I imagined kissing her, but only on her forehead. I am avuncular with her. Or try to be. She is like me, I suspect or want to believe, somewhere deep inside her, but her resemblance to me exists below the level of my consciousness and hers. Thoughts like these are why Roger thinks I'm getting senile.

How shall I tell Helen about John's ax? I don't see that I can even mention visiting John, unless I lay the blame entirely upon Alicia. It's always wonderful that what first appears to be a liability—such as Alicia's presence in the hospital—can be turned, in a nonce, to an advantage. It's the obvious course. I'll mention to Helen that Alicia and I went for a walk, and she invited me with her to see a friend in the hospital. John. I had no idea what she was up to, or who he was, and then, when I found myself in his hospital room, in the natural course of things it came out that I was Helen's friend, and so on. It all just came out—and John said what he did about the ax, and her sister; but ought I venture to bring her sister into the first conversation I hold with Helen about John? Tricky. It's Alicia's fault, I'll insist to her like a schoolboy. Helen must know Alicia dislikes her. She doesn't care a jot for Alicia, I'm certain of that, and Helen knows she can depend upon me. I care about her.

Frankly, I don't want to tell Helen any of this, as I am vulnerable to the worst sort of silly charge—being a busybody and a snoop, as well as disregarding the terms of our relationship which I tacitly agreed to that day in my car. In my defense I don't know why I felt compelled to visit John, except that I am often a trifle bored, and I try, in my own way, to make life a bit more interesting, more inventive, more like fiction than it might otherwise be—that is, I consciously do something that a character in one of my stories might, to entertain myself and my readers. It is, one might respond, my rationale. With age I do this rather more frequently.

I'd like to think this is what makes me a storyteller. My mother was a wonderful fabulist and even today I miss the sound of her voice as she turned one of Aunt Grace's visits with her into an intriguing and fantastic event, one full of danger and diversion. As when she told the story of one of her sisters visiting Boston when automobiles were still new to the metropolis. I ought not to have turned against my mother, especially when I remember those bedtime tales that were, in a way, our secret bond. I'm sure my father remained unaware of his wife's late-night confabulations. Sometimes I could barely fall asleep, thinking about all the many exciting events my mother had related. It was she who told me the stories of our family's history, which I know now were part fact, part imagination or desire. She ought to have been a writer. But unlike Jane Austen she didn't put pen to paper after her father and sisters left the room or after she finished her housework, when then, and then only, she had a moment of solitude, a moment to herself.

Instead of being a secret writer, Mother spoke in private to me, and only with me did she abandon her daily life and duties to enter into a world of her own making, an intriguing world. This must have been what impelled me to become a writer, to enter into a world of my own making, a world of literature. I ought not to have turned against her, but then I was a teenager, not much younger than Helen is now. I'm sure Helen has turned against her mother too, though mothers are different for boys and girls, I should think.

I am utterly susceptible to intrigue, my own and others. It relieves my boredom and fills my mind with puzzles and problems that I must solve. I play games, one would say in the current lingo that Helen uses, but I do not want ever to hurt anyone. When I am drunk, it is a different matter. Drinking releases both the worst and the best in me. It heightens ordinary perceptions, dulls my sense of existence as sheer repetition, and alleviates a growing and gnawing ennui, though only temporarily. Sometimes, and it's a feeling I can barely describe, sometimes I am at a table and someone begins to speak and I feel, oh no, not this, oh, not this, not again; and inside me, in the pit of my stomach, I sense I am dying, that the words being spoken by the other are in fact drawing my life from me, bleeding me. At other times I feel I cannot breathe, that I am being suffocated, that the breath of life itself is being stolen from me and I am being buried alive.

Normal boredom is not so dramatic, of course. I became bored with life when I was about thirty-five. It was then that I recognized that there wasn't more to it than there'd already been, and that it would go on and on in a similar manner. I took to my bed for a year and then, years later, moved to Greece.

I move slowly along the dusty streets, watching my shadow, which is more nimble than I. The sun still holds itself firmly overhead, glaring at us mortals, at me and my shadow. Me and my shadow . . . Me and my shadow. Fred Astaire, da-da, and my shadow, strolling down the avenue. In my mind's eye, I wrest the pearl-handled cane from my arthritic fourth-grade teacher, Mrs. Wheeler, and stride across the unpaved avenue. No one notices my dashing movements, for this dance is internal, not of this world, and in slow motion. Time moves so slowly here. Time is a tortoise, not a frog. Take my hand, I'm a frog in paradise, just a frog in paradise. Da-da.

The stores close for several hours during the heat of the day. Shopkeepers dawdle as they pull down the shutters. Salespeople dally among themselves, talking in groups. Their bodies are relaxed, planted in the moment; they are not rushing to the next appointment. In cafés the old men—dare I say that, they may be my age—sit at plain wooden card tables, wearing frayed jackets, and play tavoli, their white heads bent in concentration over the board, their fingers jiggling their worry beads. Small glasses of ouzo may be gulped down between moves, yet none of them ever seems to become drunk. It is a marvel to me. Their wives are at home, attending to their small houses or carrying roasts to the baker's oven. The men have their cafés. The women meet in the tangled alleyways between their houses, and they exchange news. Do they complain about their husbands? Nectaria, who takes care of me and the hotel, Nectaria knows all the town gossip. She is the queen of this part of town as Alicia is the queen of our community.

The covered market is open. It is so grand and plain, so complex and simple, such a home of opposites, of everything and nothing. I could become dizzy merely from the pungent scents and mellifluous rumble of voices. So much life exists here, it bubbles forth from the stalls. Today it excites me, satisfies me, whereas on other days the very same scenes, sounds and smells might bring me to an exhaustion I despair of, to an aggrieved alienation. I love the displays of fruit and vegetables, the range and array of colors any nineteenth-century artist would have envied. Green and purple figs, brown and black olives, ocher nuts, golden raisins, thick white yogurt—some feel it is the best in the world—gray and pink fish. I dislike looking at the various fish, but not as much as looking at octopuses. A cornucopia of delights with none of the razzmatazz of modern life, just a marketplace, just a meeting place, something ordinary to all who live here. Why trade this ordinary beauty, this everyday luxury, for supermarkets. Yet this is how life has gone in the West, and though I am in the West, even in the birthplace of its civilization, as the Greeks love to boast, I am far from its most avid practitioners, far from total modernity, from the city, the sophisticated city I know, love and hate, the city that thrills and repels me. I miss it sometimes but as I grow less agile, I am aware that merely walking down Fifth Avenue would afford so much less of the pleasure it once did. I couldn't walk it as I did in my youth. Why has life gone as it has?

I sigh deeply, audibly, and buy figs, picking each one carefully. I shop only at the stands that allow one to touch the fruit and vegetables. I prefer yellow figs; they are sweeter than purple ones. The market people know me well. The good ones let me do as I please. I take my time but this is hardly a demand here. I am thankful for their familiarity. I talk with Sultana, who has sold me the figs, about some kittens she has and think to ask Helen if she'd want to adopt another. Yá sas, yá sas, I call out, leaving the market. Yá sou, Horace, kali mera, Sultana calls out in return.

The harbor is quiet at this time of day. I eat my lunch rather late, usually in my rooms, an old habit I can't or don't want to break. I look up from the street. Helen's not on her terrace and her curtains are drawn again. Is she being a naughty girl? I'll have to pay the piper with Alicia; no doubt she'll invite me to tea again, which will be more like an inquisition. It is very odd, I'm completely conscious of this, it is odd that I went to visit John, but I could not help myself, and that's what I'll tell Alicia. I had a desperate need to know. Then I'll add, I'm bored and unhappy, and I will complain about Yannis and pluck at the strings of her heart. Then we will discuss men and love and perhaps she will confess her infatuation with John. After all these years—we have in many ways grown up and old or up and down together—she will ultimately forgive me. She must, as our town is too small for petty enmities.

I open the door and find Yannis on the bed, quietly reading, which I like him to do. He may even be studying to please me. I feel a rush of affection for him and walk over to him on the bed and ruffle his hair. He turns and smiles and I believe he may even feel some real affection for me. Would sex now spoil this precious moment? Lust rises in me and my sex responds, rising too. Yannis undoes my zipper and gently strokes me, until I reach a delicious orgasm. I am with Helen's John. I am a young man with long hair like his. We are lying side by side and I am as beautiful as he is. Yannis doesn't want me to bring him to orgasm. This may have been an entirely unselfish act or a mercenary one. But I am happy. I have for a moment forgotten myself, what I truly look like, how foolish I may appear to others and myself.

Yannis moves from the bed. He leaps off it, with terrific ease. I feel old. I am old. Yet, and this surprised me, for I did not expect aging to be like this, my desire continues to be and has remained and remains the same as if I were thirty. It may not be the same as it was when, at seventeen, just a ride on a bus produced an erection, when desire always settled in one's genitals. No, not like that. But with age, desire suffuses one's whole body, one's whole being, and is so much more difficult to satisfy. In a way it is more clearly life itself, life itself that is desire, that is as elusive as fantasy, amorphous fantasy.

I pride myself on being an older man who can rise easily on occasion. I must repeat this to Gwen, which reminds me of why I invited her here. How good it will be to discuss the intimate details of life with a true friend who is, in her way, as strange as I. And she is only twenty years younger, not forty years or more younger than I, as is Helen. Gwen has reached the age of truth. I like to think of my forties that way—the age of truth. And what will Gwen's truth be?

I must ask Nectaria to find a room for her since it won't do to have her stay here. I have my habits, my routines which are fixed, to some extent, although they can be broken every once in a while. There is not enough space, in any case, and Gwen will want her own room, I'm certain. I hope she is no longer using sleeping pills, for they make her cranky in the mornings. Gwen has dreadful dreams, replete with monsters and odd forms of execution, and years ago she became habituated to sleeping pills and has taken them off and on ever since. I've never asked Helen about her drug usage; I assume she partakes now and again. But Helen does not behave as if she uses downers, as Gwen calls them.

As I ruminate on Helen and drugs, I'm struck by a brilliant idea—I could write a crime story based on the alleged suicide of a twin. Pills, of course. The truth of how the twin died will become the object of Stan Green's quest. He must discern whether or not the twin had a natural unnatural death, a true suicide, or whether it was foul play, and the surviving twin sister—I'll make them twin brothers, to disguise Helen—actually and cleverly did her—him—in, by mixing up some pills, let's say.

How can I think like this? I am a grotesque creature.

CHAPTER

7

I walk to the window and discover Helen standing on her terrace, looking in this direction. I wave and we agree in sign language to meet later for dinner. She seems excited. Could she possibly have found out about my meeting John the other day? How could she? That is paranoia.

Nectaria has set up a shower on the roof for those of us who have been here forever. It is remarkable how being on the roof, on top of the world, as Yannis likes to exclaim—his innocence exists in such expressions—on top of the world and naked as a buck, with the sun still strong but not hot, with cool water drizzling down one's body, how one feels safe and clean, truly clean. Pure. I soap thoroughly and scrub here and there, over and over. A Lady Macbeth I am not, because my hands are clean, there is no blood, not even a stain, no visible sign. I am not, I convince myself, a bad man. And when I towel off and breathe the fragrant Cretan air, air that brilliant ancients also breathed, why I know myself to be in a line of humanity of which I can be proud. I wrap my terry around me and descend to my apartment.

I splash my face with the after-shave Gwen sent me, English Leather, which is, I am sure, one of her subtle jokes. I put on my lemon-yellow Brooks Brothers shirt, my yellow-and-white cravat, my white linen jacket, and I am as good as a Graham Greene character or even Greene himself. I often like to dress for dinner, especially after having been rather solitary. In a sour mood, Yannis will stay home, but he will show up later, as he usually does, I am sure. He ignores me as I leave the apartment, but I am inured to him at the present moment.

Roger is seated at a table far from Helen and me. He seems to be in a pensive mood. He's reading a Greek newspaper. He is unhappy, poor dear; he supported the junta and its regime, and liked to say that on this he and the Greek people agreed. Both he and they, he will still insist tiresomely, knew the country needed the restoration of order and a strong hand. What battles Roger and I have had about the censorship of news! Roger could be reading about the wreckage of a Bronze Age ship, recently discovered off Hydra; it is thought to be the earliest known ship-wreck ever found. Probably Roger wishes he had gotten there first, to grab the spoils.

He and I barely nod to each other. It's a mode either of us might adopt which means nothing. Helen has clipped her hair back and seems even younger and more vulnerable. Christos bends over her and takes her order, looking down her shirt, I think. She doesn't, of course, wear a brassiere. Occasionally Helen glances at Roger, who has also only nodded to her; she is not used to this from him. I explain, not caring if he hears, that this is not unusual for Roger and she must not take his behavior personally. She says nothing.

I ask what has she done today. Helen has taught two English classes. I believe she landed the teaching job by lying; she must have told the school she had a college degree. It's a real drag, Helen says. Her students have to learn how to write formal business letters; it's in the syllabus, and she must follow it. Her students are grateful for each bit of information she imparts, Helen thinks, as if one of those bits might transform them into rich Americans. This is how they model themselves upon America. I jocularly suggest that when Ari Onassis and Jackie Kennedy married, they were anointed the king and queen of Greece, and, in a sense, they have encouraged this avariciousness. I go on about Onassis' having an unhappy, jealous daughter; it augurs badly, I say. Helen has compassion for Christina.

I find it hard to be sorry for the very rich, but when I was Helen's age I was also more generous. I bet Christina kills herself, Helen says knowingly. Suicide? I repeat. She nods and strips her fish off the bone. I could prolong the discussion about suicide, but I am too guilt-ridden to do so. How could I even think about a book based on Helen's misery, her alleged misery, that of the suicide of her sister or the murder of her sister, her twin? I swallow my wine and pour some more. To wash down my guilt. Helen may be very, very rich. I hadn't seriously considered that before. I know that Roger has. He has a nose for such things.

She is not disturbed by Roger's impolite behavior. But how does she see him? I wonder. Perhaps she is also undisturbed by John's near suicide. She seems to be. But how could she be if it may parallel even slightly her sister's, her twin's?

In profile Helen's features are perfect. The blue sky, darkening swiftly now, surrounds her moodily. It is as if she were untouched by the cruelty and meanness of life, by the sailors, by John, by death. Perhaps everyone is until one reaches a certain age. That must be it—at a certain age the burden of everything that has happened to one in life achieves a critical mass; suddenly it collapses upon one and, bearing down heavily, weighs one down, and one experiences the enormity of it all. And then we understand. If we do. And with that, the pungent sensation of aging commences.

Still, Helen's reticence marks her as special if not unique, like a piece of art. I treasure her though she undoubtedly has a flaw, not unlike the golden bowl. I'm not sure what her flaw is or how to judge it. Yet I know she has one, perhaps many. These will deepen with age. But she has time, a great deal of time. It is pleasant to sit with her, to let time drift. I am spending her time. I look with her toward the sea. We are silent for long periods. She respects silence. She may be mulling things over or thinking of absolutely nothing. I do find her reticence akin to art, as art makes order out of chaos, and I think there must be a great deal of it in her life—chaos, that is.

The sea stretches before us. I meditate upon the artists, like Turner and Monet, who painted sky and sea, who were bewitched by the grandeur of nature, its unfathomability, its mystery. Nature hides the sea's deeper life from us; normally we see only a watery surface. A painting reflects that surface, containing the chaos we fear beneath. I rely on art and need order, but I'm not sure that Helen does, in the same way. Or if she does these needs haven't yet made a definite impression on her character. She never speaks of art, of paintings, just of music, movies and television, and books, occasionally. At least she reads them.

Sometimes I look at her and remind myself: Helen was born when you were past forty, Horace, or she was born after the Korean War, or during the heyday of the abstract expressionists, which would mean nothing to her. Both aspects of the thought interest me—how old I was when she was born and that she wouldn't care about that art movement or even the Korean War. I was moderately opposed to the Korean War. I was not indifferent to the abstract expressionists, though I was not convinced by them, either. They were so male, for one thing, and I distrusted their blatant masculinity. I admired the surrealists, Duchamp especially; he broke new ground. One saw the surrealists about New York in the forties, during the Second World War. In my heart of hearts, I have to confess a preference for Caravaggio, Matisse, Edward Hopper, and Cézanne. Where would the cubists have been without Cézanne!

In some ways I am in favor of what is new, almost on principle. I will argue this principle to the death, especially with Roger. Pop art was a welcome change—it leapt out when life was so dull, during the Eisenhower years, but it blossomed a little later, I remember. On a visit to New York in the sixties I saw marvelous art exhibitions. Gwen took me to the Factory, where I felt shy, and hung about awkwardly posing, and never did see Andy Warhol. I don't think I could have managed it. I would have had to behave reverentially and he wouldn't have found me attractive. But the boys around the Factory were wonderfully attractive, if somewhat frightening. The ambience was immensely different from that of the Cedar Tavern. Very perverse, but I enjoyed it even if it intimidated me. It was most assuredly a different intimidation from that created by those masculine painters with their burly arms and broad backs, who boldly discussed their paintings and their women—but mostly their paintings—over shots of Scotch and chasers of beer.

I assume Helen appreciates Andy Warhol, though she has mentioned only the group he spawned, the Velvet Underground, not that she ever saw them live, she explained to me. I am used not to seeing things live. Helen has never been to the Cedar Tavern. She has a dim recollection of hearing about it either when she was posing or when she took an art class from a bearded man who wore work shirts, a costume she found funny. By funny I think she means many things, but I'm afraid to pry too much.

It was the beginning of the time when Helen abjured any kind of naturalness and had dyed her hair and pierced her nose, for a nose ring. The nose ring, a stud, horrified Alicia. Smitty wears it less often these days, but when she does, it's worn indifferently, almost as if it were meaningless, and perhaps it is to her. How Alicia went on about it! It fits Helen, though, to transform and mark her body. She is a bold canvas on which everything appears to have landed with abandon, with splatters here and there; and her scars, most invisible to the eye, and marks, tangible and intangible, about these nothing must be said. And no, no explanations will be given.

From her point of view, it may be that we've known each other all our lives, but mine is so much longer than hers. Yet this may account for her not needing to reveal herself to me in any specific sense. When Helen does reveal herself, she does it without guile, as if dropping her clothes before an audience of art students meant to study and render the female form. Along with artist's modeling, she has done go-go dancing and stripping. Do you miss home? I ask her, as the sun dips low, peeking slyly above the horizon.

Helen first left home one summer when she was sixteen; she left it without regret, it seems, and casually mentions having taken up with a couple of guys and having gone on the road with a friend, hitchhiking. It is nearly inconceivable to me that she has actually done these things. Helen stripping and hitchhiking. When she attended college, briefly—and though they were not speaking, I gather—her parents paid her tuition. What did and do her parents think of her? Did John, does he, want to protect her? Do men still want to protect women, if they ever did?

Roger has been joined by a blond Adonis. It is not true that I take Roger's castoffs. It is nearly opposite to the truth, not apposite to it. The blond may be Manolis, one of those feminine boys who fled to Athens. He's matured excellently. Roger will take him in for a while, I know, then tire of him. Roger is a coquette, more coquettish than Helen has ever been, I'm sure. She glances from me to Roger several times, but says nothing. She is observing our scene and sometimes I feel queasy about this. She sips her coffee and asks, rather innocently, Does Roger pay him?

He may, I answer, disconcerted. I'm not sure why this question irks me. Perhaps she thinks I pay Yannis too. I won't ask, though to a girl who has stripped for money this might not mean very much anyway. I change the subject abruptly, but she is unperturbed. I observe that she appeared to be excited earlier, when I saw her on her terrace. Had something happened? I ask. Helen stops eating. It was weird, she begins, which always signals to me some fresh revelation. She was reading and felt happy. She was happy for no reason. Nothing was really different. Yet she seems to have experienced a sudden rush, a release. Everything might be all right, after all. She knew suddenly, she said, that she could be whatever she wanted, because she could simply make it up. She felt freer. The past didn't matter really. It was just a story, and she could always change the story. She asks if I have ever felt like that. Before I can respond, she says, with relish, that the only other time she ever was as happy was when she was watching a movie whose title she has forgotten, but it was as if she were a movie with a happy ending. Helen laughs quietly, her hand covering her mouth. I tell her she's had an epiphany. She laughs even more.

Now she looks twelve. Unbearably defenseless. Part of her mask has dropped, and she's stripped bare or stripping. She may reveal her true self to me. I don't know what else to say to her. I ought to say something else but the expression on her face reminds me of myself at her age. I remember, even sense, my youthful expectation of life's limitlessness, my naive belief in possibility. I would not have compared my self or my happiness with a movie's end, but looking at her, I feel the crush of memory. And, as if memory were physical, it forces me lower in my chair. I drink more wine. I feel queasy, aware of an unspeakable emptiness below my heart. I take her hand and say something to the effect that, yes, Helen, everything will indeed be all right. I shut my eyes so that she won't see that there are tears in them. But she pats my hand understandingly. It is suddenly darker. She is barely visible.

Impulsively, to pluck us from this dangerous and lugubrious patch, I announce what I meant not to tell her. I tell her almost comically, making light of it, that I visited John in the hospital, with Alicia. I emphasize the accidental nature of the visit, my surprise as to his identity and their connection, and so on. You're kidding, Helen responds, and then grows pensive. She adds, If you're not, it's unbelievable. It stinks.

Stinks? I hadn't really expected her not to believe me. I don't see, I answer, why you're so angry. It's simply true. I had no idea, and frankly, dear, I don't like being told that any of my stories stink. Helen withdraws into herself for a while, but she doesn't leave the table. I question why I care, of course, why I allow her feelings any importance at all. She's just a young girl who knows nothing; and surely it is I who invests her with power.

I study Helen and recognize a child, hurt, alone, anxiously searching, looking at the sea and the wide world, which I know is smaller and more inpenetrable than the object of her gaze suggests. Attempting to dismiss her doesn't work, as I genuinely like her and am attached to her against my better judgment. In a state, I nervously consume another glass of wine, nearly gagging as it goes down. Helen speaks at last and claims that she doesn't like liars very much, even though she lies sometimes. "I lie. People lie all the time. But you should admit it." In this moment she reminds me of Gwen.

I've never been able to admit I've lied, to anyone. I'd rather die, and, muddled and soft as I have become, I can't stand her indignant scorn. Oh, Helen, I sputter, I don't see anything wrong in my being interested in your friends and your life. It is not precisely prying.

I am appalled to hear myself sound like a father or mother. John is no friend of mine, she insists with annoyance, he wasn't really even a boyfriend. He's a worse liar than you. Then she pauses and asks if John is trying to move in on Alicia—to move in on rather than in with, I note. Her delivery is flat; it's a sophisticated voice, with little inflection. It's a voice I hadn't yet heard, from her. I am taken aback. I visualize Helen in the city, urbanely testing her young tongue in tandem with similarly dressed girls, who sit in clubs with boys like John. They are clever and wild, the girls Gwen wrote me about. Helen may indeed have been one. When I was her age, I would have been frightened to death by people, young women, like her. It's especially her psychological astuteness that unnerves me. She taps her cigarette on the table, and I light it for her. She looks me directly in the eye. I try not to flinch.

Helen seems to be weakening. After all, I am her only friend here, I and Chrissoula, who can't really talk to her. But now Helen falls silent again. Her silence may deepen into a resolve not to speak. So I do, after drinking another glass of wine; I make myself vulnerable to her. Unquestionably I want to appease her.

Ultimately, Helen, I offer, in the end everyone knows everyone. I don't know why. It must have to do with age, with how the world grows small conceptually as we grow older. We are connected whether we want to be or not. We are all connected. I toss this out, quite off the cuff, but the reasoning will serve, I hope. Then I follow with the connected notion, to my mind, that physicists deem an equation elegant when it's executed particularly well, when it is beautiful, and that makes science close to art. Do you mean, Horace, she interjects, again in that sophisticated voice, do you mean, to you, John and I make an elegant equation?

It is not like Helen to draw paranoid conclusions. I don't know what you mean, Helen, I answer. I am not Machiavelli. Helen agrees that I am not but goes on to remind me that I am a writer. She's known a couple, and even had one in the family, but no one really famous. My mind races through some possibilities, but her last name—Nash—only brings me to Ogden, and I'm sure he's not in her family. Helen may be traveling under an assumed name, carefully hiding the identity of a famous father or uncle, or grandfather. I don't know why I need to, again I'm being impetuous, but I ask, Do I remind you of your father, Helen? She stares at me quizzically and then answers that I do, but only when I ask questions like that. He's a shrink, she says. Helen swallows her retsina in one gulp. A shrink, I repeat after her. A horrible word, I think. A shrink, I say again. Helen adds, Children of shrinks are really fucked up. And, in the definitive way she has said this, it is as if she were bringing to a conclusion my own queries and thoughts.

I nod in agreement. It's as if we are and are not discussing her. She has already told me that she is, as she puts it, fucked up, but now I think she's being ironic, at least in this very moment. This is getting heavy, she says, with a half-smile. Yes, I know, Helen, we are not supposed to get heavy with each other. She laughs again—Helen often does when I use her argot.

It dawns on me that she has told me next to nothing about John and her, only that John is a liar, as am I. She is most definitely artful, and I am still curious. John was a sort of boyfriend. They are not friends. I feel more sadness welling inside me. Children leave each other without a second thought. I was; I did. All those wonderful men, those friends, lovers, and I'll never see them again. Each face is a drop of memory that is diluted by time and dissolves; nothing rests or stays still long enough to form into a clear image. They've drifted away, or I did. Helen doesn't realize how precious all those moments are, and John—how beautiful he is, with those violet eyes and soft lips. I'd hold him to me forever were he mine. I'd love to make love with John. I gaze at Helen vacantly. Perhaps. With her, too. The thought scandalizes me. Am I blanching? Would this idea horrify her? Probably not. I have learned over the years that only one's own thoughts can ever genuinely shock one.

I swivel in my chair, pull myself up and talk to Helen pompously, as if giving a lecture. I suppose I feel the need to appear sensible and knowing, because I am wondering at myself, questioning whether my friendship with her has somehow to do with a kind of frustrated heterosexuality, though I think it hasn't in this case. I am not attracted to her. I do accept Freud's notion of an original bisexuality. Certainly in dreams I've desired men and women, even simultaneously, yet in life I rarely ever find a woman sexually attractive, sexually desirable.

I explain to Helen that art makes virtue out of necessity—the artist must do what he does; he can see no way other than the way he sees. That is vision. Science, on the other hand, makes necessity itself a virtue—that is, it says that nature is beautiful, even though it is cruel. Niels Bohr once told his colleagues, I heard, that the task of physics was "not to find out how nature is, but what we can say about nature." This is much like writing, I go on. Physicists designate equations elegant when they serve many functions, which is part of that beauty. That is what elegance is. I'm defending my earlier assertion, and some other position, my position vis-à-vis hers, but I'm not sure what hers is, except one of disbelief. And she must never guess that I have had, even for the most minute second, a nanosecond, the slightest trace of desire for her. I would never act on it. Am I an old fool like Lear? "O heavens, if you do love old men . . ."

Drunk, teetering on the maudlin, I pursue an ambiguous line, but I cannot stop myself. I cannot go home now. I know I should. The white wine is gone, much of it swirling around my brain. Helen is most certainly by my side. I am close to her, but what does that mean? Am I really close to anyone? It must be the alcohol that has produced this phantasm—that I could bed her, could desire her. I feel not a trace of lust for her. It is all a product of my imagination, mental activity—an inventive kind of willfulness, in a sense.

I focus as best I can. She's probably not concerned yet with elegance, and may never be. It's odd how quickly one becomes or feels drunk. It's true—to me, her father's being a psychiatrist serves a function; Roger over there with Adonis serves another; even Alicia, who is not here, annoying, marvelous Alicia, serves a function—she appears at the wrong times, as she did in the hospital. But what function do I serve? Am I content with thinking of myself as a storyteller? Isn't that too easy?

Wallace, who has just arrived—this I observe with a start—he serves no function whatsoever. He is inelegant. A clod. No, a succubus. The Dutchwoman is with him, propping him up, and with them an aged stooped creature whose face is covered by a beard. I squint and squint. It's Stephen the Hermit. This is quite extraordinary, I exclaim to Helen, that man hasn't been out in years—not in company. He was once exquisitely beautiful, so beautiful. A great beauty. How did they manage to capture him?

Helen turns to look at him and giggles, as she should. It's as if I were describing Tarzan. Tarzan was English, wasn't he? Stephen is English, a scion of colonialists; I would bet on that, were I a gambling man like Rhett Butler. She probably hasn't read *Gone with the Wind*. She must have seen the movie. I am effervescent, giddy, and at the sight of Stephen, light-headed if not light-hearted. Words almost dance off one's tongue when one's mind is addled by drink.

They're coming our way. It's been ages since I've seen Stephen. Roger is coming over too. It's a feast. I feel festive, ebullient. More drink. I call out, Wine for everyone, Christos.

Stephen sits down beside Helen. It is hard to believe that he was once a child movie star. His mother was Hungarian, I believe, his father terribly English and rich, but for some reason or other, Stephen was raised primarily in Rome. There a director cast him in a role and he quickly became a child actor, whose adorable looks were beloved by a nation that worships its bambini. The early attention did little good for Stephen, as he grew up surrounded either by doting nannies, a narcissistic mother, or film crews paid to pander to him. And what does a child know, father to the man.

My word, Stephen now—a sight to behold, a sorry sight. I can't quite believe my eyes. How low a man can sink. Roger and Wallace are arguing about politics, so I needn't join in. I can observe the scene.

Helen is rapt. Weird Stephen, in good form, is talking to her in a respectable way. He flails his arms every now and again, but is in most ways well behaved. English eccentrics are wonderfully odd. Even though he is completely mad, he still retains some of the manners of a gentleman. I hear bits of his monologue; it follows in a seemingly logical order. Perhaps he does make sense much of the time, but as I never see him, how would I know. He makes sense in the forest, with no one to hear him out, and we all judge him so harshly. I am ashamed of myself and turn to face Helen and him. They are blurry shapes. They are good people, I know this in my heart.

I listen wholeheartedly to Stephen, moving my chair closer to his to catch his every word. He has no money, as he has been cut off by his family, almost entirely; naturally they disapprove of the way he lives. He pushes his hair back—long, unruly hair—which exposes more of his face, though there's nothing to be done with his beard. Helen takes my hand, she must know I'm drifting in and out of this world, and squeezes it every once in a while. Sweet Helen. Sad Stephen. The authorities cut off his electricity some months ago, and he lives in a house without light except from that of candles which he's set about his place in tin cans. He'll die by fire. I know it. I feel it. The house will go up in a second, and he will be destroyed, burned to death. No, asphyxiated. It seems inevitable.

An impish smile plays on Stephen's lips. He is exuberant. He declares to Helen, as if exposing a great truth, his great truth, that he has discovered electricity, how important it is, how electricity is magic. He ecstatically enthuses on the power of Light and God, that electricity running through thin wires and cables is the lifeblood of our society. He'd never realized before the way that God was a part of everything, but seeing dots of electric light in houses around the world was proof of God's power. His mother and father had tried to control him through the telephone, but that was not the fault of God or electricity. His daily life was once absorbed in switching lights on and off, and he rues the day he complained of that activity as simple repetition when in fact it was central to his life and all life. Now, without this routine, it's as if he were doing penance. Lighting candles makes him wish he were Catholic but still he misses the radio, the voices that spoke to him and the world. The BBC, the BBC World Service, he can't live without it. He bellows: I love electricity. I love electricity.

Roger, Wallace and the Dutchwoman laugh, first in horror, and then raucously, in morbid delight. Stephen looks about only to discover them laughing at him, staring at him, as at a comedian or worse. He grabs his book bag and shuffles off from the restaurant, walking in long angry strides around the harbor until he is well out of sight. The mirth dies a self-conscious death. Wallace explains that he wooed Stephen out of his ramshackle debacle of a house with the promise of a good dinner. Roger, ever the one to know more than anyone else, Roger insists that Stephen cribbed all of that from Nijinsky, and that he's not mad at all. Just playing possum. Like Pound? Wallace goes on again. Roger notes sarcastically that even madness is unoriginal. I simply won't hear any more of this, I think.

Wallace says that Stephen eats scraps these days. Roger harrumphs caustically. Poor Stephen, I declaim, and, in Roger's direction, ask, have you no pity? I reach for my glass but can barely lift the drink to my mouth. And to think that, by comparison with Stephen, Wallace now seems sane. Roger bothers to respond only with, You're drunk, Horace. Then he turns his chair around so that his back is to me. But where is Helen? She has disappeared. Has she run after our Nijinsky, our Stephen?

Yannis as usual has managed to appear from nowhere, like one of the Furies. He is begrudgingly at my side, but where has everyone else gone. Have I been talking aloud again or thinking to myself? Where is Helen? Yannis grabs my hand and pulls me out of the chair. He walks ahead of me, leaving me to putter along after him. A great rage wells in me. I want to strike him, to hurt him. I mutter something. He looks at me as a wounded animal might, but what have I done? I am infuriated by his reproach. I throw down some money, I throw it down on the ground in front of him. He turns again. There is on his face an expression of disgust so great that I must avert my gaze. Surely he cannot hate me that much. This is a dream, a poisoned vision.

CHAPTER

8

A yacht named *Viridiana* docked in the harbor the other day, a sleek white sailing vessel off of which my friend Gwen alighted, sleepily. She met the owner in Iráklion and took up his offer to sail here with him—a French-Greek millionaire—and his wife, who's just French, and assorted guests. Gwen tells me the vessel sleeps twelve, all in one bed, and I can't decide whether or not she is joking. She remarks that I've been away from the States too long if I don't know.

Gwen is in fine shape, thin and energetic, yet she somehow exudes, at the same time, a soigné world-weariness. While here, she announces, she will work only on her tan, and me. Then she laughs. Gwen hugs me, not too tightly, and mentions being beat but not a Beat, not ever, and later, something about missing the beat or the boat. I'm not sure. She talks very fast, she always has. I'd almost forgotten that.

It's a tonic to see her, smoking cigarettes, drinking coffee, running her tongue over her lips, patting her knee impatiently. Lulu—she calls me Lulu—you're looking well for a beaten man. She is capable of using one word or metaphor all day long, in as many different ways as one could. Gwen views Yannis through her jaded eyes, and it is as if I can see him through them. I know she is suspicious of him and our arrangement, as she is naturally suspicious about everything, and certainly exaggeratedly so about affairs of the heart. Gwen has often remarked she has no heart for the heart, that hers just ticked over and died, stopped beating ages ago, that she goes through the motions. Her heart's wound up, ready to spring, like a dog on a bone, but really it's only the motions, the emotions. Statements of this kind often issue from her, but in fact she continues to fall in love over and over again, even if heartlessly. She has carried on an affair with a friend's husband for years. I've nearly given up men, she confesses. But I'll never quit smoking.

I lead her to her room, which is one floor below mine. A bouquet of flowers carefully arranged and placed in a locally made ceramic vase has been set on the white dresser. Nectaria put the flowers there, to welcome Gwen. I think Gwen is surprised and pleased. People who expect bad or poor treatment are usually overcome by kindness. I would never allow anyone but Gwen to call me Lulu.

It's so nourishing to talk with Gwen. We talk and talk. I embellish the stories about Alicia and Roger, and then offer my tale of Helen. Gwen listens, scrutinizing me, getting the story. Her lips caress and hold tight a Greek nonfiltered cigarette. Her dark eyes, which slant upward, are narrowed. When I've finished, she repeats, You've been out of the States too long, Lulu, you're becoming one of those expatriates. She waves her hands in the air, indicating, I suppose, a dizzy expatriate, a confused one. A predictable expatriate, she explains. Then she adds, Horace, girls like Helen are a dime a dozen. Pish-posh! I exclaim, like a character out of Dickens.

It's been some time since I've seen Helen on her terrace, and she hasn't come for dinner at Christos' restaurant. One of the beauties of this place is that one can make oneself scarce, it's true. One can disappear at will, for a time. Yet Helen may be angry with me. It is no fault of mine that John is living at Alicia's house, surrounded by bougainvillea, and that he is cared for by such a lovely older woman, though to me she is a younger woman. Isn't everyone younger than I? Helen may need to blame me, but I am blameless. Of this event, anyway. The last time we dined, in the condition I was, I may have blurted out something about suicide, about her having had a twin who died. Too much time has passed since then. A few days' absence is normal. And though, prior to Gwen's arrival, I was furiously at work on my crime book, I was unsettled and concerned about Helen. I thought about her and that evening, and then repressed it. I said to myself it is nothing; but then I dwelled on her and it again, and yet I did and have done nothing. Actually I have been waiting to hear from her. But now I think I will send her a note. I will also ask Yannis to go to the market and buy her some flowers to accompany the note. I don't think this can be viewed by Helen as another one of Horace's impositions.

With Gwen here, my absence from home seems poignant. I've been here nearly as long as Helen's been alive. I might become annoyed at Gwen's harping on my being out of touch. No doubt I am, whatever that means. With the zeitgeist, with American life and day-to-day reality, whatever that may be, with the city, the polis. Politics were not why I left America. I'd lost my lover of many years. I had a publisher, a contract, books to do. I was tired of everyone and everything, just as I am now, come to think of it. I had a little money to play with, as I was and am privileged. I loathe people who hide their means of support, though I am no Marxist. I identified during the sixties with James Baldwin, especially when he fled to France, and though I'm not black, and he's years younger, and I didn't suffer the poverty and discrimination he did, I felt close to him. I still feel close to him because of these things and certain details like our bulging eyes and predilection for men. I always thought I'd meet him, but fate has not been kind to me in that respect. He's a marvelous writer and much misunderstood. Gwen knew of my feelings for him, and she's the only person I ever told. She's met him. Gwen knows everyone. She is more than twenty years younger than I. I must ask her how Baldwin is these days. If anyone would know, she would.

The sea is remarkably calm now and the only sounds one hears are small waves slapping gently against the harbor walls.

It is quiet, peaceful. The States is a maelstrom. All those products, and people and clubs, and TV shows. I watched television once only. It gave me a headache. There is some noise here of course. On Sundays the army marches around the harbor. Gwen will watch the parade, laugh her sharp little laugh, and flick the ashes of her cigarette. I never would have marched in protest marches. I couldn't, carrying a banner proclaiming, "U.S. Out of Vietnam," or "Women's Bodies, Women's Lives," and not because I don't believe in the truth of both, but because I abhor the idea of wearing a placard or button. I hate to think that a phrase could in any way, even for an instant, define me. That I could be summed up that way is appalling, absolutely terrifying. I immediately conjure a tombstone upon which my life is reduced to an engraved epitaph.

I am more than a little ambivalent lately. Gwen has never marched, I'm sure of that. Were I to ask her she'd arch one eyebrow and shoot me a certain look, as if to reproach me for reading her so badly. She and I share ambivalence like a biscuit we might break in half for tea. She's more angry than I, I believe, but her anger is carefully muted through sarcasm. This may or may not reveal some truth beneath. I'm sure she still fights, verbally, as she always has, especially when she's tied one on. Gwen loves a wickedly good contest, one of wits, of course. For her there is almost no other contest, except perhaps for love. The love of a bad man, usually.

Some fights must be fought—the Civil War, World War II. I would have liked to have been at Stonewall as a fly on the barroom wall. But I hate physical violence. I was not brave enough, when I was living in Boston, to go on a freedom ride to the South. I drank a toast to them in Gwen's apartment in Cambridge; she drank and said nothing. I cried when King died; Gwen wrote me that she was so drunk that night she lay down in the gutter on Canal Street. But it was not at all clear whether her drinking was in relation to King's death. She allowed that to remain ambiguous. About matters pertaining to civil rights or to the fact that she is black, she has, over the years, said little, almost nothing. I am sure she carries all this within her where she nurses her secret self, the self that would not rest easy in the company of whites, not even men like myself whom she loves and trusts. But I don't really think Gwen trusts anyone. Her cynicism is deeper than the sea out my window and beyond. I can't bear to think about it. I wonder if Gwen's script—Dark Angels—holds these secrets, these surprises, exposes the Gwen I am not privy to. I've often thought that, that her true self and outrage would find release in her personal writing. I wonder if on this trip she will show me any of it. But I know, in my heart, beaten but still beating, that she will not.

Gwen is asleep in the room beneath me. Her proximity provides a homey comfort. That Gwen represents for me a kind of security and sense of rightful place is odd, as she is edgy, always on the edge, always about to fall over to the other side. I sigh audibly and look out again to the sea and to Helen's terrace. It is empty. The sea is choppy.

It is beautiful here. Gwen must or will surely recognize that. Truth must be beauty. Beauty its own truth. With a full heart I go to the typewriter and confront Stan Green as he studies and tracks the young rich boy, stalking him, stalking him, watching and waiting for him to return to the scene of the crime. Blasting with energy I type more than ten manuscript pages. I will make my deadline after all if I continue with such alacrity. Just a little more detective-like analysis and Stan Green will nail the young spoiled criminal to a cross of his own making. I think it will be in a diary he's kept, a small book written in code. Green will crack it.

The sky is darkening. Gwen is still asleep. Perhaps she took a pill. Suddenly it comes to me that the word analyst on Helen's diary may apply as much to her father as to herself. That is, I had assumed she was in analysis, though I never inquired, and now, I remember quite distinctly, she told me her father was a shrink. Her psychological astuteness may indeed be an inherited trait, or one encouraged from birth. Perhaps placing analyst in block letters on her diary's cover was an ironic gesture. She may have been one of those children who was sent to a psychiatrist at a young age. I don't think Helen was a twin, after all. I cannot imagine that that fact, were it so, wouldn't have risen to the surface in these past months. But I do think her sister died. There was some great family tragedy, I am certain.

I know Gwen is going to disabuse me of this and upbraid me. She will most likely tell me that my fascination with Helen has to do with my being isolated, out of touch with my base, or that it comes from alienation, loneliness, or that my desire for progeny can't be fulfilled by Yannis. She'll think of something, I'm sure. I do agree—there is something strange about my relationship to Helen. Her curtains are still drawn. Perhaps she is traveling or hiding. Helen may be spending time with the Gypsy.

Gypsies pass through this way with some regularity, and some have settled not far outside of town. Thousands of Gypsies live in Greece and have for years. But I have always been suspicious of them. It's a prejudice, yet I cannot shake it. I don't understand their ways at all, and they have not yet come into my mind as individuals. Alicia has some sociological books on them. I think I'll pay her a visit while Gwen sleeps. It's still early for dinner. I'll just leave Gwen a note and toddle off. See Alicia. And John, of course.

Generally I like this time of day. Dusk elicits neither happiness nor sadness. It doesn't demand a precise response. The boats are rocking gently on the water. The slight nip in the air is invigorating. I walk briskly up the hill to Alicia's house. I knock boldly on the thick wooden door. John answers and lets me in. His neck is healed. He wears a small bandage on one part of it only, which I suppose is the place where most of the damage was done. I shudder to think more on it. His violet eyes, I detect, light up at the sight of me. How curious—he's glad to see me.

Just a short visit, I explain quickly, embarrassed. How's Helen? John asks in a muffled voice. She's well, I lie, since I most assuredly don't know how she is. He makes his inquiry at the base of the stairs, out of Alicia's sight and hearing. He dawdles, waiting for something more, some more meaty disclosure, and as he dawdles, he scratches his cheek lazily. His cheekbones are high, and today he reminds me of a foppish lad I went to school with. I want to offer other, better information and thus add portentously, She's taken up with a Gypsy, John. A girl, woman. Yeah, John snorts, what is she going to do—live in a cave? I shouldn't think so, John. I answer him with as much dignity as I can, more for Helen's sake than my own. She's much too urban for that, I insist.

I follow him up the stairs. His tanned feet are bare and dirty, and I recall following my first lover up the stairs to his bedroom when his parents were away. His feet were very dirty too. He committed suicide many years later, I heard, which also reminds me of John and his recent botched attempt. When I knew my first beau, he was furtive and guilty but he possessed a mad sense of humor. In those days a practical joker was much prized, a wicked but wickedly appropriate spoof much appreciated. I once was served coffee in a porcelain bowl, not a cup; I spent several minutes searching for the piece that holds the index finger. My friends howled as I spinned the bowl around, again and again, feeling but not looking for the handle. My friends knew I never looked at what was in front of me when I was engaged in conversation. It is the same today. Many things do not change, though we Americans expect everything to change all the time, which is why we are so easily disillusioned.

Alicia is reclining on her Moroccan couch. She's in blue, a violet blue. Her cheeks and nose blush pink and there's something indefinable about her mood. Were I a vulgar man, I would imagine she'd just had an orgasm. An orgasmic flush had spread over her precious womanly body, that's how our South African Don Juan, Wallace, might pen it. She's lost weight, I think, though I'm not really able to imagine what Alicia's body is like. She wears flowing robes and loose trousers and shirts. She waves her hands in the air grandly when making certain points. Her wrists are thin and delicate, her hands well-shaped, each finger pink and clean, her nails are covered in a clear polish. When quite still she seems active or about to be. One might call her intense. She moves with her mind. Your mind races ahead of you, Mother used to say to me.

I've just been playing the piano for John, Alicia says, and touches her brow as if the heat of playing had overcome her. She sang for me, too, John declares, looking down. I hate opera, but when Alicia sings, it's okay. How wonderful of Alicia to sing for you, John. You haven't sung for me in ages, Alicia, I complain petulantly. She smiles patiently.

Alicia is all pink and blue, like wallpaper in a baby's nursery. She hasn't sung for me in a long while. I used to cherish her private recitals, sung on nights that were gray and rainy, in November and December, when the mistral blows this way. She would clasp her hands under her breast, purse her full lips to contour sound, shaping it this way and that with ovals and circles; she emitted lovely bell-like tones and her voice transported me. I had assumed she'd given up singing, at least in company, and feel rather peeved that this scruff of a boy has become her audience.

On the other hand, this scruff of a boy is immensely pretty. Alicia and I both look at him at the same time and then look at each other. Much passes in this glance. She offers us wine, my favorite, Demestica, which I cannot refuse. My curiosity about their relationship grows by leaps and bounds. How are you spending your time, John, and will you stay here long? I inquire. Alicia directs her attention to him with an interest as great as mine. Obviously she must also be in the dark about his future plans. He swallows his wine, wipes his mouth, and says he hasn't decided, but he doesn't think he'll be here that long, because there's no way he can do his music here. Also, he says he's nearly out of money. Impulsively I respond that I need some carpentry done, if he does that kind of thing, bookcases and so on. He perks up, observing—inspecting?—me from under his long dark lashes. Those violet eyes. Alicia seems surprised or startled but not upset, I think. The question one always wants to ask of truly ravishing individuals like John is how well aware of it are they.

The wine loosens John up; he becomes almost voluble. He likes Greek food and espouses reasonable sentiments about the people, all nuanced by a fashionable coolness and a studied in-articulateness. He seems a distrustful type, I think, but like most callow youth, betrays an enthusiasm for life—against his will, I should imagine. He discusses bouzoúki music and is apparently somewhat knowledgeable about musical instruments. He talks of modalities; I think of Joyce and modalities, the ineluctability of the visible, wasn't it? What is ineluctable here? Alicia and I are ineluctable modalities, and John is rapturous dissonance. During the day, John tells me, he fishes down at the end of the pier in the harbor and catches enough for their dinner. He wiles away many hours with hook, line and sinker—and bait. A rock-and-roll Huck Finn, I suppose. The doctor cautioned him to be quiet, which is what he's doing, and of course he's not taken any drugs in weeks. Which drugs, I do not ask.

I tell Alicia and John that I have a visitor; my best friend, Gwen, has arrived, I explain, and John asks, Gwen who? Gwen Duvanel, I answer, and he says, Wow, her. She's cool, man, a scenemaker. Gwen? I say, surprised at the appellation, Gwen, a scenemaker? What a strange term, I announce, she's much more than that . . . Oh, I don't mean that's bad, man, you know, it's a sixties word, scenemaker, and she's kind of sixties, John says quickly, and, you know, she's still on the scene, and for someone pretty old, she's heavy, great.

Pretty old, I repeat to myself. I know that Alicia is also repeating that to herself and that the phrase is reverberating within her, too, somewhere.

Now I am sure they haven't slept together but that Alicia lusts for him just a little, or maybe a great deal, perhaps in a *Death in Venice* way, which I too could easily fall prey to. This thought invades me, nearly an epiphany of the negative. It feels unpleasantly real, and might be ineluctable. That is, once I have placed all of us in this narrative, I might just be determined to see it through. I am a perverse creature. But, I remind myself, I don't need John, as I have Yannis. But he doesn't and cannot negate John. Fantasy is fantasy, literature is literature, destiny is destiny. And I, I live life for art's sake.

Overwhelmed almost by the sight of John now, having articulated this desire so brazenly to myself, my secret self, I tell them I must return to Gwen, who will probably be awake and hungry.

John will come to my rooms tomorrow, he says, to see if he can do the work, man, as he refers to me. Man, I think to myself, yes, that is surely what I am. I rush to the door, as if to escape fate.

But the die is cast. I walk into the hallway, followed by Alicia; she is close beside me. I exclaim, Oh Alicia, the books. Which books? she asks. Yours. On Gypsies, may I borrow them? Of course, but I didn't think you had any interest in Gypsies, dear. I do of late, I say, abashed. Yes, she answers, of late many things are different. Alicia takes my hand. Helen no longer comes for her piano lessons, she adds almost ruefully. Have you seen her? she asks. No, I haven't. I think she is angry with me. You see, Horace, I was right to distrust her. Alicia, you distrust everyone. I was nasty to her. You were probably drunk, Horace, I worry so about you. Pish-posh, I sputter, I'm made of sterner stuff than you think.

Standing there, holding Alicia's soft hand, I think, rather suddenly, I'll have a party. And instantly blurt out, Alicia, come for a party the end of next week—won't you? And John. For Gwen. I'll invite the whole crowd, Helen too. What do you think? Alicia responds thoughtfully, What I think is, I hope you know what you're doing. She kisses me on the cheek. I look toward the living room and admonish waggishly, I hope you know what you're doing, too.

Alicia glides to the bookcase and gathers several books from the shelves. She hands them to me and looks steadily into my eyes, as if to unfrock me, then answers, much too wisely, I know as much as you do, dear. Alicia always has to have the last word.

CHAPTER

9

Yannis enters my room, agitated. His disturbance has something to do with Roger and the blond boy who was with him nights ago. Yannis is so angry I can't apprehend what occurred. *Sigá, sigá*, I say, to quiet him. Just tell me, slowly, what happened. Yannis reports that he was fishing with the blond boy, the friend of Roger, as he puts it. Roger came upon them and accused Yannis of stealing his fountain pen—a beloved object inherited from his father—and perhaps some money, too. Yannis became, and is still, infuriated by Roger's attack upon his character. Rightly so. Roger must have been drunk, I explain to Yannis, he could not have been in his right mind. I make circles with my index finger, next to my temple, to emphasize Roger's alleged craziness. I will write him, I continue in a consoling tone.

Right then and there I take out my best-weight letter paper and begin the salutation. I intend to handle this unappealing matter directly and with speed, but I will also invite Roger to the party for Gwen. Two birds with one stone; one bird to take the sting out of the other, for it is possible that this mild rebuke may be unnecessary. Yannis may be concocting the story, or something else may have transpired, which he has been canny enough to cover up through the invention of this tale. I look at Yannis, who seems earnestly angry. I don't want an all-out war with Roger; our nightly sniping is mission enough.

The door opens. Gwen has emerged from her beauty sleep. Naturally Yannis is not delighted to see her, being in a sullen mood. I too am a trifle agitated. I hate these kinds of bizarre disturbances. Also, I am anxious that what occurred among Roger, the blond boy, and Yannis may be revealed to be of a sinister nature, much darker and more convoluted than what I've heard, though for Yannis to be accused of theft is dark enough, for him. Still, my guess is that a piece is missing from this puzzle.

With Gwen present I don't want Yannis and my unpleasant conversation to proceed. I place the letter paper under the blotter. Yannis stands by my side, still looking over my shoulder, though I have stopped writing. I halted mid-sentence—didn't René Daumal die mid-sentence when writing *Mount Analogue*? Standing thus, Yannis surely is an ominous figure, or at least an unfriendly one, to Gwen. Though Gwen must be accustomed to surly and unruly types—bouncers, rock-and-roll musicians, scenemakers and the like. They probably do not disturb her, whether or not they offend her. Incivility is unnecessary. People ought to behave, to attempt first to be polite, to respect each other, simply to make the world a less disgusting place to exist in—for oneself if nothing else. Otherwise we are mangy dogs.

After a definitive gesture—I cross my hands over each other several times—I stand and look directly into Yannis' dark, angry eyes. When he seems as if he is not going to give ground or relent, I brush past him, insisting, in an aside, *Telos, telos, endáksi*, okay? He turns abruptly and stares at Gwen, glowers at her I think, then retreats into his room. I'll deal with him later.

Telos, she repeats. Quel droll. To know the end now, Lulu. Wouldn't that be marvelous? The puffiness and dark circles beneath her eyes cast her as the sophisticate, a moody one at that. She could never play the naive ingenue. They never go, she says, touching the soft skin beneath her eyes, the area she designates as her pillows of tormented pillow talk. I brew some coffee; she stretches out on the chaise longue and lights a cigarette. She is about to spin a tale for me, I can tell, and I get as comfortable as I can, hoping that my bones won't ache from sitting and that my fingers won't go numb. I treasure Gwen's stories.

In New York, Gwen was caught between two friends who had become lovers and who were fighting like mad and drawing her into the fray. Daily telephone calls lasted for hours, first one of the furious lovers, then the other, to tell his or her side of it, the recent split-up, and there were threats of suicide as well as indiscriminate pill-taking by both parties. Mandrax was the drug of choice; an orgy drug, for some, she adds, waiting for me to react. I don't. Gwen was not beyond reproach from either of the lovers, since when they made up, which was as often as they split up and as impermanent, both would vent their fury upon her. Why had she said this to that one and so on. Comical and boring, a miserable situation. One of the pair had slept with the enemy of the other, and the question was: Was her sleeping with him a deliberate attack on the other's career? Quel drag, Gwen intones.

Then there were her own intimate relationships. She was still seeing the Hunk—Gwen has a nickname for everyone—the married man. It was abundantly clear he wouldn't leave his wife, and it was also clear that Gwen's remaining close to her friend, his wife, was entirely untenable. Untenable for ten years, I remark, not without some acerbity. She ignores me as only she can.

The New York scene was appalling. Tacky. The boys were becoming younger, and she'd slept with two girls, both of whom became serious about her, the older woman, much to her chagrin. Life was dreary. The seventies were boring to her, in one way, and outrageous in another, and they were half over. This too was depressing. She was unable to get into punk. She was tired of the clubs, none was what it used to be. I'm not what I used to be, she says. She feels old, but can't stop herself from devouring whatever's around, tawdry remakes of the un-original. Rebellion had reached new lows. A teenybopper punkette spat on Gwen's neck at a club called CBGB's. She wasn't sure at first what it was—perhaps a leaky roof. She looked up but saw nothing. It happened again. Finally Gwen turned around in her seat to find the idiot child smiling at her as if she'd given Gwen a gift. Gwen was too drunk to respond. Small indignities reminded her that the times were truly silly. Quel zeitgeist.

She was drinking too much, sleeping with too many kids, or

tots, as she calls them, staying out until all hours, not getting anything done. She hadn't accomplished any real writing in months, almost nothing on her script, Dark Angels, nor had she done any research in ages—she's exploring the relationship between Emily Dickinson's spare poems and some nineteenth-century American painting. For money she was editing manuscripts for several publishing houses and was doctoring one low-budget movie script. She has written several dissertations in her time, earning doctorates not only in art history, which is her field, but also surreptitiously in American literature, sociology and German history. Gwen considers herself a ghostwriter with range. Her only release and comfort is in reading. She visits with some of the old crowd from Cambridge, but there are new friends too, who come and go.

My life is a revolving door, Gwen says, not the door itself but the spaces in between. Lulu, she opines, we're all stale as week-old white bread. We are not vrai gay.

But Gwen's eyes light up gaily when she talks about him, the great passion, passion criminelle, of her life. The leather-jacketed rock-and-roll singer still invaded her dreams and bruised her life. He was around, as she puts it, a vague expression to match his vagueness, around even if around meant only late-night telephone calls which woke her from tortuous dreams of him. He might appear at her apartment at 2 A.M., eat a peanut-butter sandwich and complain of problems with his group. She might meet him at an after-hours club where they'd talk and drink and then she'd find herself alone again, alone and high. That was all. Her feelings for him were not at all vague. They were, rather, pitched at a high frequency and quite romantic for someone as cynical as Gwen claimed to be. She is feverish about him, in fact, after all these years. I am always true to him in my fashion, she laughs dryly.

Gwen is a dry martini, shaken briskly, with a small onion, no, an olive—the green and red go well with her skin. The rock singer's habit was more for heroin than for heroines like Gwen. She knew she wasn't his type: she was too bookish, not sexy enough, too small. Perhaps, we both speculate, he likes boys better. Gwen interjects that she likes boys better, too. Maybe, Lulu, she speculates dispassionately, I'm a faggot like you. Gwen looks down at herself, taking her own measure or casing her body as if it were merely clues to herself. There is wan dismay on her thin face.

Dramatically I exclaim, I'm a Victorian faggot. Then, bending from the waist to produce a small bow, I pour us more wine. No, you're not, you can't be, Gwen goes on tipsily, there weren't any faggots then. Wilde was a homosexual, which was very avant, but he was no faggot. If he had been, he wouldn't have sued Lord What's-his-name. Gwen drags on her cigarette. Lulu, let's think of you as the Sugarplum Fairy. She chortles and finishes her glass of wine. Sugarplum indeed! Hummph, I respond, much like a foppish Father Time. I finish my wine too. I'm an Edwardian faggot, I utter finally, or I am no faggot at all. Terrible word really for us, I insist, bunch of sticks on peasant women's backs. I'm thinking of course of my day with Helen in the country and the peasant women in the road, but Gwen doesn't, cannot know this, and she arches one eyebrow.

A faggot might indeed sue Lord What's-his-name. Mightn't he? I wonder. I feel quite ill at ease, truth be told, with some of the young gay men who come here from the States from time to time, given my address by Gwen. This might be because they are so very young, chic and high-spirited, but it may be other things too. I was raised in a much different time, after all, and though I am sympathetic to the cause, still they sometimes strike me as bumptious and nearly patriotic, in a sense, to their newly fashioned identity and freedom. Their fervor I do not completely or comfortably share. I wouldn't admit this to Gwen, although she may agree, being herself no patriot about anything. Roger calls people such as these enthusiasts. I would argue with him to the death about such a term, if he used it pejoratively in relation to our brothers. For I feel I ought to experience such—a brotherhood—and yet I am disquieted by it, with the notion itself. Camaraderie has never been easy for me. In any case I am an ambivalent enthusiast. I am also too old to mend my ways, if indeed they need mending. I am not sure that one ought to be proud of anything, though I do take pride in some things. On the other hand, I do recognize that self-esteem is important.

But I am stunned by Gwen's admission—that she feels old, too old for punk and the clubs. Of course this makes her more like me than ever, and ought, in a way, to please me. But it doesn't. To me she will be—and I suppose I need her to be—eternally, even prosaically young, forever at the age I met her. She is the outrageous art history student, the life of every party, and so forth. You'll always be young, I exult, impassioned. No, no, she demurs. As if she means it, she repeats twice, I'm over the hill, Lulu. Then she laughs at herself, more for using the phrase "over the hill," I think, than for anything else. A second later, she is pensive again.

Gwen rarely smiles; she laughs but doesn't smile. I'd nearly forgotten that too. Instead of a smile, her lips might straighten into a narrow dash, a printer's em-dash—she's a literary type— or move into a grin that is more nearly a grimace. This is especially obvious, I remember, when she meets people for the first time. She is in her own way shy, I think, though most people would think her arrogant. She's terribly afraid, I think, of being in new situations and is enormously vulnerable, quite easily given to feelings of rejection. As I stare at her now, I wonder if this has to do with her being a woman, black, or both. I think I wonder this now somehow because of Helen. Helen is bold about being female, her own kind, and almost aggressive about her differences from others. She had no problem telling me that the Westerns I loved bored her. And then there is the way she snapped at those Greek men. Years ago I hadn't ever reflected seriously or thought too much about how different Gwen was and might be from me, our backgrounds and so on. Years back I didn't think about it. Perhaps it is only distance that allows true reflection.

Gwen is lounging languidly on the couch; still she's quite contained at the same time. Her feet are plugged under her bottom, her black pumps strewn on the floor. Her fitted gray suit— she often wears mannish suits—gives her a there's-no-foolishness-here image, but the wineglass balances flirtatiously and contradictorily in her hand. She has painted pale purple polish on her short nails. Lavender-blue, she calls it.

My unsmiling Gwen. It's as if she proclaims to the world, I may be masochistic with men but I'm damned if I'm going to be servile as well. Or that may be the way it is with me, what I, Horace, would say to the world had I as much courage as Gwen. For though she is terrified, she moves about and into worlds I myself shrink from. She dares herself constantly not to be afraid. Perhaps the most courageous people are the ones who are most afraid. Imagine, I think to myself, the fear of a mountain climber. Or a social climber. It is really difficult to sift other people's feelings from one's own. Especially when one feels close to the other.

Gwen has picked up one of the books I borrowed from Alicia, the one titled, simply, *The Gypsies*. She is leafing through it, reading a bit here and there. She looks at me quizzically. I tell her they're Alicia's books. Gwen met Alicia a few years ago, but Alicia and she didn't take to each other. Actually I think Alicia liked Gwen, but Gwen didn't give her the time of day except to talk about opera. At one time Gwen devoted herself to opera and ballet, one of those people who knew the best cheap seats at the Met, very disdainful of those with season tickets who didn't attend, leaving their seats vacant. Years back I told her she ought to be grateful, for she could move from her cheap seat to one of the better ones. Gwen reproached me in no uncertain terms: being grateful was not a feeling she easily owned.

She inquires if I am killing Gypsies in my next crime story. Certainly not, I assure her, nothing of the sort. It is research for myself, for a special project inspired by Helen. I explain that Helen is most likely off with a young Gypsy woman, and that I have become interested in the subject. It is Gwen's turn now to harrumph, Quel exotic. She brings up a letter I once wrote her in which I went on at considerable length about some Gypsies here, who I thought had stolen from me. I am forced to admit that I am prejudiced against them, but find this a failing in myself, I tell her, and then I go on, no doubt pompously, about how, if one studies a subject, or engages it in a serious way, it becomes impossible to hold on to the same prejudices. Gwen contends that my belief in the power of reason ought to be examined, that prejudice is not reasonable. Though I wouldn't know about that, she expands listlessly. She laughs again. She is nothing if not ironic; and I ought to take her up, I know, but I have launched into a train of thought that leads to the conclusion that we study what we hate as much as what we love. Yes, Gwen says, we study our demons. And our demons won't let us go, Lulu. For a second Gwen appears desperate, at a loss when she is never at a loss—for words at least. I don't know what to do or say. She tells me to forget it. She says she's quite all right, just a little tight.

Did I look stricken? I wonder. How I hate being given away by my eyes, by myself. I offer her some cheese and bread—the bread is a bit stale, like that metaphor she offered about her group. She eats a bit and complains that I am in no way a Jewish mother. Perhaps I'm a Greek mother, I say. Does that mean I am a father? We laugh together and some of the tension passes. Then I announce, with no little anxiety, that John, a handsome young musician, an ex-beau of Helen's from New York, will be here tomorrow to see about building bookshelves. Gwen and he will certainly meet, and in anticipation of that meeting, I must explain his presence beforehand, I believe. I don't want any more unruly surprises. Gwen shoots a knowing we've-been-here-before look at me. I expected this. I can keep nothing from her, at least nothing that is about love or lust. To deflect her curiosity, I remark, rather more loudly than I want, You're making quite a name for yourself, dear. John knew who you were. Gwen grimaces, inhales deeply and sips her wine. She asks rhetorically, because how would I, out-of-touch Horace, know if she ever slept with him. You know how forgetful I am, she says; then inquires disinterestedly, he's staying with Alicia? Such a woman. She emphasizes woman. Clearly Gwen remembers that she doesn't like Alicia, but I don't remind Gwen that that aspect of her supposedly bad memory has not suffered injury. Also I don't repeat that John referred to Gwen as old. I have no desire to hurt her.

Perhaps Gwen grimaces because she is nearsighted. She refuses to wear glasses. I have learned to accept the fact that she subscribes to Parker's "men seldom make passes at girls who wear glasses." As I said, I do believe she is very much like Parker. Gwen is vain. Often she cannot recognize friends on the street or at a party unless they are right in front of her. She uses this to her advantage—she can shun people and seem not to and can always say, I didn't see you. I'm as blind as a bat. Then she might wink. The literary line which divides her face cryptically, or critically—it is doing so now—allows her the liberty of ambiguity, or rather the solace of ambiguity.

I'm throwing a party for you, dear. I'll invite everyone. *Tout le monde*. Gwen smiles and grimaces. She hopes that I serve food, so that people don't retch all night and the next day, as they did in Cambridge that time, our last and most infamous New Year's Eve party, which ended in a near-riot. Recalling it makes me laugh uproariously. I twist or roll in the chair and hold my sides, then lose my breath and begin to hiccup. Gwen watches me steadily, with some concern. You don't laugh enough, Lulu, you're out of shape. When the hiccups stop and I catch my breath, I explain that memories have come flooding in. Of our friends vomiting? she asks, deadpan. I shake my head and start to laugh again. I was also thinking of much more pleasant things. Remember Peter collapsing into his lover's arms? Pleasant, Gwen retorts. I ignore her. Remember George, absolutely blotto, collapsing, after much Scotch and many pills, remember how he crashed upon the table like a giant redwood cut at the stem? Timber, we shouted. Timbers we called him afterward, for a long time. He's gone, Gwen notes cryptically.

Perhaps it is the mention of death itself that is cryptic. Or those times at that café, I go on, I forget the name of it now— and our arguments about New Criticism with the social realists. This in turn reminds me of a recent argument I had with Roger. He believes that a work of art's greatness can be measured by the difficulty with which it can be copied. Gwen finds this viewpoint hilarious, as do I. Roger claimed, repeatedly, as if speaking to a dead man, that a Vermeer couldn't be copied. But I won the argument by insisting that a Jackson Pollock would be much harder to copy, as it was executed not by the careful application of paint but by employing randomness. How, I said to him, my voice mounting in vehemence, just how would you copy, exactly and precisely, a splat? A three-dimensional splat at that? Gwen salutes me.

I prefer Picasso to Pollock, though Gwen doesn't. Quel stupid is your Roger, says she. How do you stay here, she asks again, if you have to engage in boring arguments like that? Please, Gwen, I answer, with more annoyance than I mean to show, let us decide that this subject is off season, shall we? I am here, that is all. You are in New York and from what you report, it is not so marvelous there either, and we will not have a pleasant time together if you keep harping on this place and its obvious inadequacies. I enjoy these inadequacies. And why not, I think to myself, enjoy them. All right, Lulu, Gwen nods, and studies me in her inimitable way. All right, Lulu, you win. You witness the demise of a scold. She suggests that we drink to our inadequacies, which we do. The matter is as much as resolved. An understanding has been reached on the subject.

The rest of the night speeds away. Somehow, attempting to envision it now, I see an image, myself lying on the floor absolutely still—I am pretending to be a log. This may have had to do with Gwen's wordplay about letting sleeping logs lie, and so forth. I seem to recall something like that. Or it may have had to do with another mention of our dead friend Timbers. Or it may have been produced when I was laughing and rolling like a log.

In the morning Gwen's pumps are still on the floor under the chaise longue. She is nowhere in sight and Yannis too has disappeared. With her shoes there, it's as if she'd melted into thin air, like the city of Oz or, more ominously, like the Wicked Witch.

Melting has a mysterious and fluid quality to it that attaches itself to Gwen, who has a wonderful plasticity to her. She can fit herself into so many scenes, as John might put it. But Gwen is not magical in the way that Helen is, I mean, not as mysterious to me. Mystery might have its roots in magic. Gwen has her feet on the ground, even if she abandons her shoes. As for Yannis' absence, about this I experience some trepidation. On the other hand, John will come soon, and would I really care to have Yannis hanging about being surly?

PART · II

THIS STRANGE

DISORDER

CHAPTER

10

It occurs to me that part of this story transpired before certain revelations, before some events occurred which disturbed my peace and the pace of this narrative, such as it is, which I was in no way able to predict or even to imagine. Looking back on it, the life I lived and am recording had been orderly and relatively contained. But at the time I lived it, I sensed myself, inarticulately, to be not quite in it, holding on rather tentatively, threatened by something, a presence or other who might be waiting in the wings, and who might make me lose my way, lose my grip. I was always at the brink of that, staving it off. Dante expresses it so elegantly: *Nel mezzo del cammin di nostra vita / mi ritrovai per una selva oscura / chè la diritta via era smarrita.* Yes, "In the middle of the journey of our life, I came to my senses in a dark forest, for I had lost the straight path."

I did not see Helen as an impediment, but took her for a miracle, my Beatrice, if you will. She existed outside my world, and so was a delicacy, an entity delicious in it, drawn into it but separate from it. I embraced her without reservation. To me she was unaccountable and yet, within limits, delightfully unmanageable. Now I see that my habits were designed precisely to control my world. And that I deigned to do so was typical of my approach to life before a certain dramatic break in my thinking, perhaps not dramatic, but one of import to me, and one which necessarily affected my daily routines. And surely one might—I will—call that dramatic.

John is due to arrive at noon. Yannis is nowhere to be found. I have already spent most of the morning writing, which included invitations to the soirée for Gwen. Yannis has not been home for several hours, not counting the evening hours. Yet this is not terribly unusual. He must have gone home to visit his mother, a widow. I believe he shares with her some of the money I give him, and that is perfectly all right with me, though he never tells me precisely what he does with his allowance. Nor do I ask. I assume he thinks I would not like it, were I to know, but in fact I do, very much, as I feel my largesse supports those who need it. This in turn supports me in feeling worthy and virtuous. After all, I am the scion of Calvinists and Puritans, an upbringing that still adheres, in some respects. In addition I have heard that Beauvoir and Sartre support the people around them, their adopted family, and I admire that greatly.

John appears. He is late but he looks beautiful. I would say as usual, but this afternoon he has a glow on. That is how my English friend Duncan might put it. Duncan would sleep with him right off, without so much as a by-your-leave. He would know just how to seduce a supposedly non-homosexual lad into his bed and into imagining that just this once made no difference whatsoever, that, no matter what, he was as good as new, still a man, that life goes on, and in fact it may not make a difference and life does go on. Duncan with his lime-green eyes and catlike cunning—Duncan would simply charm and charm and then pounce. But Duncan is younger than I, and even when I was younger, I never pounced. I am not the pouncing type. I am cautious, unless I am drunk, and then I don't care, and no one else does either, I should think.

John glances about my rooms with no hint of self-consciousness. He takes them in and I drink him in, a rich brew, a heady tonic. Some such idea wafts playfully in my mind. He is quite playful too; I am sure he is flirting with me in earnest. He measures the wall against which I want to place two bookcases. He moves gracefully and with assurance. He is a lissome lad, I think contentedly. And he seems to know what he is doing. He is even direct when it comes down to it—the nuts and bolts of daily life, the practicalities. We discuss the size of the shelves and whether I would want them all to be of equal height. I decide to have the top ones built for oversized books. John even appears interested when I explain how my library will be ordered and how it will differ in plan from that of the Dewey decimal system. Libraries reflect their collectors, and each library, I tell John, has a life and mind of its own.

Naturally talk evolves from shelves to books and to other subjects and at one moment to Helen, which is not a surprise. I am prepared for this. We are sitting on my couch, having tea. John discovers that I have not seen her for a while. I reveal the whole truth—that she and I may be on the outs—because now my subterfuge would be almost callous and surely unnecessary. John becomes alarmed, which surprises me pleasantly; his entire demeanor had excluded the possibility of his being shockable. He could not be just "a liar," as Helen had said, but a delicate young man, more complex and sensitive than she allowed. I keep reflecting upon how odd it is, how peculiar, that someone as hip, probably as groovy as John, in his colorful terms, should manifest alarm. His rationalizations for it are feeble, to the effect that it has nothing to do with him, but everything to do with her. Though I have my own doubts, I attempt to calm him, assuring him that no harm will come to Helen, who is willful and remarkably resilient. He now exhibits a grave scrupulosity, but says nothing. His expression, easily called up in my mind's eye, is full of meaning, yet ambiguous, even opaque.

I am still extremely curious about Helen's sister, and whether she was a suicide as I had surmised, and whether they were twins, which I have less belief in of late, especially now that Gwen is in town. With Gwen around I am more aware of my feelings toward her, twinnish feelings. In fact, I was in the process of writing something to that effect when John knocked at my door.

Long ago, I imagined Gwen and I were fraternal twins—man, woman, heterosexual, homosexual, black, white. But in a way these supposed oppositions meant nothing to me except as qualities that added to our specialness. The point was we were originals, that was what was most important. Nothing could really separate us. Gwen and I were two sides of the same precious coin. As Alicia might put it, we were each other's anima and animus. But I really don't subscribe to Jungian theory. It was true, though, that I idealized us, and perhaps I will always. From other sides of the tracks but on the same track, we were, and are, our own club. Gwen has often commented upon how discriminating we were in those days, how exclusive, no one was good enough for us. She was a greater snob than I in many ways.

She must have acclimated quickly to being the only black person in our group, and often the only female. She never let on what her feelings were, if any, about being singular in those ways. I knew then, and know now, very little about her other, earlier life, with her family, and little in regard to her attitudes toward or even her experience of race. In New York there was a black piano player she liked, but he too spent most of his time in white society. On one occasion I attempted to ask her. She uttered something rather abstract about being more about sex than race and disallowed, through her laconicism and gestures, I recall, any further questions, direct questions of that nature, anyway. It was a less strange remark then—to be about sex, not race, in a way—than now, although maybe not, since it was at the beginning of the sixties. I accepted her answer, as it neatly coincided with my conception of her. But in any case, I was not and am not one to press, even though I am unusually curious—this is often said of me. I have the urge to pry. Can this truly mean, as Freud suggested, that I am always seeking to discover my parents in flagrante delicto?

Gwen never wanted to talk about her family; it was as if anything said about families at all was childish or beneath contempt. She seemed to hold them in contempt. But all of us did then. She seemed, and still seems, not to think about herself in any of the ways one might imagine. This may be true of original people generally. But while she never made pronouncements about race, as if it didn't occur to her, and therefore ought not to others, I have now more than a sneaking suspicion that nothing escaped Gwen, that she always knew where she was and where she had come from. Very little escaped from her that she didn't want others to know, no matter how close one was. But this never occurred to me then. Gwen must have suffered the way one does when one lives a crucial aspect of one's life in secrecy, in the closet. She must have suffered in silence. Perhaps she still does, even in these more open times. I felt a chill and shivered involuntarily. I walked to the open window and shut it decisively. The cold air had blown in from some distant, terribly remote place outside me, outside us. Actually, I felt a bit like Rebecca in Daphne du Maurier's novel, which Hitchcock most successfully brought to the screen.

I was not terribly happy with the passage. It was likely I had not gotten it right, for no matter how I looked back at Gwen and myself, to recapitulate our past and to examine my perceptions of her, then and now, she and it—the past—slipped away, seemed just out of reach. I was too clumsily grasping at it, whatever it was, and it slid through my puffy fingers. Indeed even recent history was difficult to remember with precision. I wasn't quite sure precisely how long it was that I hadn't seen Helen. At first it seemed Gwen had arrived instantaneously, right after my telephone call to her, but now I believe more time had passed. But I was unaware of it. Time does that; I do that—refuse to acknowledge time's passing. I let it slip through my fingers. So, as often happens, I was glad to hear John's knock upon the door, interrupting my meditation and labors.

Now, gazing at John, my mind wanders to Helen, from Gwen to Helen, and to John, back to Helen, then to Gwen. I may be clumsy, inadequate, even unequal to the task of grasping Gwen and my relationship with her. Perhaps I am no longer an expert judge of Gwen. I feel, at least temporarily, unable to delineate her character and the quality of our relationship. The essential eludes me. As I watch and listen to John, I imagine too that Helen, like the grains of sand which measure time, has passed through and by, and that she may have slipped figuratively through my arthritic fingers. Though I mustn't blame my ineptitude solely on age, I suppose. I might have fumbled the ball when I was young. In any case, there is still time.

After some initial reticence, John is forthcoming. It is not hard to pry from him the secret he alluded to in the hospital, about Helen's sister and her past. He is a trifle skittish. But after discussing the shelves for a while and sitting on the couch, and after I poured us tea and observed the obligatory conversational gambits, he relaxes entirely.

It's beautiful here, he remarks, looking toward the window. I am always touched when young American men notice beauty. Especially beautiful ones. I offer him a few biscuits which ought to be fresher, but he seems not to notice. Then I mention my visit with him in the hospital and then, first putting my cup to my lips and pausing, I ask him what he meant by saying "not like her sister, man." John nods his head up and down several times, and it seems to me he is eager to divulge this information.

He speaks with an air of casual authority. Everyone thinks—and Helen indicated to him, at least obliquely—that her sister was a suicide. She was four years older than Helen, was finishing college, was obese, and very miserable. Helen and she got along all right, but not terribly well. Helen's arrival in the family was a disruption for the older one; and she was, like most children, jealous of the attention Helen received as an infant. Still she was, according to many, her father's favorite. To myself I note that, like Helen, I am the baby of my family. Helen's parents fought a great deal, and it was rumored that the noble father—for so he was viewed—was engaged in an affair with a woman not much older than the older sister at the time of her alleged suicide. There were no brothers.

The dark events were matters of great speculation, involving some rather shocking questions about the psychiatrist father and the sister and the effects upon the sister of the illicit coupling of the father and his lover. It was very nasty business. John thinks the sister was found in a bathtub. That's what he heard, but not from Helen. I didn't ask—discovered by whom?—for even I felt the need to expunge the ghoulish image that "found in the bathtub" elicits.

In my family, I remark to John, determined to be as forth-coming and open as he, we are two brothers, sons. He is older than I, I continue, and we do not get on . . . But just then Gwen pushes open the door and enters the room, in medias res, so to speak, as she did when Yannis and I were engaged in our troubling conversation.

Are my shoes here? Gwen asks; then Gwen sees John. They recognize each other. I perceive it in a flash, a charged flash. That special expression of chagrin passes over Gwen's face ever so fleetingly, and I am sure that she must have wanted to sleep with him, as I do now. A shadow hovers over my heart, an emotional storm cloud looms. It has been ages since Gwen and I longed for the same man. I think about this for no more than a second, though. I push it aside and study them. They are young. They are chatting. They are absurdly young.

Actually I am also disconcerted by having had confirmed what I suspected—that Helen's sister was most probably a suicide. It is just the kind of grotesque fact that sets my mind to work. As if from nowhere, an idea plants itself inside me and grows. I think the idea locates itself first in my head, which seems heavier and more diffcult to balance on my neck. But then it flies down-ward, toward my heart, which palpitates in shadow. It is a simple idea; and my heart beats to its rhythm: I must find her. Helen may be in harm's way. I must go to her. My heart beats fast, fast, faster, faster. She may be in trouble, it goes. She needs you, Horace, it says, find her. Find her, Horace. This kind of thinking, I tell myself, must induce heart attacks. I place my hand on my heart. It ticks. I walk about the room and sit down again.

I say nothing of this to my guests, for even in such a condition, I am conscious that the assumption of Helen's need, produced as it were by and in my body, derives from a great anxiety that may have little to do with Helen. Yet I feel that it does. One can easily hold such contradictory ideas and emotions and still pour drinks for friends, I have found.

They have not noticed my anxiety. They talk to each other aimlessly, effortlessly. They are gossiping, discussing bands and clubs. I am both relieved and annoyed. Why does one always want to be noticed, in some way? I open a bottle of retsina and place three glasses in front of us and pour each full to the brim. Let us toast—to the three of us, here in Greece together. Gwen can barely contain herself. She is almost gleeful at my inarticulateness, at my witless toast, innocuous enough for all occasions. She winks at me and John. I gulp down my drink and pour another.

I had nearly forgotten John. He of course must be as anxious as I am about Helen. Thinking this makes me suppress my anxiety about her, and I realize once more the strange situation I am in, with Gwen and John. It is as if we are framed and constrained by an uncertain and unspoken desire that lingers in the air like a perfume distilled from electricity, not flowers. I look at both of them, fixing on my visage a patient smile to indicate that I am calm, even sanguine, which of course I am not, as I never truly am. Why should one be? In the next instant, I decide that John and I should make the journey together—to find her, to find Helen. John would want to, I am sure of that. But that would mean leaving Gwen on her own. This plan could wait until after the party. I dither internally and drink.

But I wanted Helen at the party. And first things first. It—the party—can wait, first things first. Helen must be found. I glance at Gwen and wonder if she has been reading my thoughts, since I believe she can and that she is, in some sense, my twin, and don't twins know instinctively what the other one is going to do next? Don't they dress alike without planning to and so on? For her part Gwen is impassive, waiting for someone else to speak, to do something, anything, and it is clear she will not be the one to take charge, make the advance, parry and thrust. It is more in keeping with Gwen that she not be the one, but be the one who bides her time, who waits. The one who waits, a rather clever title, I think. But for what? Gwen is waiting, actively waiting, if that is possible, and John is also waiting, discomforted but keeping his cool.

How does one escape from these awkward social patches—should I stop beating around the bush and reveal ingenuously: I want you, John, or Gwen wants you, or let's be adults, or let's be children, as we are anyway, inevitably, all children. Surely,

I caution myself mentally, to do so—that way lies madness. I drink another glass of retsina. Such a vulgar wine, so raw and crude, so right, so shocking. Retsina is blatant, not reticent, and how I wish I were capable of a flagrant display! Silence, ordinary sweet empty full silence, is intolerable in the moment. Anything would be better. A scream, a cat in heat, an off-key tune . . .

What is happening back home? I ask, innocently enough. What horrible events am I missing, what terrible things has Ford done lately? Who is this man Carter? The peanut farmer has found favor with John, it seems, but Gwen refers to him as a cracker. They are off on a discussion of the Mafia, and how Sam Giancana was slain. He was tied to the CIA, and his murder, Gwen says, happened fast upon the heels of the revelation that the CIA was spying domestically, under Nixon's orders, and so forth, so Giancana must have been implicated. John seems impressed by Gwen's deduction, which I too think is clever, as I hadn't thought it.

I once remarked to Roger, when he and I had—and it is a rarity—the same thought: Great minds think alike, Roger. He quickly countered: And small ones. Even now that makes me laugh. Roger isn't all bad. No one is. Perhaps evil despots, but they . . . I am muddied by drink, muddled, that is, I can't focus and think. I study Gwen, who absorbs me into her and absorbs this scene into her as if it were already seen, and I think I understand better the term scenemaker. Suddenly I realize that since she's arrived my thoughts have been mostly taken up with her, and with John, and not actively with Helen, which is all right, I know, and perhaps wholesome. And yet, I have been thrown off the track of Helen, with whom I was engaged in something lively and new, I think, and I know she is angry with me, disappointed or whatever, like my mother, and she has disappeared. Helen has. My mother is dead. I would have hunted her down by now had Gwen not arrived.

I must find Helen. If she is not out of town, why did she not answer my note?

Drunkenly I think: Gwen stands in my way. She may have arrived here, she has arrived here, perhaps, in order to disrupt the progress of this story, its particular chain of thought, and its fascination, though that may be to the good. Or it may not be. But that is much too teleological. And why is it either one or the other, good or bad, with purpose or without? An old friend comes again into one's life and one must adjust to the changes she brings. After all, I wanted her here. And now, in a way, I don't. Is it because of John? John is captivating; it is hard for me to take my eyes from him, as from a mirror that reflects dully so one keeps staring, and still one can't perceive one's image with any exactitude.

If I were to arrive with him at Helen's door, wherever that may be, she would not like it. In a thousand ways she has made it plain that she doesn't want to see him, and how or why could I think otherwise. I must go by myself. But if I do leave, I know that Gwen and John will be thrown together, left to their own devices, and certainly I cannot count on Alicia to stand in their way. Gwen is cunning and may be treacherous. John is not mine, surely, so how could her desire for him be construed as a betrayal of me? Unless she were my enemy—a horrific thought, one of the saddest I have ever had, or ever had in a long, long time. It's the wine dementing me, demeaning me, soliciting demons to play louche tricks. They soak in a senseless alcohol-sodden brain.

In reality, though reality is, especially in my condition, debatable, Gwen deserves John. She can—ought to—have him; age before beauty. No, no, the other way around; in our case, beauty before age. Though Gwen is not quite beautiful but handsome. Also she is my guest, and I intend always to be a good host. It is an image I hold of myself, the gracious host, which must be maintained, I feel, as if civilization itself depended on it, and it may, actually.

Even now I am neglecting my duties. Hurriedly I open another bottle and pour us all more to drink. I have no food to serve them which I'm sure Gwen has already registered—Horace is starving us, she's thinking. I laugh out loud; it's amusing to think I might be purposely depriving them and that I wish them to die of starvation. They are quite thin already. It wouldn't take much to starve them. It is an interesting idea, one that might be useful. Someone could be holding them prisoner, they might be sex prisoners, love slaves, that kind of thing. Perhaps captives of a de Sade–type character, who lives in New Jersey or Connecticut, some unlikely locale, and they are bound together by his insanity, even manacled together in his faux-medieval fort. The neighbors never suspected, they would say, clucking nonsensically as they viewed the bodies being wheeled out from the dungeonlike cellar. I must jot that down later.

Now John and Gwen are discussing Jackie Onassis and Angie Dickinson, and the Andrews Sisters, of all things, molls, and their gangsters. Can Jackie Kennedy Onassis really be thought of as a moll? I ask. Such a well-brought-up woman? Gwen makes light of this, having seen many too many well-brought-up young women go to pieces, all the crowd around Warhol—Drella, she calls him—and she knows how these women trade, on a grand scale, their sexual favors and beauty, jockeying for better position and greater financial security. Gwen reports that the just-married Jackie Kennedy, when asked if she was madly in love with then Senator Kennedy, answered the newsman, No. Incredulous, he asked her again, and she repeated, No. Did she really, Gwen, I ask, did she really say that on camera? Yes, she did, I have it from a good source. Gwen has good sources.

I must admit I'm shocked, I rather like Jackie, and even approved of her marriage to Onassis. I can see how she'd like an older man. I am an older man, I'm thinking. I may be slurring my words, but what does it matter. What about Callas? John asks. Jackie marrying Onassis screwed her up, right? I'm astonished. This can't be my rock-and-roller John speaking, not about the diva Maria—it is Alicia speaking through young John. She is mad about Callas.

Hungry? I ask them. Shall we dine? Or dance? I mime a tango and mince around the room. Gwen joins in. I love Gwen. I hate myself for ever thinking her a disruption. Though she is. And so are John and Helen. Life disrupts life. I am getting little to nothing done, it's true. But the dance is life, and life is a dance, and life is a short dance, and oh, I am silly, and on and on. I whirl wildly about the room, as if I hadn't a care in the world, and right now I don't feel I do have a care in the world, only what I wish to care about. I do not wish for anything to care about. I am shockingly free. Free. Fancy-free. I come to a halt, throw my head back and pretend to strip off long evening gloves like those worn by Rita Hayworth in *Gilda*. Gwen roars with laughter and curtsies before me, her king or queen. It is as if she had been presented before royalty countless times. And even to think of countless times, of the ages of human existence, makes me sigh. I feel weak, I weaken before that august history, weaken before Gwen. I return her curtsy, and her courtesy, and snap the long invisible gloves in the air for emphasis, as if the gloves were designed as punctuation marks—periods or exclamation marks—and were oh so necessary to the sense of my performance.

John probably has no idea what I'm doing. For his sake I ought to have imitated Mick Jagger. It is for his sake I am dancing the tango of the gloves, is it not? For whose sake then am I dancing? Does one commit mischievous acts for oneself or another? Murder, a tango, a striptease. How I wish my body were beautiful! I toss myself here and there, hither, thither, and yon. My ecstatic positions are ephemeral, sublime, ludicrous, but they do have a logic, even if it is only internal. They make sense to me.

I stop prancing just as suddenly as I started, mentally patting myself on the back for bravado, nothing else. I offer to treat them both to a wonderful meal at the only restaurant on the harbor. John hesitates. Is he thinking of Alicia? Gwen notices his hesitation or reluctance. Damned hungry, she declares and grabs me by the hand, pulling me toward the door. This action leaves John standing alone in the middle of the room, with the empty wine bottles on the floor about him. They look like sinking ships.

We must go, I declare to John. John's hands dangle foolishly from his long thin arms. He himself is in some way dangling foolishly, even dangerously. Ah, I muse waggishly, a pretty boy is considering his options. He must soon come to a decision, having weighed the pros and cons of doing this or that, I suppose. He blinks, clears his throat, but says not a word, and then follows after us penitently, nay, passively. He's a young man easily led.

Will I be the leader or Gwen? Am I in any condition to lead? Actually the idea of Gwen and me as leaders is marvelous; in our present state, we ought to be inflicted on the public! To Gwen I bellow, in a mock English accent, Where will it all end? Hell, she mutters, just hell. O, what a rogue and peasant slave am I, I answer. I recite this line in the manner of Olivier, I'm almost positive of that. Dear Gwen, perverse Gwen. Perverse me. To dinner we three!

CHAPTER

11

I am losing too many nights, if nights can be lost. How do I love thee, let me count the nights. They do count, whether or not they are lost. Perhaps Gwen and the boy have scooped it up, whatever it was that was lost. I must have been asleep for a generation—accounting for the generation gap—and they have taken my—that—night from me, sharing it between themselves. What a foul idea. I don't even remember if Roger made an appearance at the restaurant when we three were there. If he did, I think he and Yannis were scowling at each other, quite ferociously. I can see their contorted faces before me. How ugly anger is! John must have deposited me at my door. Or Gwen. Or both. Though for some reason I believe it is unlikely they were together. Something happened between them, I think. Perhaps it will come to me as the day goes on.

The sun glares into the room. The curtains were not drawn. Yannis forgot to do it. I don't want to open my eyes. Not yet. But even though I think that, I do open them, just to demonstrate to myself that I can think one thing and do another. My small world comes into view—bureau, slice of sky, books on floor, and so on, and I ask myself again: Why has Helen disappeared? What is the reason? There must be a reasonable explanation. But I cannot, for the life of me, find one. I am, I decide, obsessed by this, and I know it's weird, as John might put it. I think he did put that way, the other day, come to think of it, when I talked to him about Helen. John thinks me strange, I think. Yet I must find the bits that I do not know and join them together into a reasonable, a functional whole. This makes me a sort of quilter on the order of Great-Aunt Sarah, a loathsome woman, but most talented in her homely way.

I am reminded of an unfinished piece of writing about Helen. But where is it? If only Yannis acted as my secretary. I get out of bed and shuffle through some papers and come to it.

We were at the restaurant, at my table. Helen was rubbing her foot. Then she began tapping her foot on the ground in an arrhythmic pattern that annoyed me but I did not complain. She asked about my past, friends, college, Boston, New York, as she did from time to time, and very easily did I relate anecdotes and tales that I believed she enjoyed and which I would not so willingly tell others. Helen was a wonderful listener. One simply felt her appreciation. I told her about a fatal disagreement between two artists, both of whom developed a certain kind of technique or effect. They fought about who did it first and who could claim it. Each was adamant. It ended their friendship. Helen was astonished. What did it matter, she wanted to know, who did it first? I explained that it had to do with originality, with thinking up something first, with being the first to have fostered a new idea, to have changed definitively a field—in art, in science—to have produced a theory or form, which established a new way of thinking, in writing, even a locution, and that that ought to be credited. Helen thought it was funny. She declared that she would never care about something like that. Why did it really matter who did it first; didn't it only matter that it was thought or done, she wanted to know. I was hard-pressed to get to the heart of it, to why it mattered ultimately. But I elaborated that it was important, for instance, in science, to mark the link from one idea to another, and to give credit where it was due. Human beings strive for immortality, for recognition and acknowledgment, to make their mark, to encourage progress, and to move civilization forward, I went on. Later, we laughed about the fifteen minutes any of us might be given in this regard, but my sweet young Smitty accepts this short span on the stage more readily than do I, I think. Indeed I was winded by the end of my short speech. I waxed and waned with it.

I never finished recording the events of that day and night which we spent together. What did we do that day? I cannot remember now. It's so odd what one forgets and what one holds and stores inside one, good memories as well as bad ones. The oddest occurrence of all is when a friend remembers much too well an event you have no memory of and yet it struck the friend as worth preserving, consciously or unconsciously, and in the friend's memory you are a vivacious actor in the scene.

I reread the page. What did it mean really, that conversation with Helen? As a piece of writing it doesn't seem to fit anywhere. It may not. It does not explain anything to me. But I am not sure. There may be clues in it that are hidden from me. I put it away again but this time place it in a clean new folder which I mark, Questions about Helen.

In the great scheme of unknowable things, Helen's absence is unimportant, a speck of dust in a vast and unseemly, filthy world. Still, a mystery is a mystery. I rub my eyes; they are coated, a film over them. I cannot see properly. While this may be a metaphor, it is also true that my sight has bothered me for years, and as I age I worry more and more that one day I will not be able to read, that I will go blind, and end life as one of those poor souls with a white cane who is forced to walk the streets waving it in the air about him, a spectacle who cannot see what kind of spectacle he makes. I am susceptible to humiliation, while the people I admire most are indifferent to how they appear to others. Could I, like Milton, train young people to read for me, and would I be as cruel—to teach them to read without understanding? I have no daughters. I nearly thought, I have Helen. How comic, how predictable. Now a pang—a kind of hole—lodges just under my heart, a register of longing or emptiness, which may be the same. This hunger I experience—to be full and whole. Do terribly obese people suffer this in the extreme?

Still, why shouldn't one long for eternal life? Why shouldn't one crave immortality? Or is this pang an intimation of heart disease?

Immortality is one thread in the quilt. I try in all matters to find the significant thread—or theme—that if pulled would rip apart the sweater, unravel the yarn. It's why I enjoy writing stories based on real-life crimes. People usually have motives for what they do, foolish ones, perhaps, ones spurred on by the least attractive qualities in men and women. Jealousy, greed. Ignobility. There are always motives in the crime stories I've written. Thus I can move from event to event unselfconsciously and with a degree of fluidity: someone wasn't named in a will and took revenge; he stole his girl; she took a lover and her husband found out, then murdered them both; and so on. A murder is committed or two murders, the second to conceal the first. There is a chain of events, a series of links, and one need merely trace the links back or begin at the beginning, moving forward to the penultimate event, to understand the ultimate one. Increasingly, life is not like this.

Yannis arrived home late last night, his tail between his legs. He is sporting a ghastly black-and-blue eye, a shiner, we used to say, and is terrifically vague about his lost days and nights. Lost to me, not to him, I suppose, as he knows what he was doing and I do not. Yet because of the palpable presence of John and the comfort of inimitable Gwen—at least in some respects—I'm indifferent to his evasiveness. I do not press him as I would have in the recent past. I refuse to react to his shenanigans. I do not cajole and barter. Yannis is startled by the change in my attitude: my lack of reaction has sharply shifted things for him. He doesn't know what to do to catch hold of me again. I see him thinking, plotting how to do it. It is the same look that overcomes his normally placid features when he is fishing at the harbor and something tugs on his line. He snaps to with a mixture of stealth and cunning, a tiger about to pounce, then he jerks the rod to fix the hook in the poor fish's gaping mouth. Thus is he thinking about me, with the same determined expression on his face. One day Yannis may find he's lost me, that I have not been adequately hooked. That I have not taken the bait. Look, I am saying to him, I am swimming away. You cannot catch me. You do not have the right bait and lure. And soon, I say to myself, seeing his power diminish, he may leave me—I can sustain this thought—and that will be all right. Nothing is forever, after all, except common death.

Distracted—or perhaps in order to distract myself—I choose a book from the night table, one of Alicia's, entitled *The Gypsies*, and I turn to the index, where I discover a citation for Death. Under the subheading, "Death and Funeral Rites," I read that "a Gypsy does not die in his bed . . . no more than birth, may death pollute the home." "On the announcement of death, the whole tribe begins to weep or cry out, even yell." I should have liked to have witnessed such behavior at my mother's funeral. My brother would never wail; even the need to wail and cry out would be beyond his comprehension. Actually he would be incapable of wailing, I'm certain. At our funeral rite for Mother, there were some wet eyes, and several cheeks were damp with tears, the teardrops pressed into or blotted onto the skin with handkerchiefs.

But oh I have wailed, I have brayed at the moon, I have found myself on my knees, howling. I have seen the best minds of my generation . . . and really I disdained the Beats then. Yet even I, in that funereal group, was contained, tight. In fact, I was tight. How else to get through such a sad ceremony, surrounded by the living dead.

It seems the Gypsies have a different conception of death from us. Once they bury one of their own, they forget the place of burial. That makes sense for a nomadic people, for travelers. Fascinating, fascinating, I mutter aloud—Yannis is not, I hope, within earshot. I converse with the invisible interlocutor who, I often imagine, stands near me to hear my amazement, to absorb my thinking, and to encourage and feel my rising excitement. At times I recognize that this other must be my mother, as she was the first person who shaped and shared my intellectual concerns; she did encourage them, and me.

I read on, "There remains the matter of protecting oneself

against the return of the deceased in the form of a ghost, a vampire or a *mulo*." (I look up *mulo*: "The *mulo* really seems to be in effect 'Death's Double.'. . . . He is not the corpse; he is the man himself in the form of his double.") My mother must have become a ghost, one I cannot yet see. Perhaps I have not earned the right to see her. But why not? I squint and try. I rub my eyes and try again. I can nearly discern her face, but her pale image dissipates and dissolves into the air. This would not count as her making a visitation, in any case, but rather as my failed attempt at bringing her back. Why wouldn't she want to visit me? I oughtn't read on.

A weight settles upon my chest. If I close my eyes I can see her, I can see her next to my bed, reading to me. She was a lovely woman. My unfortunate looks come from my father. I touch my nose, which is like his, bulbous. How palpable the past is! I shift in my bed as if to throw sadness off. Yet her loss weighs me down. Loss, oughtn't you be light? I find my notebook and pen, sit up straight in bed, fluff the pillows behind me, touch my back, notice I've lost weight, and, even without coffee, read on.

There are five to six million Gypsies distributed throughout our world—the book was published in English in 1963, in French in 1961. In the introduction, it states that "Above all else, Gypsies are feared . . . 400,000 Gypsies were shot, hanged or gassed in the Nazi concentration camps . . ." I skim along and my eye lights upon this: "The Gypsies represent an exceptional case: they are the unique example of an ethnic whole perfectly defined, which, through space and time for more than a thousand years, and beyond the frontiers of Europe, has achieved success in a gigantic migration—without ever having consented to any alteration as regards the originality and singleness of their race." The writer of this is a Frenchman, as many Gypsiologists, as they're called, seem to be.

It must be the Gypsy originality and singleness that attract Helen. I would venture this analysis even at this early date. Except that she is not interested, she said, in originality. But perhaps if it applied to people, she might make an exception. I take a few notes. It could be their lack of having been altered by others, of being a defiant race. But are they a race? I wonder if the surrealists, who were primarily French—or at least one could say the movement bloomed, centered in Paris—I wonder if they too were fascinated by the Gypsies. I must research this. If I believe in anything, anything at all, it is in the value of research. It is one of my household gods. These notes will go into the file marked Questions about Helen.

Yannis enters the room, carrying freshly brewed coffee. He is smiling engagingly. One must be engaged to be engaging. Engaging, engaged, these words trigger a memory that is in its own way surreal. For something surreal happened the other night— or was it just last night?—something between John and Gwen. I must concentrate. A vague pattern of sounds clusters about my ears; the memory of sound is even more elusive than that of images. But aromas have enormous vitality. And an equally vague set of images forces itself before my eyes. Gwen and John are dancing; Christos is playing music tapes on his tinny machine. Yes, I see that now. I rub my eyes. But what occurred next? I am circling about it with my mind. An engagement ring. No, a circle pin. Yes, something about a circle pin. They come off the dance floor and sit near me. Gwen is going on about how she would have worn a circle pin in the fifties, in college, that she'd always wanted to, but couldn't because she was black—a Negro, yes, she may have said a Negro, and she drew out the two syllables. Circle pins were for Breck girls with blond hair, she said. It is not like her to mention her race, as I've explained, but she was high. She is especially adamant when inebriated. John simply couldn't understand her. He kept repeating, A circle pin— man, that's weird, man. He didn't get it, he said, and made fun of Gwen for being straight. Circle pins aren't hip, I believe he announced—without irony. He was, I suppose, merely trying to be playful or amusing. Gwen wasn't having it. She pulled up her small frame—she tends to curl into herself like a cat—and hissed to John that he was a privileged tot who wouldn't know anything about what life was or was not like for her. He was, I think she berated him, a hopelessly unhip white boy, and she may have used the epithet "white Negro." Which was a fifties term, if memory serves. At this juncture I believe I attempted some witticism about how the circle pin itself might symbolically shed light on the problem. I tried my best to put it all on a different plane, but such attempts are mostly futile. She may have slapped him. I think she did. Someone slapped someone that night.

This is why I don't believe they slept together that night, although I could be wrong. Aggressive behavior is often a prelude to sexual encounters. It has been so in my life, in any case. Some insects bite each other's heads off when mating. Rémy de Gourmont, in that curious book *The Physiology of Love*, produced many remarkable examples of sexual love between animals and between insects that if enacted between human beings . . . well, perhaps they are enacted between human beings. I recall some bizarre incidents in the sexual life of bees; de Gourmont adored queen bees. About the males, the drones, his language was excessive and damning. Useless, parasitic, he called them. I'm sure Gwen may have used the very same language about some of her beaux-drones.

Isn't it odd that that particular anger, or rage or life force, libido, courses with such virulence, with such peculiar physicality, and is activated and erupts within one's body like a volcano, and that its lava—molten, heedless lust—can be aroused by the most unpleasant people? One often feels such hatred and disgust for one's partner of the night before. He may have been attractive then, fierce, pleasant, indolently sexy, whatever, and in the morning those very same characteristics appear loathsome. Sex itself can be so unpleasant. Sometimes one experiences such terrifying feelings. A good lover isn't necessarily in himself magnificent; it is that he makes one feel at least proficient or unencumbered by restraint. Oh, for those precious nights!

If she hasn't already, Gwen will tire of John, another pretty white boy, a drone, useless. She will tire of him soon. I have faith in Gwen. In truth, she desires a true connection, but I—I need only have a muse. An amusement.

I can't bring myself to work on the Stan Green book today though it is due soon. I shall be just a little late. My publisher knows that I always come through. Even my agent once telephoned from New York and said, They know you'll come through, Horace, you're a trouper. A trouper. When she said that, Gloria is her name, I imagined I was a fusty vaudevillian meant to be brought out on stage during a lull between better acts. I am wearing too much rouge. I don't want to go on—yet I have been indoctrinated to believe I must. The show must go on, Horace! This tired exhortation rings in my ears as I wait in the wings, or in the seen-better-days dressing room. Fussily, I walk out on stage and stand before a hostile audience. I bow, clear my throat, and steal the show.

For the record, I do recall another incident. Though whether it happened here or in the restaurant, I haven't the foggiest: John stole the show rather uncharacteristically. With some elaboration he spun a tale. As he is some years older than Helen, he had already spent time bumming around Europe, as he put it. He bummed around Amsterdam. This was a couple of years ago. Timothy Leary, a sixties character whom Helen would laugh at and whom Gwen knows, of course, had just been captured in Afghanistan. According to John—I did not follow Leary's travails, nor have I ever tried LSD, not eager to simulate madness, unless assured of transcendent visions!—Leary had been living under state protection in Austria. For the price of appearing on television to denounce drug-taking, he could escape the U.S. government, which was eager to imprison him. He could have lived happily ever after in Vienna, if people do live happily there. But he was restless, or his lover was. It seems that Leary's wife or lover encouraged him to adventure to the East and desert his safe house, Austria, which he did. They were immediately caught, busted in the airport, and deported to the States, where Leary was imprisoned.

This is the point at which John's story became extremely interesting to me. A man named Dennis entered the scene. He appeared in Amsterdam just after Leary's capture in the Afghan airport. Dennis said he had been traveling with Leary and the woman—Joanna, I think her name was—but he himself somehow escaped Interpol, and came to Amsterdam to broadcast the truth of Leary's capture in Afghanistan and his previous life in Algeria and so on. In fact, John says, Dennis was carrying a Leary manuscript, which he claimed would never be published in the States, as it did indeed tell the real story in Algeria— Leary's wife Rosemary's adventure with Kathleen Cleaver, for one thing. Eldridge was also there, and he was involved with an Algerian girl, much against the prevailing customs and Muslim religion. Rosemary was wretched, as was Kathleen, it seems. I would be too, I should imagine, in such a situation, and with those men, neither of whom do I find appealing. But no matter.

Dennis ingratiated himself to the Dutch artistic underground community, such as it was, along with his pallid, untalkative wife and their child. They seem to have resembled typical hippies. Then, shortly after a mimeographed edition of Leary's book surfaced in Amsterdam, courtesy of a member of the underground who felt obliged to make it available, the American edition appeared, with wholesale elisions from the Amsterdam manuscript, but appear it did. And Dennis, who said it would never see print, himself disappeared, simply vanished. But, said John, who received one letter from him, written from California, where Leary was in jail, Dennis surfaced, finally. He was lately found murdered, execution-style, in a Spanish hotel room. He'd been working for the CIA, a lowly agent, but an agent nonetheless. It was likely that he had turned Leary in, more than likely, which explained why Dennis himself had escaped Interpol. According to John, Joanna too was CIA, but captured with Leary so as to give the operation the ring of truth. Leary was not a good judge of character; LSD had perhaps made him oblivious to the possibility of deceit. Acid, John told me, makes one love everyone and feel at one with the universe. What an idea! Universal love certainly did not stand Leary well.

The Dennis story endeared John to me as much as his beauty already had. There is nothing more appealing than beauty and intrigue. Can something be beautiful without mystery? Beauty would be incomplete—ugly—without it, would it not? Mother suspected that I turned everything into drama. I am drawn to the mystery and inconclusiveness of life, which is dramatic; life is allowed to hold unwieldy surprises or at least uncertainty. Yet I demand a kind of perfection, which must be definitive—perfection is never ambiguous or incomplete. Not finding it, I seek to study imperfections as if they would reveal clues to a secret existence, one living in tandem with or parallel to ordinary existence, a life that would be complete and conclusive. Perhaps this makes no sense, but surely it explains some of my interest in crime and criminals.

I don't necessarily want always to make perfect sense; but I do want to find reason and motives. Life is crazy, Smitty more than once insisted to me; and to her, I think, the pursuit of sense, of reason, was itself nonsensical, irrational. I argued points like these many times with her, yet in some ways I had to concede she was right. But she was—is—so young. I am running ahead of myself. And running ahead of Smitty. My Smitty.

There was a grocer in our town named Smitty, and everyone loved him. He was a man I visited with my mother, at his store, two times a week, let's say, a man so jovial and friendly, he was above and beyond suspicion. But one day it was discovered that he had a dark side. I don't even remember precisely what his crime was—which is odd—but at the time, I was only seven, it shocked me into realizing that life wasn't what my mother and father, when he spoke to me at all, represented it to be. Life was filled not just with incivility and occasional outbursts and rudeness, but with the terrible unexpected, with bad people, even evil ones, and one could never trust appearances. Still, one learned one must, compelled to even by the difficulty of the task, and one kept up those appearances. One had to keep up appearances for just these contradictory reasons.

What did we all hide? I remember dwelling on that perplexing question the whole hot summer after the grocer was incarcerated. I enjoyed taking long walks by myself in the woods, where I became fascinated with worms that crawled under rocks, with what might be hiding in the forest, banal experiences of that sort. And in my imagination Smitty the grocer was always somewhere nearby, a fantastic shape, a shadow hovering near a brook, and he was ready to pounce. Children have such vivid imaginations. It is a singular, exacting and herculean task of our society to damp those down, to tame children with ice-cream cones and dreary television. Helen thinks my ideas about what she calls pop culture entirely old-fashioned. Helen.

What I want to do most of all is to find Helen. I would be Stan Green were I able. And to find Helen, my Smitty, I did and do commit myself. Mentally, that is. I wished no one else to know of my quest, as I had concluded that I could not engage John in the adventure and was sure Gwen would try to put me off it. So I was to sleuth alone, and I was to begin at the beginning. I would go to Helen's house, that is, Bliss' house, and look for clues. For better or worse I am goal-directed.

With the goal tucked inside me, I walk determinedly to the open window through which the sun pours itself promiscuously into this room; its mission is natural, part of nature, and perhaps mine is too. I am watched by Yannis, who has often seen me walk to this very window. But he has no idea, of course, what's in my mind. I look toward Helen's terrace. There is no life there. Nothing stirs at Helen's house, I announce in a stage whisper. I dress quickly, as if suddenly and urgently called to action, to move and to see for myself that rickety abode where Helen greeted and loved sailors and read books and made watercolors and wrote in her diary. I am thinking this as I pull on my tennis sneakers and throw over my shoulders a favorite cable sweater. Then, as if on a whim, I grab a sharp knife from the dining table. Yannis gives a yelp of surprise and moves to stop me, but I am determined, I suppose this is what I felt, to protect myself at all costs. None of this was conscious. Thought was liminal, a pink streak of light blushing in the sky after a crimson sun had disappeared.

CHAPTER

12

Sometimes one advances toward a specific destination with not just a sense of purpose and direction, but with a sense of what to expect, and one progresses assured in the knowledge that the world one knows will be as one knows it and has always known it. When I walked to Alicia's house the other week, I knew what I would find there. I did not know of course that her cheeks would be flushed or that she had sung to John, or for him, but I knew where her furniture would be and that her books would be on shelves; I knew how her paintings would be hanging, that there would be flowers in vases, and so on. I knew John might be there, and if he wasn't I knew he would be on another day. One exists with the sense that life goes on in a regular manner, that one can breathe because one is meant to and air is air, that hello, yá sou, or bonjour will greet one, that fruit and vegetables will be sold where they were sold yesterday—in short, that one can recognize oneself in a recognizable world. And that much of life is ordinary. Even persons in concentration camps were able to adjust, over time, to the most horrific of circumstances, having come to know the routine, which was terrifyingly and mercilessly life as they were compelled by fate to know it, to live it, for however long.

As I walked to Helen's house, I had lost this sense of assurance. I did not know what to expect, which alone unnerved me. I was already unnerved—or nervous—because I didn't understand her disappearance, but when I imagined the consequences of this ignorance, I became confused. I had never even been inside her house. Years ago, when its owner Bliss was still in residence, I visited him there, but that was a long time ago. Much as I tried to envision Helen's house, its contents, and to create it in advance of seeing it, I could not. I simply did not know what awaited me.

Now one may want to interject—part of me does—that I, Horace, sought to feel compassless, to experience the vertiginous highs and lows of the unexpected, having already insisted upon my pleasure in the unknown, having insisted upon how much I needed to invent my life, to make it closer to fiction. But I am a writer and given to such musings. One mustn't believe everything one reads, after all.

But this one must, and I would implore one to, believe. The desire to invent is not what I felt. I felt without or separate from desire. Indeed I felt blank. I have never felt blank before in my life, yet this feeling which I do not know and do not recognize must be that; it is the only way I can express it. I have felt blotto, but not blank, at least not when conscious. I have been blind-drunk, deaf-drunk, dumb-drunk.

It is different today. I don't know what to think. I imagine this is what Stephen the Hermit experiences with horrific consistency. He cannot turn on his electric lights, as his electricity has been shut off, and why this has happened—why something like electricity may be shut off—is incomprehensible to him, so he is forced to light candles and place them in tin cans, and he sits in his dimly lit room far from whatever he knew as a child in England or Italy, without secure thoughts to comfort him, disoriented, without thought at all perhaps; and he is blank, as empty as the proverbial unpainted canvas. Let me not bore you with such an image, though.

I was blank and yet I marched, in a way even happily, toward Helen's house. I have thought about this often since and decided, retrospectively, that I was emptying myself, though I did not know that at the time. I was not truly blank, I realize. Can one be? I was readying myself for an experience as fulgent as one of Blake's epiphanous poems or paintings of such. Laugh if you will. But it seems to me now that I wanted to experience mystery and not just to write it.

On the way, quite near the harbor, actually just behind it, I pass a wake. The village style or ritual for death is to set a table or two outside the front door of the home of the bereaved upon which are placed flowers, a large basket of bread, and a tray of cakes, and above this hangs a piece of cloth, a tapestry, with a religious figure woven into it. The walls here are so old and crumbly that wakes are ancient and exotic tableaux and have an especial appeal to me. I believe it was the baker's mother who died, though I am not sure. I did not take this as an omen since death here never takes a holiday; it is a most regular part of life. But as I remain a foreigner, I am uneasy in the face of it. I hate it. I despise death. It is the only natural aspect of life that I detest. Because I have no faith, Alicia would insist.

When I turn the corner and round the bend, to walk along the harbor, which is a singular joy, always and in all situations beautiful—it never fails to surprise and delight me, even now, as anxious as I am—I spy Gwen sitting at a table in front of the restaurant. Were it not for my alertness, I might have come face-to-face with her. She is at my restaurant, seated at my table, looking at my harbor, but looking at the water and the scene with her look on her face, that inimitable expression. From the way in which she is sitting, so relaxed, it is now her restaurant as much as mine. Dear, dear Gwen, how quickly she takes possession—of me, too, for how can I not talk to her, yet how would I tell her where I actually was intending to go when I do not want her to know. I do not want her advice. So I rush on as if I had not seen her and madly hope, hope jarring hope, that she has not seen me. Her look of concentration is unbroken; so great is it, quite likely she has not noticed me. I decide she has not, and even if she has, she hasn't made contact with me, and I have a right to be miffed, if I am. I'm not. In fact I hope she will be just where she is after I have finished my business at Helen's house. For who knows, I think to myself, again and again, what I will find there?

I move in haste around the wide Venetian harbor and nod my head in greeting to shopkeepers who know me and even to some who don't. Then I take my favorite shortcut, along the most narrow passage, which joins with the street I desire. Then I walk up the wide, flat concrete stairs that lead directly to Helen's house. I listen to a canary sing from its cage—I do not find their music particularly pleasant—and from a courtyard I hear the sounds of domestic bickering, muted enough that the subject of their argument is unclear to me. I am not aware of being tired, or arthritic, not aware of my body at all, though I had spent days in languorous semi-retreat, I believe, from nearly everyone.

But I exaggerate. I did expect to find something, just one thing, to be honest, and that was Helen's diary. Not expected, but hoped, I desperately hoped that it would be there, and in a way, because it was my certain hope, the predictable one, the one that anyone would have hazarded as Horace's hope, I knew, in my heart of hearts, that it would not be there. In the natural course of things, she would have taken it with her. A girl's diary absolutely would be carried with her, a precious object, faithful as a dog. Helen would never have left it behind. Apart from that, I did not have any particular hope.

The corroded iron gate to Helen's house is hidden in shadow which I take as ominous, a warning, if not an omen. I stare at it before ringing the bell Bliss had fixed there years ago, though I know no one is at home. Or at least I hoped no one was at home. Suddenly Chrissoula appears from across the lane, having seen me approach, and greets me warmly, as if everything were normal. Helen? I ask. I have not seen her, I explain in Greek, in a long time. Chrissoula nods her head up and down and then from side to side, indicating she is dubious about her young charge. She then places one finger at her mouth as if to say she cannot speak or is not supposed to. And promptly Chrissoula shuffles off, her skirt swinging about her ankles. She disappears across the lane and enters the door to her house. She takes such good care of Helen. But her behavior is odd; usually Chrissoula is garrulous.

I do not ring the bell. I walk through the exterior gate to the front door. I am enormously light-headed and, in the moment, unconscious of any specific worry. Blank, as I have already said. I push open the centuries-old thick wooden door and glance around the small ground-floor room. The house is remarkably narrow, a sliver of a house. It still has no floor. Then I ascend the equally narrow stairs which are in almost complete disrepair and most likely dangerous, so I step lightly. I always say to myself when stepping lightly, why should this matter? Am I not the same weight?

I arrive at the second floor. It is sparsely furnished and obviously disused. There are many books in Bliss' bookcases; they are in poor shape. There is a broken chair as well as some insignificant ceramic pieces. Unimportant pieces, I tell myself, ruing the fact that Bliss, though a painter, has no eye for decor and the decorative arts. I continue the climb and reach the top floor, which I know to be Helen's space, as she had called it such.

I put my hand to my nose. The smell is overwhelming. At first I think, it must be death. Someone has died, I think nervously. Helen, oh no. But it is not an awful, disgusting smell that one associates with decay and a body's rotting, just an overpowering one. Sweet and sickly, like a cheap commercial perfume. I do not appreciate most perfumes; but I love the natural scent of flowers, of roses and camelias, of course, or of cut grass on a summer's day, or newly mown hay pitched next to a red barn. I even have liked the earthy stench of horse manure. The smell of sex is incomparable.

Helen's room reeks of distress, if distress may be said to have an aroma. But the first response that bubbled inside me and then formed into a word was, Insanity. This is insane, I say to myself. Perhaps I uttered it aloud. The room is not messy in the usual sense. It is out of order, entirely. The Greeks have a word for it—chaos. Could Helen have lived like this?

First, all the walls are painted black. It is dark in here, the windows having been covered over, and I cannot find a wall socket. When I do, I flip the switch but nothing happens. There is enough light to see shapes and images fuzzily. Clothes and rags have been thrown everywhere, bits of torn paper are piled in odd shapes, unusable paintbrushes left in strange places, and on the black walls daubed in what I take to be shocking pink are ragged forms that Helen must have drawn when beside herself. Her bed—there is no bedspring or backboard—is littered, covered in stuff—clippings, pins, beads, odds and ends, junk. The mattress, which has several cigarette burns, is on the floor. There are no sheets in sight and worse, no pillow, which reminds me of something John had said about Helen's not having pillows on her bed when he knew her in New York. This did not jibe with my idea of Helen. I can't remember why John mentioned it. It will come to me, undoubtedly.

Papers are everywhere, books—Bliss', I am sure—strewn about as if a great wind or hurricane had blown through, wreaking havoc, concocting this strange disorder. Hundreds of what I take to be photo-booth portraits of Helen and her friends lie in a box next to the bed. Holding some up to the light, I can just barely see them, but am able to ascertain that her friends are in all manner of costumes, making funny, ridiculous faces—pulling a face, my mother used to say—and Helen herself is posing archly, this way and that, with hats, makeup, props. There are Polaroid pictures as well, of long-haired young men who are sullen but attractive. One or two is nude. One of them is or must be John.

Cups of half-drunk and moldy coffee on the floor are a discordant note among many discordant notes—in my presence Helen never drank coffee. Or did she? I bend over to sniff one of the cups; this may enable me to tell when she left. I do so virtually in the style that cowboys and Indians are shown doing in movies when they search for their man and study the tracks of his horse. This seemed entirely silly to me a moment after I'd done it. There are dead flowers in filthy vases and magazine pictures—primarily of politicians and celebrities—thrown about in no discernible pattern.

And that is what I am searching for—a pattern. Just as I

become cognizant of this, I look up and, as if it were fated, the wind blows through a broken window and stirs some of the papers on the bureau, which is also painted black. I walk to it. The mirror above it is covered only partially in paint. Revealed by the breeze, under one piece of paper on the bureau is another. I peer at it intently. I see my name. It is written in bold block capital letters, HORACE, just that, and under my name a few blotches or stains, and some lines crosshatched over what may have been other words. Stuck to this piece of paper is yet another. On it is writing, again in bold capital letters but more shocking: FUCK EVERYTHING. OEDIPUS WRECKS. Beneath this is a drawing of what looks to me like a duck, of all things, but it may be another creature. On the back of this piece of paper is pasted a map of the southern half of Crete. A large glittery dot has been placed on it, close to several small towns, yet not at the towns precisely, rather beside or in the middle between them. But it is really too dim in here for me to tell. I delicately take up the pieces of paper, precious and strange, and hold them in my hands. Then I walk out through the French doors—whose windows have been covered with newspaper clippings—onto Helen's terrace, where I had often seen her ensconced, had watched her from the restaurant or from my windows. Now I look toward my windows, but see nothing. I am happy that Yannis is not spying on me.

I thrust the papers up, holding them at arm's length to the sun, to benefit from its natural light. I thought I might see through them another message, a code that could not be read on first glance, especially in her room. It was dark as a cave in Smitty's room. But I see nothing, just that the paper is cheap stationery. I scratch my brow and walk back into her room, look around furtively, to see if, with another stroke of fate, some other bit of evidence would make itself known to me. I wait in silence. I am not sure how many minutes pass. But I wait, conscious of time whiling away as I stand in near darkness. And then it happens, again, a stroke of luck or good fortune: a streak of light pierces the darkness through a crack in the French doors and settles on one of the black walls. I walk over to the lighted area and scrutinize it. I discern that the forms Helen has painted are rather crudely drawn cartoons of male and female genitalia. I stare at these for a while, shocked, I suppose, by the girl's boldness—and wit. Yes, wit. They are witty drawings in their way, now that I can see them. In shocking pink—chalk, I believe the medium is. Chalk. Then I become sensible again of the stench and decide to leave, to return another day, perhaps, should it be necessary. I have no idea what is producing the smell.

I am satisfied, even fulfilled, for it seems to me clear that Helen has left all this for me. It was her way, I told myself, her young way, to leave abruptly, to split, not to explain but also not to be truly angry, as I had feared and expected. Helen is not really obvious, though she may appear vulgar or crude to one less accustomed than I to the terrible power of the imagination—and to its necessary excesses. It is true I was shocked by some of what I found. The disarray could be understood merely as disarray, as poor childhood training even, as youthful revolt, but I am determined to find its sense and reason. And I am assured that she understood that I would recognize this, it, and would have gotten it—felt, as John put it the other night, the groove, or gotten with the groove, I forget which. But most important, and with this I breathed deeply and exhaled fully, surely I knew where she had gone, which had been the intention of my mission. The dot on the map signaled the spot she'd traveled to or, I ventured inwardly as I descended the rotten staircase, it is where the Gypsy woman has taken her—to her home, there to initiate Helen into the mysteries.

Yet, and this is a strange matter, I who am so curious, I who desire nothing if not to know every secret, I was suddenly not certain if I ought to pursue her and whether I ought not to be a little afraid. Of Helen, that is. Though I was certain I would detect an underlying structure, if I thought hard enough, even in her abysmally messy room, there was still evidence of a mind and a life that was foreign to me, more foreign to me than the Greeks. While I knew that Helen was a member of a new breed, that realization, which I'd had early, had been an abstract idea in many ways. When we were together, though we often disagreed, or rather, though I talked and she listened, so that I often did not know her opinion, I did not doubt that I had made an impression upon her. And I also believed that in our souls we were in deep and profound unity. Why I thought this I am not sure, but as I have written elsewhere, she was, I assumed, like me. And again, her youth was an advantage all to itself, her youth and that special androgynous quality of hers that I find and found so compelling. Like that of an angel.

Still, however I regarded her, I had new information. Helen with the Gypsies, Helen living like a Gypsy, as my father would have put it, Helen living in filth and in a kind of insane condition, Helen drawing penises and vaginas in pink chalk on black walls. FUCK EVERYTHING! OEDIPUS WRECKS! And I suppose I must admit that Helen's being female was a new element in the equation or puzzle. It is not that I had not already noticed and regarded her as a young woman. That was and is obvious. But she was acting in ways that I did not expect from a young woman, as free of that particular bias as I had conceived myself. Thinking this, I began to feel, with some anger and anxiety, that I had more in common with Alicia than I had imagined.

Perhaps Helen's relationship with the Gypsy woman, for instance, was one that was essentially feminine in nature, which I would have scant access to. But this mental perambulation smacked of magic, witches and superstition, and I rejected this idea quickly, for if Helen was anything, she was not a woman in stereotypical ways, nor would she attend covens. Unless it was a club. I did know this. It must have been the thoroughgoing extent of her wildness that confused me momentarily. Yes, her wildness.

But I realized and had to laugh to myself about my own peculiar and old-fashioned ideas about women, hidden and buried though they were, in the way that what one learns early usually is. Consciously I didn't accept any of this trite or pernicious thinking any more than I believed that blacks were an inferior race. Still, certain responses are atavistic, and because they are recessive and deep inside one, when they emerge from places that are untouched by reason and education, they are revelatory and must be considered.

But ought I go south? I would never under any circumstances mix with voodoo practices, for instance, not because I believe in voodoo's power, but because I don't. That may be a paradox.

Order out of chaos, I tell myself, as I contemplate my return to the harbor—as I've said, I always imagine where I am going before I set off—for if one looks rigorously, one finds meaning even in chaos. One must be able to envision in chaos an emergent and eventual form. That is, one must be capable of divining an inspired plan; there is always a plan, a map, beneath the most inchoate formlessness.

I place Helen's messages in my shirt pocket and look about as if I am being watched. But I am not being watched, at least not by creatures I can recognize; later I felt foolish that I had carried a knife with me. A kitchen knife at that. I march out the door, through the heavy gate and toward the restaurant, to look for Gwen, who, I still hoped, would be at my restaurant, to be my ballast if not my oracle or sphinx. For surely the interpretation of OEDIPUS WRECKS in regard to Smitty called for the wisdom of a sphinx.

CHAPTER

13

Gwen was sitting at my table, drinking my white wine. That doesn't call for a sphinx, Lulu, she interjected wryly. Maybe a shrink. Sphinx me another drink, Gwen went on, or I may shrink right here in front of you like the incredible shrinking man. Gwen had been reading an out-of-date *New York Times*, amusing herself with the horrible news, she said. I refilled her glass, as she had asked me to do, and continued to tell her what I had seen.

I was shaken, more shaken even than I knew. I must have looked pale, white as a ghost—I am never robust though I take the sun—but Gwen didn't seem to acknowledge my shattered state. I know I was shattered, devastated, but perhaps I did not communicate that—one wears masks, after all. I wrote about it not long after.

Gwen claimed that she had not seen me walk around the harbor, the untruth of which I discovered later, to my chagrin, but that is Gwen. She does not ever simply react. She chooses her time. It was probably not the right time for her in many ways, and it certainly wasn't mine. With Helen's notes in my pocket, over my heart, I experienced an uncanny sensation—that my chest was on fire, or that my heart was burning inside me, and that racing so quickly, it had turned to flame, pure heat. My head was hot, my arms and back cold, and I longed to jump into the sea with all my clothes on. I tried to pay full attention to Gwen, but all the while I had to restrain myself from leaping into the cool waters, to quench that inner bodily fire.

Rather dramatic, I think now, more in keeping with Zelda Fitzgerald than myself, but perhaps I chose, consciously or unconsciously, to be Zelda when I wrote that, and from time to time it—the desire to be a flapper—pops up, dimply, giggly, and bee-stung, and finds its way onto the page. About choosing, Gwen quipped some years later, on my visit to New York: History chooses us like a virus. We're all chosen people. She laughed when she said it; she was speaking about being caught in time as well as being taken hostage. It was at the end of 1980, and President Carter was wrestling impotently with the hostage crisis. It was dragging on. He was a lame duck, truly. Agonizing in public, Carter became in my eyes a familiar and sympathetic creature; his pathos won my sympathy, but it was the thing the public despised him for, his weakness. November 4, 1979, Gwen pointed out, when the American hostages were captured in Iran, was the same date that the Soviets entered Budapest twenty-three years earlier. Gwen always looked for occurrences like this. She called them the puns of history, and herself, the pundit queen. She once named herself—I think I remember her doing this in Boston—yes, she dubbed herself the pundit Negro. I quoted to her from Horace, my namesake—which is a joke between Gwen and me—*Mutato nomine de te fabula narratur*. "With the change of names, the story is told about you." Sometimes Gwen went on and on changing names, as she was never satisfied, though on that occasion she sashayed, verbally, that is, around hysterical puns and history's pawns. Even history's prawns, but that was when, in New York, we were in a Chinese restaurant. We were, she noted then, the shrimp boats of history. I was nearly seventy.

At the restaurant by the harbor, I report in as much detail as I can what I had seen at Helen's—the chaos, the writing on the wall, as it were, the cryptic notes to me, and, without a moment's hesitation, Gwen advanced the theory that (a) Helen had not left any of this for me, or on my behalf, and (b) that I must not go to find her, because she did not want to be found. We engaged in a lengthy and confusing, to me, discussion of the Oedipus complex as it applied to Helen and her psychiatrist father. Gwen comically played both shrink and even sphinx, and asserted, with great moral seriousness, that if Helen knew or suspected that her father had loved her older sister better and more than her, her sister doubled as her mother—who was a shadowy figure in this scenario anyway, as no one ever mentioned her, and so perhaps she too was dead?—thus Helen might have murdered her sister, accidentally, or, more likely, merely desired her death and suffered from guilt. Of course this is—accidental murder, not mere desire—what I had originally speculated and dismissed as outlandish, not that it was accidental but that Helen had had a hand in it, that it wasn't a simple suicide, if suicides ever are.

But why, I ask Gwen, would John lie to me or concoct the manner of Helen's sister's death? At this Gwen states, waspishly, John knows nothing. Really? I respond, implicitly begging for further information. Gwen smiled strangely but knowingly. Our food arrived and she didn't immediately divulge her news.

But I knew it: Gwen had gotten the story, at least pieces of it. In addition she had gotten caught up messily with John. Alicia would be a witness to, if not a participant in, the mess. I could tell, intuit that. In the old days John would have been mincemeat to her, and Alicia, whom she doesn't respect, a small obstacle if anything at all. In the old days Gwen would have sliced through John like a hot knife through butter, as Mother was wont to say. And I began to suspect that things were amiss, that things had gone awry with Gwen, that she was anxious, perhaps even desperate about something and even in some type of big trouble. It was possible that she was running away from New York, that she was not merely on vacation, needing a respite, having taken up my invitation, but had had to leave the city, forced out by something much bigger and more calamitous than bad vibes, as John would put it. She might have become entangled in a net of intrigue with dangerous characters such as the dealers and druggies she occasionally hangs out with for local color, as she likes to say. Looked on this way, Gwen was caught in a vise or had fallen into a trap. That it was of her own making, I had no doubt, though she herself might have insisted, as I've said, upon being a dupe of history, its plaything—I believe she's called herself a Barbie Doll of fate.

Inwardly I castigated myself for having neglected Gwen over the past couple of years. I had not been much of a correspondent; I had received better than I had given. In my mind's eye, I conjured what had befallen her here. While I had been lying groggily in my bed, losing time, Gwen and John had entrapped each other, had fallen into each other's arms, but not into love. Because, I told myself, Gwen was out of sorts, not herself, and because John was a passive lad, so easily led, they had succumbed to each other. It was easy for them to wind up in each other's arms, though they were uneasy lovers; they were both at loose ends. In any case, Gwen was wound up, about something. So they had coupled. Alicia must enter into this somehow, but I didn't expect ménage à trois to be the right term for the involvement. Three Americans could never become a ménage à trois, to me. Frankly I can't imagine the three of them in bed together. No doubt the failure is mine; I lack a certain type of imagination. I am a bit of a prude. Perhaps they employed a bundling board?

Gwen interrupts my mental meanderings, my wandering mind.

He's Billy Budd, Lulu, really, Billy Budd. You see, he's good and means well but he is deeply stupid. Naïveté oozes out of him. He's like butterscotch syrup. He's almost a drugstore sundae. Bittersweet naïveté—he drools it. He's sweet but thick—and of course, you know, drop-dead gorgeous. When we left you at your door—you were out of it, Lulu—I'd already slapped him. You probably don't remember, you never remember the vicious moments, Lulu. He went limp, like a kitten, and I saw the scene immediately. You know, one of those masochistic Catholic boys who wants his mother, anyone, to treat him like dirt, to punish him, to tell him to clean up his room—that must be why he followed Helen here. I'll take bets she whipped him and chained him to his bed. And he loved it.

At this I went pooh-pooh, involuntarily, a reflex, and then lifted my eyebrows, the way she usually does. Gwen just snorted, the way she does. In any case, according to Gwen, John's not sure who Helen is, or what her history is; she's told him things, but he doesn't know what to believe. John met up with her again in Athens by chance; they'd had a scene in New York, but nothing heavy. Anyway, he thinks she's incapable of saying anything straight. So he's not sure what's what. Helen first told him her sister died in a bathtub in a college dorm, but when Gwen questioned him, John admitted Helen said something else later, about the sister nearly dying. It may have been a nervous breakdown but Helen is very secretive, especially about it, because she has a shrink for a father, Gwen suggests. The sister may have nearly died at home, of an overdose of pills the father stored all around the house, like candy. Gwen calls it an occupational hazard. John and Helen traveled to Crete together from Athens, but she never wanted him as a boyfriend. He did try to kill himself, that's true, but it wasn't about Helen. John was adamant that he didn't really care about her; it was because his mother wrote him a letter saying that she'd finally seduced the parish priest back home, and his father knew and was going to have her committed. Isn't that too much? Gwen exclaims. He's impotent with Alicia, Lulu, which makes sense . . .

Instead of blurting out, again, But why would John lie to me? I ask, but what about Helen's abortion? I am impatient. Gwen never inquired.

I can't imagine he'd care, Lulu. Or if he cared, he'd never admit it—he's too cool, rehearsing hard to be cool. He's a lapsed Catholic, after all, and it's his mother he's in love with. And she didn't abort him, at least not in the usual sense, n'est-ce pas? Alicia is the perfect mom but that's why he can't get it up with her, it's obvious. Quel obvious. With us, anyway, it was a long night and then day and then night. He was all right with me, not for long, but he was able to, as we say, enter, to do it, and then he cried. It was bad and sad. He collapsed on me and whimpered like a puppy. I don't think I could go through it again. We talked. Or I talked.

Gwen galloped on. She reminisced about sex with the mentally sick musician she loves, for eternity, it seems, how great it and he were, how disappointing bad sex was, then she backtracked and recalled that Alicia had been waiting up for John, so that she—Gwen—was a surprise, yet Alicia took it all gracefully, at first.

We had civilized conversation, Lulu, some laughs for a while, we drank ouzo and ate bread and cheese, that mestizo—your get-your-goat cheese—fabulous. The evening was pleasant, if a night like the one I finally had could ever be considered pleasant, even in retrospect, or if any night is pleasant, Lulu, considering the peculiarity of modern nights.

Ultimately I believe Gwen segued to pictures. I suppose it had to do with her conjuring pleasant images after describing the pleasantries between her and Alicia. Gwen finds art restorative simply because it isn't life or even like life. The more artificial it is, the better Gwen likes it. She admires Warhol precisely because of the falsity of his work, which actually makes it true, to her way of seeing and thinking, which is not mine. To her Warhol is the modern-day equivalent of Rembrandt, doing precisely what the Dutchman did in the seventeenth century—painting the rich and advertising them and their possessions. She's rather adamant about all this. I don't see it her way. Gwen next expounded on "Le Déjeuner sur l'Herbe"—perhaps the three of them, Gwen, John and Alicia, had had a nude picnic on Alicia's floor?—and how that painting made Gwen crave, to eat ravenously or to make love, because in its center was an empty space as great as lost love, a hole that the figures created through their position, they encircled it, and had I never noticed it . . . ?

But the mention of absence made me think of Helen and about whether or not to leave immediately for the south. The phrase— the south of Crete—had a resonance it had never had before. The South. I was lost in thought for a moment or two, and then, as if a heavy curtain had been pushed aside roughly, I perceived an expression on Gwen's face that alarmed me. I had never seen it before. At least I was not aware that I had.

Are you all right? I ask her, furiously turning my attention to her, to focus on her, on her pain, her putative trouble, her fugitive absence from New York. I believe this surprised my dear friend. This sudden intensity may not have been like me. Or perhaps it was irregular for me to admit such concern.

Gwen assures me she is absolutely fine and insists grimly that it is because she can laugh. But she was not laughing when she spoke.

I can always laugh, Lulu, and as long as a person can laugh, a person can survive, in a manner of speaking, even as one is peaking, which I am. Peaking, peek-a-boo, here comes another gray hair. It is funny beyond endurance, n'est-ce pas? Sometimes I laugh myself to sleep. Sometimes I laugh so hard I begin to pant and lie panting on the floor, hysterical. Completely hysterical. In the best sense of the word, of course. This is the flip side to my unhappiness, ordinary or otherwise. It can always be said of me, Gwen maintained her sense of humor. It could be a badge, a badge of honor, or it could be engraved on my tombstone: She's grave here but she laughed until she died. I have fun, Lulu, I really do, in spite of my misery. I am determined to stay amused. I hate to be bored. To liven things up—this will horrify you, Lulu—I even smoke grass occasionally, though rides on subways, which I avoid as much as possible, subway rides are très treacherous. When I'm stoned, people look like so many different kinds of animals. And I can't stop myself from laughing. People's faces are très bizarre, aren't they? We're all jammed together—one great jam in New York. Here, the faces are so boringly similar except for what colonialism the cat brought back. You could call that the return of the oppressed. For me, alcohol is the superior high.

With that Gwen drains her glass of its wine and eyes me expectantly. But, I ask, is there anything objectively wrong? Are you being hounded by landlords, drug lords, have you done something unspeakable, is there something appalling, so awful that you're not able to break it to me? I guffaw nervously, so that neither of us has to take the question seriously. She chuckles merrily, then again looks glum, her lips turning down to that fateful position, the grimace, which is her natural pose, her normal expression in repose. This guise of normality quiets me, and I feel at ease. I refill her glass and mine.

We look at the harbor. The moon is resolute and unshaken above the horizon line. The night is eerily peaceful, and for a long while we hear only the slap of the waves against the wharf and the strains of bouzoúki music in the distance, probably emanating from the sole disco in town—one of the young Greeks had opened it, though bouzoúki music wouldn't have come from there. I don't know where the sounds are from.

Lu-lu, Gwen pronounces grandly, even portentously, letting the two syllables linger, nearly languish, on her tongue, Lu-lu, of course someone's after me, someone's after you too—Mr. Death, and he's carrying a big scythe, swinging it in huge strokes across the landscape, he's wearing a gray gown—I adore gray—and he's marching across Atlanta, the city's on fire, like Watts, or he's coming in from the wheat fields. Save me, it's a Grant Wood painting. It's titled: Death doesn't take it on the chin. Death isn't on the lam, or death goes out on a limb, death's limber and portable . . .

Stop, stop. All right, all right, I command, laughing. I exhort her that, yes, death is certainly marching nearer, but to me, not to her. You are still a child, I tell her, just one of your tots, an amazing, adult child. To me, you always will be. And in the natural course of things I will pass on to my reward before you, and you will dance at my funeral. I want you to, I implore her, in addition I want you to wail. That is my plea. It will even be in my will! Then I take Gwen's hand in mine and and hold it tight.

Gwen's hand was like ice in my own. I will never forget that moment or that sensation, her small, icy hand in my hot puffy one. As the moon, implacable in its unearthly place and as perfect as an illustration in a fairy-tale book, shone down, Gwen made light of death with more of that invocatory talk of death's riding in from a fiery Atlanta, but I think this time she improvised upon another theme—Mr. Death was traveling Greyhound and absolutely everyone on the bus wanted to die.

It was my belief that that night Gwen and I invoked—no, provoked—death, woke him up, that we stirred that specter of mortality. He had been sleeping quietly above our heads. Death needn't take the shape or form, or need the time, one thinks it will. Gwen taught me that. For instance, she had often insisted that it was an act of hubris on man's part to have created perspective, to have placed the eye, and by dint of that to have placed human beings, in the center of a series of lines and planes, in the center of being. I remember well that Gwen scowled exaggeratedly at my use of the words natural and human nature. She mocked the idea of the natural order, which she did, and had done, over the years in conversation with me.

Pointing to the stars ironically, Gwen contended—no, contested—with the sky and with me yet again. The so-called natural world existed only as a reproof, only to taunt us human beings, to tease us, for weren't we the ones to conceive of Nature to begin with? Hadn't we invented it? Innate is inane, don't you think so, Lulu?

Then, under the imperturbable sky, Gwen metamorphosed. She became stunningly solemn. She whispered into my ear, as if there were someone else sitting at our table, someone who ought not hear her confidences, that it was not so long ago when she had realized that she had been waiting, but she had not known that, waiting for someone or something, and now that seemed ridiculous. Life did not have meaning or purpose, she knew, but perhaps it required an investment, an act of faith. But she had so little—and here she grimaced—of that tender capital. Gwen claimed it was too late for that, for her. I denied it. I told her she had all the time in the world.

All the time in the world, I pontificated. What things I pronounced and with what surety! As much as I didn't hear Gwen, I didn't hear myself. But I am racing ahead now. When logic is no longer a comfort, it's hard to keep orderly the sequence of events. But I suppose she did know then what she faced, what had to be done or confronted, and had come to visit me in order to tell me, but she didn't, not then, and instead, perhaps, Gwen involved herself with John and Alicia, in some grotesquerie calibrated to stymie the ugly and the ineluctable. She referred to it, their affair, as a grotesquerie, and I suppose it was—one meant, I assumed, to frighten away malign spirits. Which ones precisely, I hadn't a clue. Whatever clues Gwen dropped for me were laid much too subtly and well, or, as she might put it, were dropped down too deep a well!

CHAPTER

14

I dreamed last night I knew precisely how to finish Household Gods. I was at the fourth and last part, which meant that the book was in that many parts. Its design, the whole, had been revealed to me. But I could not actually see what had been revealed, for the writing was faded or always, somehow, illegible. I was continually frustrated. Because travel was involved—I was moving from place to place—the dream seemed to imply that I had to find something or someone, Helen, I presume, before I could finish my book. It was most assuredly the strangest dream I've ever had. There was something about death in it, my mother's death, I think, but it may have been my own. While I accept the Greek version of destiny, or fate, as in tragedy, when one's end flows from one's flaws, from hubris, I abhor the idea that one's life is fated. Fate in its Californian manifestation—horoscopes and astrology—is anathema to me. So it struck me as bizarre that my dreamworld was invaded by something like a fate. But then I was engrossed in the Gypsy book. And doesn't Freud say, if I remember correctly, that dreams are concoctions, condensations, of what happened during the day.

With Gwen, the evening and its events dangled delicately from a string, twisting this way and that. There was no plan, no plot, and one seemed not to have any intentions at all. Time always behaves like that with Gwen; it is stretched and fuller than with others, with whom time is less substantial, less rich. Time is more intense in Crete. It is unfortunate that we were interrupted—first, and rather rudely, by Roger. Then by others.

Life is interruption, a series of interruptions. In fact, The Interrupted Life could be my memoir's title. I jot that down in my notebook and reach for the Gypsy book once more. But I am disquieted. I have to act, to take action. I know what I have to do. In a sense and inwardly, I have made my decision. I have just not yet moved. But I know I must and that I must persevere; I must not perseverate. Agitated, I call out to Yannis, Please come here and bring the heavy bond paper and envelopes and the party list; I'm disinviting everyone. The party was supposed to have been held in two days. I had vacillated long enough, primarily about whether to cancel it and risk offending Gwen, in whose honor it was being thrown, or to go ahead with it and delay my search for Helen. Somehow, all along, I knew I would put it off. It is a funny thing, human nature. One knows and yet pretends one doesn't. But why?

Resolved to act, I also hoped to make Gwen understand my decision. Also, I thought petulantly, as I was handed the writing paraphernalia by a sulky Yannis, I had had enough conversation last night to last me a lifetime.

I write what I hope are gracious disinvitations, each calibrated to charm its intended, the recipient, but I can't help recalling, even recapturing, those incendiary conversations, and how, first, Roger slid up to Gwen and me, barging into our fragile dialogue without so much as a by-your-leave.

My word! I exclaimed, my word! Roger, you've taken me by surprise again, sidling up to us like one of those poisonous snakes in Texas. Three converge there, I believe. Roger sat down, though he hadn't been invited, and I reminded myself that we were three, too, and I hoped Roger wouldn't take that up. Thankfully he replied, Six or seven of the deadliest snakes in the world are found in Australia. Do you like snakes, Gwen? He faced Gwen and studied her expectantly, as if he were about to test her in some way. But Gwen—too smart to fall for Roger's impetuous nonsense—swallowed her wine and wiped her thin lips with the back of her hand. It seemed a rude gesture, almost a Neapolitan insult. It was in any case oddly severe, which Gwen can be, oddly severe. Finally, she answered with two words: Some snakes.

I don't know why, foolishness or inebriation, but I started to tell Gwen, in front of Roger, some curious material about the Gypsies. I had dipped further into the book, and what had immediately caught my attention was etymological—the word "Gypsy" first appeared in English in 1537; also, there was no word for Gypsy in their own language, Romany. But more, I went on, and this related to my absorption in the subject of death, I explained that Gypsies believe they were Christ's bodyguards. The myth was that two Gypsy bodyguards had become drunk, had left him unprotected, and this is how he came to be crucified. Roger looked smug. I disliked him intensely in that moment.

Gwen knew someone of Gypsy origin, of course. She had spent time with Django Reinhardt's nephew, who was, like Django, a musician. He was blond and fair, and given to wearing black leather from head to foot. It was a story about feet or boots—his boots—which Gwen narrated for me, though Roger sat near us listening; for in a sense she spoke only to me and subtly ignored him. He did not care; he stayed, as if an observer at our table. I will never forget the story.

Gwen had traveled to London some years back—I hadn't known she'd been there then—and resided in a squat, a house taken over by hippies, I gather, to which the Reinhardt boy had come. There was no romance, but she loved to listen to him play the violin. She said he had talent, which for Gwen was a rare compliment. But then she was partial to musicians, and may have been in London precisely because her musician was there, but I didn't ask. One of the house dwellers took an intense dislike to the Gypsy violinist. And for some reason or other, one afternoon Reinhardt disappeared. Later, as the house dwellers or squatters were having tea in the kitchen, they heard the strains of a melancholy tune. It was Reinhardt, playing the violin. He had gone to the roof of the house, as if to play for the world, Gwen thought then. The roof was in disrepair. Gwen recalled vividly the moment the violin music stopped. She heard a series of squawks. Then one black leather boot descended through the ceiling of the kitchen, which was at the top of the house. The English fellow, a poet, the one who disliked the Gypsy violinist, yelled, "That's the Gypsy. He ruins everything he touches."

A marvelous story. I could easily have imagined and placed Helen in a seat of honor at that tea party, as if the poet were the Mad Hatter. Roger harrumphed but eventually smiled. I didn't trust any of his reactions that night, and I think I was right not to have done so. Roger was about to say something to Gwen, but just at that moment, by which time we'd all had a great deal to drink, and Yannis had shown up, the South African poet, Wallace, and his amour, the Dutchwoman with the guttural name, arrived at our table from out of nowhere. This was Gwen's first meeting with them, and after it, my memory grows weak.

Wallace was entertaining. Yes, he was. I'll admit that, and even I found myself rapt as he told a story about—now, who was it? H.D.? No, it was Djuna Barnes. Wallace insists of course that he slept with her. It all comes back. No, he didn't sleep with her. It was another poet who had, a homosexual, Wallace declared, a surrealist, Charles Henri Ford, in fact, and it was his story.

Djuna Barnes wanted to interview Hitler, and as she was friends with a man named Putzi Hofstingel who was close to Hitler, was his art adviser, something like that, she thought she had an inside chance. Barnes went to Munich to see him. I don't know what year it was, Wallace left that out. Putzi was in love with Djuna, and, Djuna told Ford, Wallace says, that while she never made love with Putzi, he once hugged her so tightly, he burst a vein in his penis. At the time of the burst vein, Putzi and she were in New York; his family's business was art, they ran a large art emporium. According to Djuna, according to Ford, Putzi was a marvelous piano player who often played for Hitler. Djuna never did interview Hitler.

This anecdote was the prelude to, the means to, the most persistent and abiding of Wallace's impassioned literary concerns. He added something about T. S. Eliot, the old possum, having written the introduction to *Nightwood*, which appeared in 1936, and went on about Barnes' discussions of race and religion in that difficult novel. What about the Jew as he appeared in *Nightwood?* Wallace challenged. What of the Jew? Roger demanded. A heated and drunken discussion about art and politics ensued, and Roger, who sides with the formalists, and Wallace, who does not, went at each other like cat and dog. In this case it is hard for me not to think of Roger as the dog; I prefer cats. For my part I can see both sides, and as long as the work has quality, which is indifferent to politics, I can appreciate it.

Wallace returned us to life before World War II and enumerated a list of great and not-so-great literature that was antisemitic—book after book. D. H. Lawrence's *The Virgin and the Gipsy*, for one. To set a different tone, usually unsuccessful, I brought up Jane Bowles' novel *Two Serious Ladies* and ventured that nowadays few would notice that one of the two serious ladies was a Miss Goering. Surely that had relevance—the novel was written when Hitler was in power, published in 1943, and Jane Bowles was Jewish. One didn't, I reminded all assembled, easily admit to being Jewish then. I glanced at Roger, as it was for his benefit that I remarked upon hidden Jewishness. Roger didn't wince, blanch or even wiggle in his chair. Roger ought to be a CIA operative.

Thinking about it now, it could have been many kinds of hiddenness I was referring to, even kinds of hiddenness that were predominantly hidden from me. The significance of Gwen's race to her, of Roger's and my homosexuality, of Wallace's time in mental hospitals for having opposed apartheid. We were a ragtag band of inhibited outsiders, each a secret and keeping secrets from the others. And ourselves, I suspect. In our own idiosyncratic, careful ways.

I can remember just one other incident. Gwen snorted something about Hitler's having been a great dancer, which, she ex-

plained, was a line from Mel Brooks' movie *The Producers*. I had
not seen it, nor had Wallace. But he took exception to Gwen's
insouciance. Indifferent to him, Gwen was hitting her usual cut-
ting stride and was swaggering full tilt, certainly by the end of
that long evening. I was, as I noted, reassured. And yes, Roger,
I believe, did finally get to Gwen, at least he annoyed her, but
I cannot remember how. Perhaps it is true, as Gwen often asserted, that I never remember the truly vicious moments. If so,
I am a lucky man. Indeed today I am content. Human beings
have no real memory of physical pain, I believe, yet psychical
pain can plague one. Perhaps I am one of those happy few who
can wipe clean from my fleshy slate even traces of nonphysical,
verbal abuse.

I finish my notes of regret, and call again for Yannis, who takes
them from me with a brazen nonchalance. I refuse to acknowledge
his disrespect and ask him to hand-deliver them. Letters of regret—though what's being regretted I'm not sure. No one will
care. Had there been a party, there could have been regret. There
could have been all manner of trouble, given that confluence and
cast of characters. It will come, the party, its stickiness, its aftermath; but it will not have come now or when it was expected to
have come. It will have been delayed. The future perfect—plus
perfect?—is an interesting condition, a tense little delved into.
The future is not of course perfect. And in the notes I haven't
let on what I'm about to do; I have let that hang mysteriously—
they would expect as much from me, I am famous for this kind
of thing. It's all in character, they will say. I have written that
I will reschedule the party and, indeed, I will, when I return.
No one will care. Perhaps Alicia will. She'll be most curious.
But I don't have time to visit her to explain. And besides, John
is ensconced in her house and I cannot possibly let him know
my plan, for surely he'll want to accompany me, even though
Gwen said he cares not a fig about Helen. I don't entirely believe
Gwen, or rather, I am not certain that her interpretation of John,
or his interpretation of Helen, is accurate. I am in fact entirely
suspicious and dubious. He could have been pillow-talking.

The truth, the ugly truth, is that one can only surmise and approximate, without any exactitude, what even one's very best friend bases his or her analyses upon. Conversation is the least propitious way to discover the truth. It is uncontrollable. Why do we do it? Why do I do it? One says it's only talk, but in fact I think talk is dangerous. Vernacularly speaking, I get into more trouble talking than by doing anything else. Others have great adventures; I merely speak. That's the long and short of it, as my father would say. He was, conversationally, the short of it. Linguists theorize about the human need to communicate, the creativity of human beings in daily speech and language, and about the inventiveness of language, all of which clarifies and elaborates upon the idiom "talking for the sake of talking." Talk is neither simple nor obvious. Human beings are perverse and complex. We can lie. We can be mistaken. One would never accuse an ape of being mistaken. Sometimes, when I am in the midst of one of those human inventions, I cannot imagine what it is that is being communicated. Although I can well believe that it has all been created on the spot. It cannot be controlled, can it?

Several papers spill off the bed and onto the floor—I have small bundles of paper as well as books at the foot of my bed, but I can assure one and all that I am not deranged and horribly messy like the eccentric Collier brothers. A lone sheet finds its way from its obscure position under the pile to the top, to visibility; it is something I wrote which I haven't looked at in a long time.

Roger is an uncontrollable character. His ability to concoct, to invent, ought to become legend, for nothing else about him will live on. Or I suppose that might be said about me. Yet at least I've published more than one book, even if under a pseudonym. We like to say—Alicia and I—that he is a parvenu who pooped. I will make Roger known (isn't this the rationale authors always offer to their "subjects" when they commit them to print?), but I will not give him feats of daring and derring-do. I will present him as he is, warts and all, just as Chaucer presented the Wife of Bath.

It is astonishing—appalling—to me that I could have written such nonsense. What was I thinking about? Still, I like the co-incidence of its appearance, as its theme, about what can be controlled, aligns with my present contemplations. But I must cease contemplating, if that is what I may name these idlings, and get started. As usual I am temporizing. May I permit myself, with good humor, of course, an allusion to Hamlet?

I have to tell Yannis what I intend to do and why I am venturing off. He will never understand. Should I ask him to accompany me? How can I explain my trip to him? I think I should ask him to come. He can say no, but at least he'll have been invited. I haven't been attentive to him lately and that is wrong. Last night he sat nearby, in his usual position, but seeemed more aggrieved than ever. Roger and he cast each other the occasional furious glance. I don't want to hurt Yannis. But in truth, I don't want him with me. I need to be alone. It is something I must do by myself.

I get out of bed and move around the room in a flurry of impotent activity. I am confused. I am enormously excited and anxious. I feel happy. Eager and expectant, like a young bride, I am about to go where I've never traveled before, and truly it seems like an adventure of the sort a young person might embark upon. This may seem silly but, for an instant, as I prance about the room, I remind myself of Alastair Sim playing Scrooge in *A Christmas Carol*. The Scrooge who has renounced his mean ways. I feel alive in a way I haven't in years, even more filled with vitality than I was when I went to Helen's house the other day. Was it just the other day?

There are things to do. I have a mission. I march to my desk to make a list. Food, clothes, money, the necessities, I write these words down with a flourish, with determination. And as if doing automatic writing a sentence occurs to me, and I write it as well, for it may come in handy for Stan Green, if not for me: Curiosity and fear are partners in crime.

And then yet another thought rushes in, as if to fill the space vacated by the previous thought, which, once written down, can be forgotten. But this set of words is more complicated and not merely a decent or provocative sentence. Why it comes to me, I don't know. Gwen may have told me it: In 1896, when dyslexia was discovered, the disease was called word blindness.

I write word blindness in capital letters. It seems to have something to do with my peculiar dream, whose oblique effects have not completely left me. Household Gods is to be in four parts, and I could not read some of the words in the dream. I may be suffering from word blindness. If one is dyslexic, one has difficulty reading, because one flips letters upside down or reads backward, and so on. Perhaps my book is back to front. Perhaps the last comes first. More generally, of course, it could mean that I am not seeing something I ought to see. Some speak of spiritual blindness, I could be afflicted with word blindness. Didn't I emit the words, My word! My word! to Roger when he came up to Gwen and me? How does that fit? The dream was definitely ominous. Perhaps I oughtn't drive to the south. Practically speaking, what if I can't read the road signs? I add to my list: sunglasses! At least my humor is intact.

Gwen's won't be. Gwen will actively dislike my cause. She will have thought she had talked me out of going to find Helen. Helen Wheels, Gwen dubbed her—hell on wheels. She insisted, ada-mantly, that Helen wouldn't have hitched a ride on a donkey with a Gypsy woman, but, like any punkette, would have driven to the caves or wherever in a fast car. Gwen has no faith in Helen. She is probably jealous of my regard for her. I can certainly understand that. I am jealous of her regard for others—even the sick rock-and-roll musician. But I'd never admit it to her. I have much too much pride. We are, both of us, in some strange way, under each other's skins, and luckily we are not in any conven-tional sense in love with each other.

Yannis will take the news badly too, but unlike Gwen, he will mope. Gwen will pull her small self up, let fly a few caustic comments, and in my absence read a book or two. She will continue to dabble in John and Alicia. But to what extent is Alicia involved? If she is. That was not clear at all.

The leather weekender I haven't used in years is a familiar and long-lost friend. A sight for sore eyes. I've had it since college. I'd never throw it away. I'm not sure how long I will be away, perhaps a week, and I toss into it a number of shirts, two pairs of trousers, socks, and so on. I briskly collect my toiletries and another bag, in which to carry books and notepads. But which books to take? I race to my shelves and grab a few travel books—as well as a map of Crete. But I'll need to go to the tourist bureau. I throw in Miller's *The Colossus of Maroussi*, Stein's *Writings and Lectures 1909–1945*, and *The Selected Writings of Sydney Smith*, an early nineteenth-century favorite of mine, and of Roger's, too, unfortunately. Credit where credit is due—Roger has a few good points.

I dress hurriedly, sip my cold coffee, bite into a roll, then leave my apartment. At the desk downstairs, I grab the mail, glance cursorily at it, tell Nectaria that I will be leaving for a week, watch her expression turn sour, or a trifle grave, and walk to the harbor where, as ever, its beauty overwhelms me. The simple life that I love. Yet I know that that simple life is not simple. I merely love the illusion of simplicity that it provides me, which is the paradox.

Many of the stalls at the market are shut or closing. It is late in the day. I rush to purchase bread, crackers, hard cheese, apples, olives and several bottles of water. The elderly Greek men, with their leathery and weather-beaten hands and faces, are unperturbed by the likes of me, moving here and there. Life for them goes on, characterized by its regularity and lack of interruption. Their games of tavoli involve them and they are intent upon moving their tiles around the board. It is strange to think now, but I often do, precisely because of its incongruousness, that when they were very young, mere boys, they may have been sexual playmates, just the way the boys are now, and one of them may have been the girl.

I reach the tourist bureau just in time and gather up as many maps as I can. The woman behind the desk is phlegmatic but warms to me slowly as she sees with what excitement I am planning my trip. She offers me, gratis, a booklet on inns and hotels that I may need. I thank her profusely. The drive, if direct, is not a long one, but I want to scout towns along the way, along the coast road, and even go off the main road, to wander into the hills and dales. I want to see if I can chance upon Gypsy encampments. I want to spy upon their way of life, upon them. Helen could be anywhere, after all, though the map she left on the dresser is evidence of her intentions, at least her intended destination.

Now it is growing dark, and some of the breath of life ebbs from me. A sunny day is transformed into a gloomy one. I cannot help it; dusk sometimes makes me mournful. The bank is closed. It is too late to set off on my trip, but I do not want to eat at the restaurant tonight, and see everyone, and have to explain anything. A few drinks and I could tell all. As if chased by a flock of reporters, I hurry back to the hotel and find Nectaria. She will bring me a meal in my rooms. I am safe. Except that I must tell Gwen and Yannis. But where is Gwen? She is not in her room. No matter, I tell myself, I'll write her a letter; that is easier, in any case. She must be with John, and Alicia. And Yannis too has disappeared again. I am alone in my room. Happily, alone.

I take my place at the large open window and watch the sky change subtly, imperceptibly. It is night's magic. Nectaria brings in my dinner and I thank her. The wine is blissfully cold, the moussaka, hearty. I am content once more.

Sitting by the window, with the cacophonous and comforting sounds of harbor life playing on my ears like incidental music, I open my book. We non-Gypsies, I learn, are designated by them as *gadjo* or *gadje*, for whom they have nothing but contempt. "The proper meaning of *gadjo* is peasant, farmer, with the pejorative sense of 'clodhopper,' 'yokel,' or 'bumpkin.' " To the Gypsies, we are the sedentary ones. To these wanderers, nomads, travelers, we are ones who do not move, who are fixed. My eyes fix on these lines. Sedentary indeed.

Instantly I am overcome with exhaustion, and nearly close

the book. So weary, even my eyes are tired, but I do not stop reading. I sense that I must go on. I flip to another chapter. "If the Gypsies have no system of writing, as we usually understand the word, they nevertheless use a very full list of conventional signs which enable them to communicate visually and in time. This secret code is called the *patrin* (from *patran*, leaf of a tree) . . ."

It's pleasing to discover that *patrin*, their secret means of communication, is linguistically close to the English "pattern." As this sentence is at the bottom of the page, I again nearly close the book, but resist, fight my weariness, and continue reading. "Each tribe has its own distinctive sign, and it is the chief who is usually the holder of the sign; and this sign is a secret." Then down to the bottom of the next page: "Thus a Gypsy woman will be the first to go into a farmhouse on the pretext of selling items . . . or to tell fortunes." She will find out family secrets, important family matters, recent illnesses and so forth. "As she is going away, she will scratch on the wall or mark with chalk or charcoal signs which only her racial brothers will know how to make out."

These signs allow the next Gypsy to reveal closely held family secrets to the amazed family. How clever, I think.

Ultimately the full import of what I have just read reaches my clotted brain. "In chalk or charcoal." Chalk. The chalk drawings or signs on the wall in Helen's room may not have been made by Helen. They may have been drawn or penned by the Gypsy woman. This was the break I needed. What I ascertained to be penises and vaginas could have been messages from the Gypsy, written in her alphabet or code, which I don't know and would never even be able to guess.

I am stunned. It is such a good story, and so mysterious, and I haven't even made it up! I am in thrall to it, and frightened by it. For next I learn, as I study the pages before me, that Gypsies use herbs and plants and all manner of vegetable and animal matter for spells, to achieve various results. In a flash a picture of Helen appears before me and I see a small silver ball attached to a silver chain. The necklace hung around Helen's neck the last night I saw her. It may have contained a plant, a potion. Ridiculous, Horace, I tell myself. Still, weird, foul, foreign herbs— or worse—may account for the dreadful smell, the aroma that suffused Helen's room. That awful odor could have been produced by rotting vegetable matter, spoiled organic stuff, and have been a potion meant to cast a spell, over me perhaps, and which I may be obeying even now as I read. My acute exhaustion? A potion to do what?

How crazy I felt in these moments, how bereft of the means to know what the truth was or to judge my experience in and of Helen's room. I cannot adequately signify or express it. What I can articulate is that it was, and is, in no way like me to have thought I could be subject to a spell. Or, indeed, to believe that I was the victim of a plot. I was the one who confabulated, who wrote plots, the one who knew. Yet the logic I used proceeded in this manner: I may have been under a spell because even imagining that I could be, or to have believed myself to have been, made it seem more likely that I was or could have been. It was not like me, not at all like me, to entertain such nonsense.

I did not completely accept any of the above, but I did allow it, seriously. I passed a sleepless night on account of it. I would awaken startled, as if shaken by Yannis, and think, What if it's true? In rebuttal I would answer, You are a fool, Horace. Then I would place my head on the pillow and try to fall asleep, counting from one thousand backward. (Both my parents were insomniacs.) Yet the persistent and disturbing idea—that one could not know what one did not know—recurred. I awoke with a start to the question, What if it's true? But it was truer to say that I didn't know the what of it, what was what, the what of the question.

PART · III

THE PURSUIT

OF SENSE

CHAPTER

15

I begin the journey south on a blustery Cretan morning. Though I passed a relatively sleepless night, fraught with doubt and un-answerable questions and, upon waking, feel enervated, I am committed to my task and resolved to be focused. I have always been resilient. As one gets older one knows how to pace oneself; it is one of the few comforts one has. The clouds are moving anarchically, to match my own eager and jumpy spirits. For my eyes alone, they perform wicked tricks, and the heavens above compose messages set in skywriting. I am filled with a peculiar, nourishing hope. I will leave this city I love, my adopted home, to itself.

As I drive through it, I wave to a few of the shopkeepers who stand in front of their places of business. I remember that I owe Lefteris a courtesy call—he repaired my radio, but refused pay-ment. That means a game or two of tavoli and some ouzo. The baker and his wife have just set out the freshly baked bread for the late-morning crowd. I almost can't bear to leave, drawn to the ordinary drama I know so well. But I am in search of Helen and, I would have to say, high drama.

Earlier I had gone to the bank, the liquor store, paid a few bills, and had also written a note to Yannis, which I left for him in an envelope, with some cash, on the mantelpiece. I gave the letter meant for Gwen to Nectaria and kissed Nectaria warmly on her rosy, full cheek. I assured myself of two things: that I had chosen the right path, though it might be risky, and that matters at home had been left in a good state. The right path and left in a good state . . .

To the left or to the right? I ask myself at the first significant crossroad. Dante positioned Beatrice to his left and Virgil to his right. Left is faith; right, reason. Reason and Faith, I hoped, would be my traveling companions. I do not beckon God, I hold to no religious faith, of course, but I am imbued with my own brand of secular faith. Is that reason? And therefore redundant? It is a good thing that at the last moment I threw in not just extra paper but my portable typewriter. I can write in longhand but prefer to labor on my old manual.

As I drive farther from home, everything seems very much behind me. Literally, it is behind me. To tell the truth, I find myself peeping into the rearview mirror often, anxious that the nameless things of daily life will catch up to me or even overtake me, things that I want left behind. I am not completely sure which things. The light-headedness that I have lately been experiencing accompanies me, an invisible but effective agent. I am in a new, nearly alien state of mind; I am convinced it is all to the good.

A pleasurable, indeed delicious, aspect of travel is that one may choose a variety of routes, some slow, some fast, some straight, some curved, and so on—the enduring metaphors of the journey theme. I go left and next turn right. Possessing a good sense of direction—is this genetic?—I can always find my way, except when inebriated. So I know that if I take this road, I will end up at that road, and then I know that that road will lead me to another, and then another, and in the end all will be right. If one knows where one is headed, so to speak, one can get there, especially when blessed with a good sense of direction. My mother often asserted this and I believe it as if it had been cast in stone, like one of the Ten Commandments.

All roads lead to Rome, I caution myself and chortle aloud. It was the Venetians who were here ages ago, not the Romans, and they settled in Crete ages before the still-dreaded Turks conquered it, and would an ancient Venetian have claimed that all roads lead to Rome or not? Or just when would a Venetian have begun to claim that?

I journey along the coast road, then turn south past Galatas, though I could have gone the other way, in the opposite direction, which would have been faster. By taking the road I have, I avoid being in the proximity of Souda Bay, where the naval installation is, and I would rather, and do, travel miles out of my way just to bypass it. I detest that part of my Sunday morning when the naval band from Souda marches around our peaceful harbor and makes a ruckus that could wake the dead. I am so glad that the military government is out. It is not that the parades halted, but when the colonels were in power, there was an arrogance and pomp to the Sunday parade which it now lacks.

This reminds me of another argument I had with Roger. Though he supported the junta, contradictorily he was dismayed when the monarchy was abolished and King Constantine deposed. In part, I repeatedly told him, the junta had formed in opposition to Queen Frederika and her son, Constantine. Still, Roger likes royalty—the English line in particular. He likes pomp. I have eternally insisted that even an Anglophile such as myself must agree that having a monarch is an anachronism of the most bizarre kind, entirely unsuited to a modern democratic state and a modern mind. Roger claims also to like strong leaders, men of decision. Roger fools no one. But why think of Roger now, as I set off on a new road?

While I don't care to hurry, at the same time I experience a strong sense of urgency. And too it is in my mind, almost disproportionately, that I must leave myself, and the trip, open to chance. This is a chance operation, I say aloud, in hard-boiled style, and again indulge in a spur-of-the-moment directional decision. I even wonder whether or not I will better appreciate the abstract expressionists after this trip, since it is to be based to some extent on randomness. My perambulating may be a whimsical foray into abstraction. But its randomness is under my control; that is, I am in charge of it. I decide when or if it is this road or that that

I take. I am, I tell myself, the agent of change, my own travel agent. After all, even Jackson Pollock, whom Gwen likes better than I—she has far greater sympathy for the barmen, as she calls them—even he, to some extent, controlled randomness through his execution of it. It is not as if anyone at all could have just walked up to one of his gigantic canvases and thrown paint at it.

A stream of cars passes me; sometimes there are many, sometimes few. Cars usually pass me. I drive quite slowly. Carts drawn by horses do not pass me, though. I remember horse-drawn carts in my hometown. They were still in use when I was a child, after all. How strange that is to consider in this day. Greek men on World War II German motorcycles with sidecars overtake me; the Greeks glance at me and my Volkswagen bug with amusement. Were I to have any, my passengers would become infuriated because of my caution and lack of speed, though Helen didn't when we drove to the mountains that day. But as I am alone, with no passenger, no one to answer to, I am free to do what I please. But why, I wonder, should I be thinking of this condition as a freedom, as if it were rare, when I live alone and essentially answer to no one?

Yannis is there but not there. It is true that I am never unaware of his presence, of his odd and occasionally sinister gaze that can so brutally penetrate and pierce me, my soul, if I have one. His look can pin me to, or in, a moment. It is painful, dreadful. It has to do with one human being being seen by another and one or both being able to understand in that all-too-human instant something intensely peculiar, even deranged, about the other. There can be no recording of the vague exchange, no document left behind, just one's experience of a naked expression, of being naked, in an impropitious moment. It is chilling and unsettling to be caught unaware. It is probably why many people prefer to live alone. I remember Gwen telling me that a man she was seeing caught her staring at herself in a mirror, as she pushed her hair from her forehead and studied her face. She realized that in that brief moment he discovered something about her, her narcissism, her paranoia, her incessant insecurity—in regard to him as well—

all of which she would never have wanted revealed. He didn't telephone her again, though they had been seeing each other off and on for two years. Gwen was relieved. She felt that neither he nor she could have borne the burden of what had passed furtively between them.

It is strange to break off a relationship in that manner, but then that is the way it happens. The break is sudden and sharp but seldom clean. And, to prove my hypothesis, Gwen is one who lives alone. One Who Lives Alone is another good title. I pull over to the side of the road and jot that down.

Looking at the map of Crete, at the road ahead and the environs, I am struck again by the island's magnificent geography. Most of the major roads appear to halt in the middle of the island, because of the treacherous mountains. The mountains defy one and all. This is extraordinary country, rugged and violent. Its landscape is unexpected and invigorating. With my eye and finger I trace on the map the many possible courses—possible worlds—from which to select, and decide, again on the spot, to quit the road I have been taking and head toward the coast road again, so as to travel near the sea and around the exterior of Crete. It was what I originally had planned but then for some reason rebelled against, even though it was my idea. At my age it may always be one's own ideas, however hackneyed, that one rebels against.

I don't particularly want to drive through the mountains, and of course the roads do come to a halt disastrously and one would have to backtrack here and there, to meet up with the right road, and in a sense one would be much too directed by the terrain. One is by the coast road too, but one does not experience it in just that way. Besides, if Helen were with the Gypsy, or on her own, mightn't she want to see the beautiful coastline? I start up the car, plot my new course, and turn around, to begin again. The scenery is magnificent.

I wish I could keep my mind on it. I am not one who can keep his mind on what is actually before him; I am more involved in what I see in my mind's eye. It is prosaic but true. I tend merely to register the physical world, my surroundings, but then, in a matter of no time at all, have in view a whole range of associations—a mountain range, if you will—which looms in front of me, and off I go. I might consider the mountains in the distance, their rough beauty, how purple they appear, but the color purple might lead me to the term "purple prose," for example, which then always brings to mind Alicia and how Alicia has been written about.

Alicia. I see Alicia when I first knew her. She is young, willowy, graceful, nearly ethereal; her face is before me as if pasted on the windshield. Years ago she took a trip into the mountains, which she did not invite me to join. A friend had arrived from France and she devoted herself to her—another opera singer, I believe. Alicia is a devoted friend, one capable of loving. There are few of those. I easily slide to the opposing concepts, and to Stan-Greenish thoughts, to hate and betrayal. I ponder anew what I have often pondered before. These repetitions are as annoying as they are compelling and absorbing. If Alicia hates Helen, as she seems to, what is the true reason? Has it anything to do with Helen? What exactly are Alicia's feelings toward Helen? Are they murderous ones? Would Alicia murder Helen? Would Alicia be capable of murdering anyone? And why not? What about Helen? Would she have strangled her sister for her father's love or his fortune, though he probably has no fortune—a psychiatrist earns well but not spectacularly. He may have inherited a great fortune. Just as I would have if my father hadn't lost much of his, if there hadn't been the Great Depression, and if and if. And what of Gwen and Alicia? What of them right now? Where does John sit in the equation between them? Is John sitting or reclining right now, is he recumbent on a bed of silk?

John. The idea of him arouses in me a range of emotions, a mountain range of feelings, of highs and lows, a violent, lusty landscape, which can be quite uncontrollable. The one thing one cannot control is lust. But it is what we most often control, or are controlling most of the time, or are most controlled by. I don't want to think of him, he is not on the map right now. He is not on my course, and I have not plotted him there. Isn't it odd, the two significant meanings of plot—one having to do with a conspiracy, the other with a story. Perhaps all stories are conspiracies. But there, my paranoia is showing. I am happy to be alone.

In real life one cannot find the single, unmistakable, absolute event or fact that drives everything and everyone forward. It is, this motive, what makes a compelling if thin narrative, for the stories I particularly admire relish ambiguity and happenstance. One character meets another—the servant is there, so Raskolnikov must kill her as well. How does it take shape that someone, even someone like me, will do the unexpected? I hope to work these ideas into Household Gods. Is it now, at this precise moment, that I joke to myself about being off the road yet again?

It is well past lunchtime. I have arrived at a small village and spy a taverna that appears to be open. I pull up to the side of the road and park the car. I am not thinking anything special as I am hungry—famished—and a little tired. The owner leads me to a table on the terrace. A breeze blows and the air is fragrant and rich. It is more than comfortable here, it is pleasant, and its pleasure is ordinary, inexpensive. Overhead is a trellis, a grape arbor. All is as it should be. This taverna, this scene, is in no way extraordinary. It is, and I am, comfortable, yet something is missing.

I order grilled sardines, a salad, and a bottle of mineral water and the white wine I drink. Fortunately they have it. After one glass, I am tranquil. With the second glass, I am impatient and want more wine and, I suppose, action. John might put it that way. I can almost hear him pronounce it, can imagine his lips loosely forming the words. Horace, you want action, man. I do want something or want for something. For lack of a better word I will name this luck. If I were lucky, a Gypsy would appear and sit beside me at this table. As this does not happen, my meal is unadventurous and undisturbed. Even disappointing.

I drive toward the coast. I don't care to stop or to make a detour. I see no strange encampments along the way. Had I chosen the faster way, I would already have been on the southern coast, quite near to the dot on Helen's map which signified where she had probably gone. But I am not sure if that is the case, or if she had been the one to leave the map lying there, with its mark. Thinking about this is ludicrous, in one way, and confusing in another. I drive, plagued by the uncertainty of it all, and of how this isn't and wasn't like me, to go flying off in pursuit of a mere girl, even one like Helen.

I am discouraged, but hasten to encourage myself to have patience. If Gwen were with me, no doubt she'd caustically remark that I need patience but need more to be the patient. I'd bet the conversation would take such a linguistic turn. I would bet that, were she here to take the bet. I swing around on the road, the road to Mandalay, to somewhere. I am indeed going somewhere.

Gwen says one always goes somewhere, even if it's nowhere. She entered into psychoanalysis in the late 1960s, but rarely talks about it seriously, or at all, with me, in any case. It is another of her secrets. It may be something that she could share with Helen were she not so antipathetic to Helen, and why is that? Wouldn't it be beyond coincidence if her analyst were Helen's father? The idea excites me. Such a fact might easily have created in Gwen the extreme distrust and dislike of Helen she has. It is much too farfetched. It would serve a certain kind of plot. Or fate. Though I do not accept the concept of an externally derived or driven fate, I remind myself that the root of fate—*fatum*— and story—*fabula*—is the same, *fari*, which means "to speak," and, in the past participle, "to be spoken."

One cannot fail to see that there is a way in which a story and a fate proceed similarly, the causes for action or inaction lying within the character as well as within the environment, the conditions surrounding the characters, those the characters were born into. When the situation seems too unlikely, the reader will no longer willingly suspend disbelief, will not accept the outcome. The reader will demur: it does not seem that that could have happened. Didn't the Victorians change the endings of particularly wrenching tragedies? In a sense, the story itself has a fate, which must be discovered or discerned first by the writer. Yes, that is so, I think. But Helen's father as Gwen's analyst wouldn't do, except as a fantasy. I suppose I oughtn't to have finished the wine. Still I did mix the wine with water. *Fateri* means to acknowledge, to confess or admit. Confession is rooted or yoked to fate and story, which makes ultimate good sense. Confession and admission—neither do I do easily or at all. Yet I know they are always a part of what I write, even if inadvertently.

I have no idea where I am and pull over to the side of the road to check the map again. I seem to be going in the right direction. I rarely get lost.

Arriving at Kissamos in just over an hour, or perhaps more—I am not timing myself—I decide against stopping. But I do enter the town and drive along several streets, to scan the scene and the people. The stores are similar to my town's, though the town itself is smaller. Here people beep their horns rather too insistently.

Uninspired, I continue on my way. My mood shifts, swings down, and I am suddenly overcome by a vexatious idea: I will never find anything or anyone, not the Gypsy, certainly not Helen. I have been on this journey, this adventure, not even a day. It is like me to indulge in hopelessness, in a futility so great I could not imagine a future different from a lackluster present. (I note that future and futility may not have the same root, though future in Latin, *futurus*, means "that which will be," which implies fate but not through its being spoken.) This limitation is probably why I am a writer. I do not want to confront the severe differences between what I would imagine and set on paper, and what I might find should I venture to live it, to act upon or to enact it. Mother called me a dreamer. She said it affectionately, even though she knew, as did I, that that very quality was what caused my father to abandon me, in a sense. My mother's voice had a clear, bell-like tone. Dreamer, Horace, you're such a dreamer, dear! Even now her words ring like the sweetest of chimes.

Oddly enough, reflecting this way restores me to a better frame of mind, because it is like me to think such things, depressing and poignant as they may seem to others. The familiar is a comfort, whatever that may be, the most inconsequential thing, something insignificant to anyone else. One often cannot explain it to others or even to oneself, still one knows it somehow. Something that would appear to be nothing to a friend is precisely the big nothing to oneself. Now that's a good title, The Big Nothing, another one for Stan Green. I drive even more slowly so as to write it down.

The sight of the coast, too, restores my spirits, though I am wondering with some regularity by this time how Yannis is and whether or not Gwen has read my letter and how well or ill she will have taken its contents. Of course I cannot know this, and while it is useless for me to conjecture about it, I do. A particularly stirring view of sky, sea and mountain pricks my attention and I drive down a small road that will take me nearer it. This road is unpaved and rocky and I drive less than a mile, whereupon I reach a clearing and park the car. I get out, stretch my arms and legs, and allow myself the pleasure of contemplation. I am not certain where I am.

I must record an incident that were I reading this I should probably not accept it as fact. But it is true. In this lonely area, off the beaten path, as it were, and without a thought in my mind, I came upon first a Gypsy woman, not the Gypsy woman, but one who looked as if she could have been her mother, or at least a relation, and then her children, or children, and some Gypsy men. They appeared from nowhere, at least I thought that for a moment, until I realized that I had by chance come upon an encampment. My excitement cannot be measured. It was a dream come true. I was lucky. Still it is really not so strange, as there are at least eighty thousand Gypsies in Crete.

Happening upon them like this, I am shaken, almost breathless. I had no plan, yet, I exhorted myself heartily, that is the plan. From what I had read about them, I still did not know what to expect, nor had I been tutored or prepared in the ways of greeting them. I knew I wanted them to know instantly that I was not like the others—the *gadje* for whom they had disdain, yet whom they also feared, from whom they might steal or at whom they might sneer.

I decide that the best action is inaction—I will do nothing. I will wait.

With my back to them I stand looking at the view for some time. I have no way of knowing if they are looking at me. I think they must be—at the least they must be aware of my presence. It is better just to let them study me, without any intervention on my part. I am not frightened in the usual sense, my heart is not pounding, but I am very much conscious of the fact that there is only one of me and several or many of them. The odds are on their side should things go awry, I remind myself. On the other hand, I am strangely sanguine. They will quickly learn that there is nothing to fear from me.

It is growing colder and getting dark. I turn, not too quickly, and walk back to my car. I grab a bottle of ouzo. Without hesitation and with a cheerful alacrity, I carry the ouzo to the older Gypsy woman, who seems to be the clan's matriarch. There is a younger woman, a girl, beside her, I see now. She is bedecked and bejeweled, wearing a striped dress that looks like a bathrobe I once had. She herself is very like a photograph of a Gypsy I once saw in a New York gallery, I think. They both are, in fact.

The older woman stares at me and accepts my offering. I then announce in Greek that my name is Horace. She nods. Then I state, also in Greek, that I am a gadjo, living in Crete, but that I am originally from America, that I was born there. She appears to be startled, I suppose by my declaration that I am not a Gypsy, for of course she knows without my telling her that I am not one of them. What I was hoping to do was to indicate that I had some knowledge of them, their language and ways, that I was not merely one of the stupid sedentary ones. But after her initial surprise, the woman breaks into peals of laughter and repeats what I have just said to the family, even the children—all have gathered about us—and then she slaps me brusquely on the back. With surprise I too realize that my presentation of self is humorous and chuckle along with her, with all of them. The oldest of the men—the chief of the family, perhaps—opens the bottle of ouzo, from which we all drink. Glasses of many types and sizes have appeared as well as a large pitcher of water. I mix my ouzo with water by the light of a lantern that hangs above us.

Several rounds of liquor are consumed in a short time, which is characterized by liveliness and gaiety. At some point we all move into a large caravan that is parked behind a clump of trees and bushes, and along with the ouzo and raki and other liquor, which one of them had brewed, there is also some food. I am thankful for that. I am also grateful to them for their hospitality. I can sleep there should I want to. That is also lucky because I should not drive.

The men tell stories; they take great pride in their narrative skills. The storyteller, I know from my reading, is beloved among the Gypsies. In the community, the stature of a man is to a large degree determined by how well he speaks. One of the stories told is about why the Gypsies are the smartest people on earth and another has to do with why the Gypsies steal. The former is long and involved, the latter short and devilishly ambiguous. When Christ was to be crucified, a Gypsy stole one of the four nails meant to nail him to the cross, the one meant to pierce Christ's heart. Before he died, Christ, out of gratitude for the Gypsy's theft, stated that forevermore the Gypsies could roam the world and would be the only people free to steal. All the Gypsies laugh loudly at this story. I smile but am confused, perhaps contrite, as this is the very attack that I—and others—would have mounted previous to my brief study of them. It is an awkward moment, but it passes quickly with the arrival of more food.

One of the young men is most intrigued by my desire to find Helen and asks many questions about her, some of which I am not able to answer. What is her birth sign? Will she have children? Where was she born? What is her mother's name? There is a general discussion about which of their younger women could be with her, but none of them think it likely that they know the young woman. The fetching young man—he is hardly more than a boy, I think—has a ready smile, an easy smile. He is winning and charming, with none of Yannis' surliness. Even so I decline a card game with him; I have never been a great fan of cards, though I bear a poker face. After I disclose that I am a writer, he shows me some papers which have to do with a Gypsy organization and a conference that had been held in 1971, to press the world for Gypsy rights. About this cause he is impassioned, and he speaks a good, grammatical Greek. He has had some formal education, I think. Though I believe that is contrary to Gypsy dictates.

I am most interested in this young man—his name is Roman—and his involvement in his people. It is, in a sense, not unlike my own. Do the Gypsies, I finally ask, now agitate for their own country or state? At this they all laugh, and one says, how gadje that is of me, or something of that kind, but in a friendly manner. Roman explains that some Gypsies want a territory where they would not be forced to be like everyone else and to obey laws and rules that are not their own. They hope to escape harassment and persecution. We are already a nation, he explains for my benefit, and in Romany, I believe it is, and then Greek, exclaims, All Roma are brothers! Immediately an argument ensues among them about the Gypsies' having conferences at all as well as questions about their submitting to organizations, which also are seen as gadje. This is stated succinctly by the older woman.

But the argument is cut short. Roman takes out his violin—he can play too!—and I am reminded of Gwen's association with Django Reinhardt's nephew. A melancholy and haunting melody fills the caravan. Even though it is a cold night, we drift out the door, and one by one everyone dances under the moonlight. First the young woman in the striped bathrobe sways and claps her hands and strikes a tambourine, and even the children, who are still awake, join in. I too dance. It strikes me that I do not know how the night will end and about that I am nearly ecstatic.

Feeling inconceivably like Noel Coward, I whirl about alone, but then dance with the older woman, whose crinkly amber eyes remind me, and this is uncanny, of my mother, who would have been shocked by the comparison. But does anyone know anything other than by comparison?

The next morning I awake, and all about me is commotion and movement. My head pounds ferociously. Immediately I am in a panic, as I am disoriented by my new, strange surroundings. I attempt to calm myself. Sigá, sigá, I intone silently. I lie quietly in the makeshift bed. I think again of Gwen, who can always reassure me in her no-nonsense way. Where is she now? What did she once quote me—something from Mao Tse-tung, about it's always being darkest before it is black.

My Gwen. She insists that if one remembers one's dreams one can shake off the night's bad news and rise up—at least leave one's bed. I force myself to remember my dream; I often forget. It comes in bits and pieces, one entailing the next. Ah, yes, I see it now. It must have been influenced by the Gypsies. I too am wandering and homeless. Then I am in a room. It is depressing to inhabit, with a single light bulb hanging from the ceiling over a cotlike bed that is unmade. It is the kind of cheap room one might have found on Forty-second Street during the forties or fifties, or in novels about the people who live in those sordid places. I would never. I leave the room to roam about a large building. I take an elevator, which fits one person only, but I must pull a rope in order to make it move. Come to think of it, it is like the freight elevator in the building where my father had his office for many years. And had his secretary! The elevator door eventually opens—I am afraid that I will never reach the right floor—and I walk into the hallway. I am near the principal's office. It seems to be a school.

That is all, but there is a good deal of anxious wandering in it. I assume it has to do with looking for Helen. If I were Gwen, I might become the punster and enjoy the movement from roam to Romany to romance. I did think, last night, of Bizet's *Carmen* when the Gypsy girl in the striped bathrobe danced. The word "Gypsy" comes from Egyptian—the Europeans thought the Gypsies were Egyptians when first they encountered them, hundreds of years ago. They don't look Egyptian to me. I would like to jot down all these thoughts right now, but there is too much bustling going on about me. I finally move and arise from bed and stick my head out the tentlike structure I slept in. I am in my pajamas, but how I got into them, I do not know.

By the fire is the elderly Gypsy woman who spots me and, in a loud voice, announces that she will read my fortune. Suddenly I remember that, in my dream, the elevator could not go up; it could only go down. That is most ominous. I want to tell the woman that I abjure any kind of fortune-telling, but feel it would be discourteous to do so. I walk toward the group and the fire, my blanket tied around me. Roman, the winsome lad, hands me a cup of strong coffee and a sweet roll. He also hands me a postcard dated from World War II, a well-known photograph, of some Gypsies being captured by the Nazis. I thank him solemnly.

This morning the old Gypsy woman is draped in many layers of clothing, her body lost under the colorful fabrics and scarves that enshroud her. One scarf, of bright blue and green, is tied rakishly about her forehead and covers her gray hair. I have no idea how old she is. Perhaps my age? Silver bracelets dangle from her plump wrists. She takes my left and right hands in her own and pats each palm, as if the skin could be flattened, stretched and unfurled for better reading.

"Ah!" the woman exclaims, "ah! You are in someone's mind, someone's heart. You are in their dreams. You are needed. You are looking for someone." She stops abruptly as if stung by a bee. She peers closely at, nearly through, it seems, my palms. She shakes her head from side to side. The woman continues: "I see something . . ." But then she stops again and removes her eyes from my palms to seek my eyes, into which she stares intently, even angrily. She lets go my hands, sharply. They drop to my sides pathetically. "You cannot see," she intones. "You do not learn. You only look for the right things." Then she turns away from me to poke the fire.

Her fierceness is stunning. Though I accept nothing that she has spoken as the truth, for I reject prophecy, and remember all too well how much I myself spoke last night and how much I drank—every Gypsy knew I was looking for Helen and much more—I am rather disconcerted. It is early in the morning to hear such things. Probably it is Helen who dreams of me, who needs me. If I were to believe any of this, and I do not. It is as if I were thrust into that scene in *Macbeth* when the three witches chant over a steaming caldron. But one sentence particularly provokes me. "You only look for the right things." It seems a paradox, for how does one know ahead of time what is or will be the right thing to look for?

Pondering a paradox, with a blanket wrapped around me in the midst of an encampment of strangers, I must be a foolish spectacle. Perhaps it is—I am—an amusement to the others who stand nearby. Embarrassed and ultimately annoyed by the old woman's presumption, I decide to leave that very instant. I return to the tent where I slept to dress and gather my belongings. Then I make my way around the group to offer thanks for their hospitality.

But I am arrested in my departure by the young man, by Roman. He begs me to allow him to accompany me on my journey. Under ordinary circumstances I would have said yes—I had already begun to imagine that I could be this clever young man's teacher, and he my amanuensis, and that he could benefit from my worldliness and knowledge, and so on. Gently I explain to him that I must be alone on this trip. His disappointment is palpable and I nearly relent. But something holds me to my conviction. Instead I offer him my address. I write it down on a small piece of paper and urge him to visit me soon. He takes the piece of paper and folds it twice and tucks it into the pocket of his shirt—he is dressed, by the way, like any young Greek man; no one would know he is a Gypsy. Then he pats his shirt pocket, which is over his heart. He pats it several times. He stares deeply into my eyes. My heart leaps. I am astonished, even mesmerized by this display of unexpected affection.

We are not alone. All this occurs in the midst of the group, who are no doubt aware of us and this encounter. What do the Gypsies think of me and of this intimate, if not romantic, episode? Suddenly I wonder if they know or suspect that I am a homosexual. Would it matter to them? I cast my eyes about the campsite. Everyone is going about his or her business. Probably they think I am rich. That may be all that matters. I do not know.

Together Roman and I walk to my trusty old car. I note their two new Mercedes parked behind some trees. As I get in, Roman holds the car door and tells me he will visit me, absolutely. And soon. He touches my arm. I am more than touched. "Look for Helen well!" Roman calls out as I drive away. "Make a good journey!"

By offering Roman my address, didn't I, I think with pride, demonstrate to the fortune-teller that I don't always look for the right things? Am I not taking a chance with Roman? Is this merely foolish pride?

In the privacy of my car, I repeat his name aloud several times. Roman, Roman, Roman. With a start and a great deal of pleasure, I realize that in French his name is the word for novel. And it is the French who are fascinated by the Gypsies and who, I believe, dominate the field of Gypsiology. I experience a deep satisfaction that bubbles and flows through my languid body like lava down the side of a volcanic mountain.

CHAPTER

16

It was only later in the day that I was able to record some of the impressions I had gathered. I felt privileged to have been in the Gypsies' company. Though I had momentary doubts, I was mostly assured that they liked and accepted me. I did not know why. Perhaps I held steadfastly then to what dear Gertrude noted about the writing of *The Making of Americans*: "Whether they are Chinamen or Americans there are the same kinds in men and women and one can describe all the kinds of them." I was not afraid that the Gypsies would steal from me or kill me. I didn't know why, either. The simplest explanation was that I did not want to think these things, things I would ordinarily have thought. It was also true that up until that night I had had no real or intimate experience of the Gypsies and had, prior to Helen's friendship with one and my reading about them, maintained only predictable and prejudicial notions about them.

I drive all morning, mulling over last night's events. I let each one sink in thoroughly. Roman is an exquisite, even extravagant event. How is, I ask myself, a character like an event? I stop for souvlaki at a roadside café where I warmly greet the owner, whom I don't know. I am in exceptionally good spirits. I am not at all hungry and nibble listlessly at the pita bread and meat. As any good Cretan will, the owner returns my solicitude with his own. He offers me a game of tavoli but I explain that I am in a rush. Frankly, I cannot concentrate. I merely glance at the open book before me, Stein's lectures, and decide to follow the fastest route to the south, so as to arrive at my destination—that dot on the map—before nightfall.

The village that is nearest to the dot on Helen's map probably does not have a guest house or inn. Often one can rent a room from a Greek family and indeed, when I arrive there, this is what I set about doing. I park the car on a deserted side street; there appear to be hardly any streets at all. I walk to the only store, a general store, that is open and ask for help. The young woman who owns the store has a room to let just below, in the basement, and so I am in luck. There is a restaurant a mere half mile from here and a beautiful beach, she tells me. Her name is Partheny, which means, curiously enough, "little virgin"; her husband is dead and she wears black, in the tradition of the Cretan widow, but I would guess she is only thirty. She also tells me there are many Americans who pass through, but yes, she believes she has recently seen one with a gold ring in her nose.

The village is a crudely built, almost barren place, not likely to be invaded by the hippies from the caves at Mátala, which is considerably south of here. It is such an unprepossessing, scrubby spot, with a few ratty flowers and trees dotting the cement sidewalks, I rue the fact that this is the setting for my rendezvous with Helen.

I move my car to a space in front of the store and carry my suitcase, groceries, liquor, and typewriter downstairs. The room is sparely furnished, but has a sink—the toilet is in the hall. There is just one light hanging from the ceiling but the sheets on the cot are clean enough. There is a table on which I place my typewriter. Quickly I remove it from its case, roll in a piece of paper, eager to bang out as fast as I can—my fingers are stiff— all the strange and marvelous events which have transpired since I left home.

Perhaps I ought this instant to go in search of Helen, but it is nearly dark. Also I am exhausted, having slept so little the last few nights. Might it have been Roman who undressed me and put my pajamas on me? I muse about this possibility—who else could it have been?

Overtired and somewhat frantic, I commit the following to

paper: The large-screen television is on annoyingly all night. The children occasionally gather around it as if around a hearth. I am surprised that television is so central a part of their lives and I suppose I am even surprised by their having electricity. Roman has watched television all his life; his favorite programs come from America and he talks fluently of them. I admit I never watch it and he—they all—are astounded. At some point the old man calls out that the Gypsies are the smartest people on earth. And then he relates a tale to prove it. I can recall it only generally. Forty not-very-smart Gypsies were sent into a forest to do a job— cut down trees—and instead they bought sheep and used up all their money. Then they fell asleep, but no one Gypsy wanted to sleep on the outside of the circle, so all night they kept changing places, and by morning no one had slept. They lost their rope and axes; thirty-eight of them fell into a ravine and died. The other two—something dreadful happens to both. But the last— this is most amusing—the last dies because he wants to look at his private parts, which he has never seen. By now he is carrying a torch, but he leans so far forward, he falls off a bridge into a river and drowns. The Gypsies who died, says the old man, were the foolish ones, the scatterbrained ones. It is lucky they died, he says, for all the others who remained and didn't go into the woods, they were the intelligent ones. All the stupid ones were gotten rid of, and that's why the Gypsies are the smartest people on earth.

I pull the typewriter paper out of the machine.

The Gypsy's desire to look at his genitals is something I'd never come upon before in a folktale. It could be, in a sense, derived from the Narcissus myth, but it's base; rather its base is focused lower. It could also have to do with masturbation. My hand settles on my crotch, and I speculate, lazily, about whether they obey the same laws and prohibitions that oppressed me. I close the typewriter case, though I would prefer to linger and wander in the luscious maze Roman's interest in me has provoked. But I can't find the energy. Fully dressed, I lie down and fall into a blessed, restorative sleep.

After my nap, I wash, shave, splash cologne on my face, and change into clean clothes. Refreshed, I walk in the direction of the restaurant the little virgin mentioned. I have some anxiety that this might be the night I find Helen, and though I have been planning for this, or at least praying that it would happen, I haven't the faintest idea what I will say to her. In truth I am unprepared, for what in the world should I say to her?

When I enter the restaurant, I find no one I recognize, just a few Greeks and several Germans.

I order taramosaláta, grilled fish, salad, and wine. The view is not spectacular, not mind-blowing, as John might say. I'd nearly forgotten him. I am relatively calm and eat the bread, which is fresh, and fish-roe spread, downing every mouthful with a gulp of cold, dry wine. My appetite is back. Just as the grilled fish arrives, the door opens. I stiffen, expecting it to be Helen. But it is not. I open my book and try to read, but a disquieting idea invades my overwrought brain.

If I don't accept the Gypsy's prophecy, or prophecy in general, ought I to continue to read about or study them? If I reject their ways and ideas, can I learn anything?

I drink more and continue along this mental path, which now engrosses me. For perhaps this is what the old Gypsy woman meant. If so, I tell myself, I am accepting at least some of her wisdom and ought to be allowed to go on. But didn't T. S. Eliot become an Episcopalian, an Anglo-Catholic? Don't most medievalists eventually convert to Catholicism? Jews, Protestants, all? It is a conundrum.

I make my home, my bed, in a rational world, but I awaken in an irrational one. That might be a good line for Stan Green, though perhaps too refined. Is it any less rational to consider accepting this, the Gypsy's prophecy, for instance, than Eliot's acceptance of God, his submission to faith? Perturbed, I rub my eyes. How is it possible to think about something one cannot or does not understand? Prophecy? The writing on Helen's wall? My experience with the Gypsies has affected me. I hope it has made me a better person, a more human one. I sigh audibly. The Germans glance in my direction.

My dinner finished, and my exhaustion acute and abiding, I pay the bill. But courtesy demands that I meet the owner of the restaurant and his family. I explain where I am staying; at the mention of Partheny's name, the owner's wife lifts her head up sharply, indicating, in a Greek gesture, a strong no. I cannot inquire why. Probably she dislikes Partheny. Of course, a young and attractive widow is always feared in a small village. But that is not the story I wish to pursue. I do let them know I am pursuing Helen and describe her. They too think they have seen her, so I am certainly on the right track.

Partheny welcomes me back as if I were Odysseus. I hope she is not matchmaking. It is a lonely life she leads. I smile and return to my subterranean abode where she has placed a vase with flowers. It sits on the cheap dresser, inadequately providing beauty to an undistinguished, indeed dismal, room. But in Partheny's small gift is such richness that I sit on the bed and weep. I do not know why. The events of the last days have weakened me. I sit motionless on the bed.

Her gift of daisies and narcissus dislodges a buried incident from my days in college, when a friend with whom I had had a quarrel and to whom I no longer spoke left flowers in my room. In just the same way. Then too I wept, uncontrollably, and yet we never again were friends. Pride, I suppose, or callow youth prevented my making the rapprochement. I wonder if he is alive. Life is endlessly sad. To be sad is to be human. To be human is to be sad. With such bathos do I nearly slip out of consciousness. But just before I do, for which I am oddly glad, I hear Roger's bawdy voice. He shouts gleefully, Blow it out your asshole, Horace.

In the morning, Partheny knocks on my door and carries in a tray with coffee, a boiled egg, bread and jam. I thank her profusely. Behind her is a little girl with a ribbon in her dark hair. She has a child and is not alone, I tell myself. I eat and dress. I am in a common-sense sort of temper. I will walk to the beach this morning and see what's what. I straighten my bed and march up the stairs. There is a young man—he is French, I believe—standing close to Partheny. He is nuzzling her neck. Suddenly they become aware of me. She smiles, with some embarrassment, but much less than one expects from a Cretan widow. Clearly he is her lover; it is no wonder the woman at the restaurant last night shook her head no. Partheny is breaking with the custom of her village, indeed, of Crete. She is either brave or foolhardy. She might, and this is Stan Greenish, yet not farfetched, end up dead. I am simultaneously relieved—I am not part of her marriage plans—and worried. The consequences of their actions could be dire. Does the young Frenchman know this? And will he behave responsibly?

I rid my mind of these concerns as soon as I shut the door behind me. Partheny must know what she is doing. But do I? That must be faced. I amble along the gravel-and-tar street. Pebbles stick between my toes, making walking a nuisance. I despise sandals—one's toes stick out in such an accusatory fashion—and yet I refuse to ruin my tennis sneakers by wearing them on the beach. I do treasure the ocean and excitement mounts inside me, welling up in my chest. It is how I think birds feel when mating, or what nature intends for them in the winter when they puff themselves up to keep warm. I often compare myself with birds because of my thin arms and legs and slightly rounded stomach.

I pass the restaurant. The family is on the terrace. I call out to them—Yá sas—and they greet me by name. Then I continue on my way and, after not too long, perhaps another mile, I reach the path to the beach. It is down a rocky incline. I fall just once but do not hurt myself. There is no one in sight and I make my way to an isolated cove where the water is clear as glass. Tinted glass—it is the palest of aquatic greens. I drop the blanket which Partheny has lent me onto the warm sand and remove my trousers and shirt. I am of course wearing bathing shorts; nude sunbathing is for the French and Italians. I smother my skin in suntan oil. I pay particular attention to my face, to my nose especially. Now I gleam and glisten like a Greek god. I unpack my bag, which contains a towel, a flask of water, books, pen, paper, and a small but powerful telescope.

I intend to read and sunbathe. Then I will go for a swim. Ten laps would be fine. It is so far south here, the sun beats mercilessly upon my head. I put on my blue yachting cap and sit up. I look out as far beyond the horizon line as I can. That is an old game—trying to see how far one can see. But how does one know? After a while—it is extremely hot—I walk to the water and rush in, determined not to be cautious. I do not want anything to stop me. The water isn't cold. I swim ten laps, I think. It is exhilarating to be in nature in this way.

I return to my blanket and towel off. It is an utterly peaceful site. I am oblivious to everything but the luxurious lassitude physical exertion and sun cause. I peer through my telescope but see no one in the distance. I douse myself again with oil, lie down, and place my arms over my eyes. I am close to sleep. The air is still. Jupiter and Poseidon must be holding their breath. The waves lap sweetly, blissfully, at the wet sand. I drift off. I am not sure how many minutes go by.

I become conscious suddenly of something that is near. It rouses me. It is present. Opening my eyes but temporarily blinded by the noonday sun, I perceive a human form. Gradually I can see, but I can hardly believe my eyes. More strange than my chancing upon the Gypsies, who had been in my mind and on my map, as I had wanted to chance upon them—a matter of controlled randomness and, therefore, not unaccountable—is what happens now. Rather, who happens now. That this meeting occurs on an obscure beach in a town not important enough to be on a map makes it all the more improbable. But, for all of that, it happens.

Standing above me is Stephen the Hermit, the ex-child-movie star, the lunatic, the man who loves electricity. Details of his biography mount one on top of the other as he smiles down at me. Tall and thin, he looms over me. I have not seen Stephen since that night when he ran away from the harbor, humiliated by Roger, Wallace, the Dutchwoman, and me, too, I suppose, his meal left behind uneaten.

Stephen lopes over to the space beside me and throws down his towel. He positions it not too close to mine, providing us a wide berth. As I remember it, he suffers from claustrophobia and fears all manner of intimacy, which to him must promise and threaten suffocation. Imprinted on his oversized towel is a salmon-pink flamingo and the words "Miami Beach." The colorful and incongruous souvenir towel is in marked contradistinction to Stephen, who is in no way like the tourist who might sunbathe on beaches there. It is unimaginable—Stephen the Hermit strolling on Collins Avenue, traipsing into a hotel catering to the nouveaux riches.

Is there a meaning to his appearance? My mind races along these lines—he is an apparition, then a presentiment. A ghost, someone who has come back from the dead. He has, in a sense, been dead to me. To the Gypsies he would be a mulo! But frankly and quite simply, his presence is first, to me, were I to be completely honest, intensely annoying and implicitly a rebuke. There is something about his accidentally turning up in the place I desperately and urgently needed to find that is irksome.

I glance at him casually, I hope. Stephen is settling himself down innocuously, patting his shoulder bag—a striped and shabby cloth affair—and placing it neatly on his towel. The bag bulges. What could he—of all people—be carrying in it? Still, taking him in anew, and seeing him thus, I scold myself for my initial lack of charity. At least he has not been consumed by fire. He is safe and, from the look of him, eating well.

Stranger to say, once I have gone through a compendium of negative responses, I am happy to see him. I have always liked Stephen and have maintained a genuine if distant affection for him. But one would think he were a long-lost brother, so pleased do I become to have his most unexpected and unusual company. Of course I know from my reading about the Gypsies that to them we gadje are brothers, sedentary brothers. I smile to myself—and we are sitting! Normally, as I've already mentioned, I do not espouse or experience brotherly feelings. I dislike my brother intensely. Stephen, though, is nothing like my brother. I suppose, also, I am somewhat guilty about not having chased after him that night. It was unconscionable of me. What could I have been thinking?

Stephen bounces up and again smoothes the creases and wrinkles in his blanket, for rather too long a time. Will it ever be right? It seems that it never will. Perfect, perfect, he murmurs. His sounds are more like purring than speech. At last satisfied, he stations himself at the edge of my blanket and stares down upon me again. He is grinning. It is disconcerting, but then one expects bizarre behavior from a hermit. I sit up. Obviously he is pleased to see me, too. He is in much better shape. He has washed recently. He is wearing cut-off blue jeans, faded but not in ruins, and he has trimmed his unruly beard. Actually one can now recognize how handsome he is or was, how nature once endowed him generously. Stephen had the kind of looks that could kill, as Stan Green would put it. His looks surely brought him an early fame and caused an equally precipitous fall. His looks may have killed only him.

"Welcome, welcome," he exults. Up until this moment, no words had passed between us. After this hearty salutation Stephen flings his arms out as if to embrace me. He doesn't, as I am sitting. It is merely a gesture. I stand up and embrace him, which surprises him. Perhaps this is somewhat uncharacteristic of me. Nevertheless, he doesn't run away, which is good. In unison we both sit down again upon our respective blankets and remain so, side by side, for quite a while. The uncanniness of his appearance in this lonely spot forges my silence. And also it is pleasant to be with an old acquaintance to whom one does not have to speak or to explain. Stephen does not, and would never, ask me why I am here, what brought me to this place, and why should I inquire it of him?

He is scooping up sand with one hand and depositing it into the other. He does this over and over, compulsively repeating the same action in the same way and in the same rhythm, until I feel on the verge of nausea. It could be hunger. Or it could be the sun beating down upon me. Like me, Stephen may be at a loss for words or without any pressing need to converse. That is typical of him. No polite colloquy for Stephen. With him, as far as talk goes, it is feast or famine.

Sweat pours from him. The English, I believe, have difficulty taking the sun. He is turning beet-red. Stephen leaps up and races toward the sea. As a child might, he swings his arms exuberantly and runs crazily—his legs going this way and that—then he flings himself headlong into the water. I marvel at his joyousness and strangeness. And to think, we are here together.

I change position, so that my back is to the sun. I clasp my knees to my chest. Stephen has always loved swimming and diving and will be in the water a long time. I watch him frolicking. He may think he is a dolphin. Such a harmless soul, now, but when he was younger and eminently presentable, men and women alike flocked to him. He toyed with them and cast them off and about with nary a care. I watch him swimming back and forth—he is shouting and singing ecstatically. I look again at his absurd beach blanket. Where did he get such a thing? And his shoulder bag. What does he have in that silly bag? I could, I think playfully—without his ever knowing—search it. I could go through its contents. This mischievous idea plants itself inside me and takes root. He would never know. How would he know?

Without fanfare or further ado, I reach for the bag and stick my hand in it and bring out its contents. A book on electricity, a copy of *Aesop's Fables*, a leather purse with a few coins, a red bandanna, sunglasses, pen, and . . . Helen's diary. The book with ANALYST inscribed on its cover. This is it, I exclaim to myself, heart beating, this is it. Astonished and alarmed, I shove everything back into the bag and then place it again on Stephen's blanket.

But I do not and I cannot relinquish Helen's diary. I will not. It is mine. I ought to have it. I smooth Stephen's blanket to return it to its previous pristine condition.

I have never before stolen. Never. Not since I was a small boy and then only a trinket. It meant nothing. I glance anxiously, shiftily, toward the sea where Stephen still swims, innocent of my theft. But why should he have her diary? Why Stephen? Then it comes to me. Yes. How stupid of me. The last night I saw Stephen was also the last night I saw Helen. So she must have gone off with him, which I did consider then. Helen followed after him that very night and did not go off with the Gypsy girl. Or all three joined up and ventured off together. But I cannot ask Stephen what happened, and obviously Helen is no longer about, as he has her diary, and I will not surrender the diary. About this I am adamant, even indignant, and I certainly don't want him to know that I have gone through his bag. Of course I could replace the diary in the bag and hope that the whole story would spill out, and probably a story would—but Stephen cannot be counted upon for a reliable report, and I would not have Helen's writing, her own words. Besides, the diary—I keep thinking this—belongs to me. I am insulted that he should have it. I stare at the book. I cannot open it now. Who knows what will be in it?

The sea and sky, the sand, the view, all this is as it was, but I am not. I do not know what I am. But I know I have to leave. I must get out of here before Stephen finds out what I have done and what he is missing. For surely he will miss it and know. Still, I remind myself, he is so crazy he may think he lost it. He would never suspect me, Horace, of such an outrageous and scurrilous deed. Not Horace. This calms me and enables me to contemplate the situation and to devise a plan.

Yes, I see it now. I can grasp it. Stephen is here as he arrived at this place with Helen, who left abruptly, the way she can. Alternatively it was he who was living at Bliss' house, with her, or by himself after she left, so it could have been he who made the map and the drawings. But whatever, whatever, I repeat to myself, Helen befriended Stephen, that is as clear as the pellucid sea, and they disappeared together, at least from my purview. These facts square with the evidence, with the diary, its being in Stephen's possession. These things clearly show themselves; they are demonstrable. A fact is a fact, after all. One must confront reality.

I place Helen's diary in my shoulder bag and gather my belongings. I straighten Stephen's blanket again. I know exactly what I will say to Stephen. I cannot—and do not—run away, for that would make him suspicious. Upon Stephen's return I will tell him that I am sick and must leave the south and drive home, as quickly as possible. I will say it is my heart. He will be sympathetic but I will not let him help me. I will tell him I have left my pills at home. Strange to say, but as I concoct my cover story I do begin to feel queasy, as if I might have a heart attack. The best cover, as Stan Green knows, is honesty. No one should blow an honest cover. Didn't Joseph Conrad once write that all a man can betray is his own conscience?

Stephen returns. In short order I tell him I am ill. He is dripping wet and not ready for my revelation, which is perfect for my plan. Before he can utter a word in response, I hurry off and leave him with his towel on his head. I march to the path that leads to the road and even more quickly thumb a ride—I have never before hitchhiked—to Partheny's store. I throw my things together and shove them into the suitcase. I pay my bill— scarcely thinking about what she will make of my sudden departure. Then I jump into the car and drive like the wind—or in any case with more speed than I ever have—toward home and safety. It is possible, I realize, that Helen did not give Stephen the diary. He may have stolen it from her. That is just as likely. In which case, I am no more a thief than he.

I arrive home in the early evening. The return trip seemed to have taken no time at all.

CHAPTER

17

Inside my apartment, at last in the secure confines of my rooms—I note Yannis has not tidied up since I left—I can breathe again and relax, somewhat. The door locked and secured behind me, I walk in shadow to the windows to draw the curtains. No one must know I have returned. Upon entering the hotel I instructed Nectaria not to tell anyone I'd come back. Except for Gwen and Yannis. Nectaria will bring a meal to my room. Dear Nectaria.

Only after the curtains are closed do I switch on a light. I settle into my favorite chair near the window and hear once more the music of the harbor. Yet nothing alleviates my anxiety. Helen's diary—the stolen treasure—awaits my perusal. It is a prize and will be my reward, I tell myself, though reward for precisely what I have not yet ascertained. For the journey, for my labors, for my concern, for my relentless curiosity? All the way home, I was able to refrain from pulling over to the side of the road to read her diary then and there; this was accomplished by admonishing myself that I ought to be in the right place to do so, that all must be right—the setting and so forth. I do not like dark, dreary places for reading or eating. On this point I appreciate Sydney Smith: "Better to eat dry bread by the splendour of gas than to dine on wild beef with wax candles." My objective was to dwell in a place of peace and quiet, I told myself, and then, and only then, would I—and would it be proper to—immerse myself in Helen and her diary.

With a stiff drink in hand, I study its covers carefully. There is silver glitter sprinkled and glued onto the back cover. On closer inspection I notice that the word "analyst" has been scratched upon. I swallow the Scotch then pour another shot—the tawny liquid toasts my innards. Then, for good measure, another, and only then do I dare open the book.

Gingerly I flip through its pages, from first to last, to get a sense of the whole. Some pages are nearly blank, with just a few words on them; some are covered with magazine pictures, a few words glued on or over the images. Other pages are filled with doodles and scribbles; most are writings, scrawled in an intense, vertical script. There are photographs and news clippings. The journal is in bits and pieces, cut up and pasted, like a collage. Like her room, I say to myself. At first glance Smitty's diary— though I have nearly quit using that name—is a messy, disorderly affair; though, like her room, it may have its own rhythm and order. Helen is a very young woman—just a girl, really—and not a writer, after all. Thus I prepare myself.

I begin in earnest. Her diary starts at page two, for page one merely gives her name and address, in New York City, under which is emblazoned in gold ink, READ THIS AND DIE. I down another shot of Scotch. While these words are chilling, unnerving, they are also sophomoric, touching and comical, something common to adolescents. The diary is undated and may have been begun before she came to Crete, but I am not sure.

On the second page is a quote: "Take a walk on the wild side." Beneath this is a picture of Jane Fonda. Helen has scrawled *Klute* next to it. The movie played here; I was intrigued by Fonda's portrayal of a prostitute, who was shown in session with her psychiatrist. It was a frightening film—she was stalked by one of her clients. Fonda's having visited Hanoi during the war in Vietnam was an outrage to Roger; one can barely mention her name to him. He will fulminate for hours. Opposite is a photograph of Helen and another girl, posing extravagantly; the two look about fifteen. The other girl is pursing her lips. They are both wearing black lipstick, I think. Next, two pages of line drawings that appear to me to be sexual organs.

I'm walking somewhere maybe a park on my way to something, a date with O., and I see a man, a father, with his child, a girl, and the father's struggling to carry something that has to do with his work and his child's welfare. So I help him by carrying one side of it—like a car hood or counter—I carry it on my shoulder and the child is in the middle between us and he and I do all the work. Then we have to run and I'm afraid I'm going to drop my side. Daddy REX.

I am reminded of OEDIPUS WRECKS, written on the piece of paper I found in her room.

Picked up J at CBGB's—the Dolls—the usual / Told J he could follow me all night if he wanted and he did, all night, followed me everywhere, and he was there in the morning. And it was weird. Told him, lying the way I can, told him I was in a theater class and studying to be a great actress and I was trying to be someone else just for an experiment, to see if I could. Like the Method. I'm not really like this I said. He got really really FREAKED, it was funny and he tried to act like he knew what was happening. Just felt like it.

Was this "J" our John? If so, their relationship had a rocky beginning. Why would she want to experiment in that way? One cannot understand why he would have followed her here, if he did, based upon this piece of evidence. But one must never forget, or underestimate, how perverse we humans are. A quote from Rainer Maria Rilke follows, from the *Duino Elegies*, I believe.

But what are they doing here, these acrobats, a little more fugitive even than us? Who are they trying to please? What sadistic will compels them from earliest childhood to perform such violent contortions? Rilke

Helen has marked his name only, which, as I proceed through the diary, or scrapbook, is, I see, her usual mode, though occasionally she does state the source. I am rather surprised by her liking Rilke; but I remember that when I was young he appealed to me, too. I haven't read him in ages.

Headlines or captions dot almost every other page; I suppose this kind of thing is popular in her group. For instance, on the page just mentioned, at its top, is inscribed "Perpetual Outpatient."

I'm going to blow up and explode and die a thousand times. Every day. Sitting on a nuclear bomb. What's the point, everything is so stupid such bullshit it makes me sick.

There follows, after this outburst, a series of phrases:

Courage between legs
Spaced out
Walking the dog
live evil
Kill for Peace
outsider insider
fuck the sixties
fuck prohibitions

These are not written in her hand but appear to have been clipped from newspapers or magazines. They are accompanied by matchbook covers that have also been cut up. The phrases may represent and be typical of graffiti; Gwen has mentioned in passing its popularity. A headline similar to any one of these phrases sits at the top of pages dense with Helen's intense, vertical script and functions, I believe, as a title for a dream or story, though it is often difficult to distinguish one from the other.

Looked more second avenue than any 20 year old should, skin on ankles actually drying up ALREADY so I bought socks and later I told him and he said he would have given me a pair, they would've been too big anyway. His arms, no arms could keep me warm enough, couldn't hold me long hard tight enough.

This is titled: "Trouble is Love." I wonder if the "he" was John or another. Like most teenagers, Helen is concerned with love.

There are several lists scattered over the pages—things to do, buy, chores—and these are interrupted by quotes and headlines of the type already noted. I turn the page and find a lurid paperback cover, for a novel by—of all people—Colette. It depicts a scantily clad young woman with a long-haired black cat at her feet. She, the coquette, wears hot-pink stiletto heels. "Colette's *Claudine*. Shocking and Delightful. Part woman, part child. Ruthless and sensual as a young cat." It is an Avon Book, and at the time it was published—I would guess the late fifties—cost only thirty-five cents. I can well remember when paperbacks cost that little. Those times are gone.

Next, there is a sequence of doodles, all geometric shapes: squares, rectangles and intersecting triangles; above these, EMOTIONAL SLAVES DON'T TALK. More magazine clippings of images from films, including one from Sergio Leone's *A Fistful of Dollars*. Below it, Helen has printed in bold letters: "Make a movie NOW everything's a movie." The Leone image is pasted beside a news clipping about a man born with two heads, and beneath this collage is an item about the Watergate burglars as well as one entitled "Some Who Believe in a No-Work State." On the next page a photograph of Helen and another young woman— her sister? Helen is holding a camera. Her sister is frowning.

There follow a few clippings about the plight of Patty Hearst that detail her kidnapping by, and her professed allegiance to, the Symbionese Liberation Army. Helen has inserted two pictures of Hearst—indeed the infamous bank-robbery image itself. Helen might identify with her, in some way.

On the opposing page, in carefully rendered block letters:

It was a queer, sultry summer, the summer they executed
the Rosenbergs, and I didn't know what I was doing in
New York. Plath, The Bell Jar

I remember that terrible day. I remember it as if, were I to walk
through the door, I would discover myself in a bar in Cambridge,
with my friends, arguing about treason and the death penalty.
How poignant and odd that Helen, who wasn't born then, should
have chosen this particular line. Just below it is a telephone number painted in what I take to be nail polish, a repugnant orange.
Perhaps the number indicates the person who gave Helen the
Plath novel, as a present, though from what I know of it, the
book is depressing, not her best work. I have not read it. I believe
the book is a roman à clef and has to do with the suicide attempt
of a young college woman, which of course might have reference
to Helen's sister. But who turned Helen onto, as John would
say, Plath?

> Amelia Earhart. Dupe. First lady of the skies.
> She had no guy holding her down.
> No one could clip her wings.
> She was no bird in the hand.
> She is no living thing now.
> Patti Smith

Helen has underlined "no living thing now." John might be one
of the many guys who would hold her down and clip her wings.
But why is Earhart a dupe?

> Script: He and I on the street. He does something I don't
> like. I kick him. He holds me. I laugh. He picks me up.
> I wrap my legs around his waist.

The title for this fragment is "slap kiss / kiss tell."
   Next, two postcards of the harbor here, as well as some ad-
dresses of friends who are scattered around the States—Califor-

nia, New York, Arizona. There is a scrap of a page torn from a book: Jacqueline Susann's *Once Is Not Enough*.

> Linda looked thoughtful. 'I agree. There must be some conversation before you leap into bed. And when a man invites you to his apartment, it's for just one thing. Somehow it's different if *you* invite him up for a nightcap to your apartment. You're in control . . .'

On the opposite page, in her own hand:

> Diploma: Emblem of knowledge. Proves nothing. Orgasm: Obscene term. Radicalism: All the more dangerous that it is latent. The republic is leading us towards radicalism. Dictionary of Received Ideas.

She has now definitely arrived and settled in Crete. The postcards are evidence of that; in addition the definitions from Flaubert indicate Smitty's having read Bliss' copy of *Bouvard and Pécuchet*. I do not believe the Susann novel is in Bliss' library. If it were, would Helen have torn a page from it, destroying Bliss' property? I have never read a book of that kind, to its conclusion. She has found it compelling enough to clip and preserve. Surely Helen realizes the thoughts in it, though in some oblique way relating to her experience, are idiotic, and the writing boorish. Yet she places Flaubert and Susann side by side, which is most peculiar.

> She made her sister cry and didn't help her because her sister made her cry and she even felt good and then felt guilty of course of course but later she saw she was just a bastard too just like her. I'm the bad one, I'm so bad, I'm being so mean to her and him.

I assumed she had guilt feelings in regard to her sister. But who is the "him" in this instance?

More pictures of friends. Another postcard, a charming view of our harbor. Another list of things to do. More visual embellishments, including pictures of rock-and-roll musicians who are called The Talking Heads and The Modern Lovers.

> Twenty one today. NO one knows. Feel like the oldest person in the world. Went to the mountains. Later saw Kostas. We fucked. Letter from parents, happy bday happy bday, come home, finish school ETC. Telephoned W. She says everything is great. No TV. Would watch anything. Even the Waltons.

Was it her birthday the day I drove her to the mountains? And she said nothing, not a word. Which Kostas? Helen is a strange girl.

> Detective Electric announced a short circuit we might blow it so they stopped at the doorway to destruction. Call the exterminator—not a weird electric woman if you don't WANT AND NEED STRANGE CHARGES and she put her finger in his socket and up went the rocket, and they became an old flame.

On the page opposite, in bold letters again: DO THE OBVIOUS and STRAIGHT FROM THE UNCONSCIOUS. In her normal script: "I miss my dog." I assume Helen is Detective Electric. She misses her dog. Her family must have had a pet, a dog. I wonder suddenly what became of the kitten she was taking care of here. I pour another Scotch and turn the page, to discover:

> Most of our sentimentalists, friends of humanity, champions of animals, have been evolved from little sadists and animal tormentors. Freud

Of course it is not strange that one finds Freud cited in her diary, as Helen is the daughter of a psychiatrist; also Bliss has, I know, several volumes of Freud in his library. Following the quotation from Freud is a color photograph of a transvestite, in high drag. There is also a picture, captioned "Marvin Gaye"; he is dressed in a tuxedo and singing. I have never heard him sing but in this picture—his arms are outstretched and his palms up—he seems to be a crooner. Underneath his picture are what appear to be his lyrics: "Love just comes and it goes. That's the way love is." And, on the next page, "What's going on?" Gaye's name is cited again. Is he gay, I wonder.

During one short phase in my young life, I liked to play dress-up and wear my mother's clothes. I believe it was when I was six years old. But Mother discouraged me. I was, in any case, quite content to dress as a boy. I am not sure that I completely understand transvestism and the desire of some men to masquerade as women. I did enjoy, from time to time, though, the secret drag clubs our crowd frequented years ago. We were influenced by Christopher Isherwood; no doubt some of us liked to imagine that we were night-crawling in Berlin in the twenties.

Can't stop frightening thoughts. Some angel came to visit me and I was scared because I don't believe in angels and she said that's why I need your help. She was carved in stone but she could move and in the background there were millions of graves.

What are her most frightening thoughts? Is this a dream? A story? I want to race through the journal—not really a journal, a jumble—to find something definitive, something that is her own interpretation of an event, perhaps, something that is explanatory. I do not know what it might be. But there is more of the same, odd phrases and lists, names that I have never heard of. A calendar with the dates of her last periods, I determine, and a list of colors—blue, lavender, gray, green, just a list, which makes no immediate sense to me. Unless it has to do with her stab at watercoloring.

Then Dr. Brodsky said: Delimitation is always difficult.
A Clockwork Orange

Burgess is certainly in Bliss' library. Bliss knows him. *Orange* is a cult book. Burgess was most likely influenced by *Finnegans*

Wake; I thought it remarkable that his book found such success with the young. But didn't Helen once tell me something about this issue of delimitation? I pour myself another drink. I think someone demanded of her that she delimit. Who was it? Her father? She rarely if ever mentioned him. I remember now. Her college guidance counselor did, when Helen was called to her office for a consultation. It must have been just afterward that Helen left school. The woman insisted to her: Delimit, you must delimit! But when did Helen tell me this story?

> W wants to be me and I won't let her. She hates me
> sometimes. I hate her. I love her. She loves me. The way
> I don't know her I always won't know her and she knows
> me in the way I think she knows me, to really know—

I abhor split infinitives. This passage must refer to her complicated relationship either with her sister or with a friend. A rather different kind of writing, I think. Were she beside me now I would explain to Smitty that one's family—and one's friends—plagues one throughout life. Near to this entry is a picture of a rock or punk band called the Ramones; Gwen mentioned them in a letter. They are a motley crew of unhappy-looking boys, with long hair and small dark glasses. Surly types. On the opposite page is a picture of a dog. I suppose the dog is hers. Is she cunningly commenting upon the Ramones?

> J makes me sick, the liar, he's a total fuck up—

This cryptic assessment of John is accompanied by a single squiggly line and then a list of words: "punk junk gag hag lag jag did dit dot dope hope mope hip yip yippies." And so on. I wonder if this might be labeled graphorrhea—a mental illness marked by the writing of a long succession of meaningless words.

> I'm at a picnic and she won't speak to me and I try to be
> nice but she's in a disgusting mood and I can't really do
> it whatever it is I'm supposed to do and my parents ignore

me. My friends too. What did I do wrong this time? Later I phone Iggy Stooge but he's busy.

HELL WHERE DOES HERPES COME FROM ANYWAY?

In the water there's a rock it's huge and it has the profile of a man but not the same man as before and nobody else sees it. Then everyone goes for lunch and there are different rooms and bigger and smaller ones and everyone knows everyone else but I'm an outsider. I say to someone I'm going to make movies but they don't believe me, and the place is a movie set and then Crete, and me, I'm just trying to find a place to live and no money and some awful guy I slept with is on the set too but I'm standing next to the director and feel okay with him, very close to him. The Who is playing loud and some woman is singing, not Daltry or Townshend, and I don't even like them anymore, and she's screaming something about her mother who's famous.

The first may be a dream or a real event. Does she have herpes? I had gonorrhea once but never syphilis. I have been lucky. Surely the second paragraph is a dream. The boulder may be the one in the harbor which does jut out, but does not, to me, look like a man in profile. I am unfamiliar with the Who; the name is amusing. Is Helen's mother famous? I think not. Unless she is using her maiden name. Practically speaking—and this problem has more than once vexed Stan Green—it is much harder to trace women if they assume their husbands' names. Divorce is a further complication.

Next, there is a news item and a picture of another group—whom I have heard of—The Jackson Five. Gwen interviewed them before they made a trip to Ghana with other black American musicians. I believe it was Ghana.

You want evidence I want ecstasy.

Beneath this is a photograph of five men in white laboratory coats. One holds a device of some type, the others are studying it intently.

> I did poison him. I can tell cause he's looking at me now. Phoned N in the city and told him and he said he never knew I was like this and I explained that certain things are for me alone and I know they're probably just in my mind which isn't mine in a way and I don't act on everything anyway. Always feel like a hypocrite. S is really funny, really out there. He read to me and told me these weird stories about his family, crazy, I don't believe everything but it doesn't matter—I thought mine were nuts but his are the worst, it's amazing the guy is still alive, and he also told me a fable—he's into Aesop—about the jackdaw and the eagle. The jackdaw wants to be an eagle and tries to do what the eagle does but can't. The jackdaw gets his claws stuck in a sheep's fur and he can't fly and then a shepherd captures him and cuts his wings off. S says it's about how you realize who you are only after you aren't that thing anymore. He crashed on my floor.

Might I be the person whom she imagines she has poisoned, but why? That cannot be the case. And surely I was right about her and Stephen having become friends and his staying, or crashing, with her. Who is "N"? I once studied cryptography, hoping to serve as a cryptographer in the war. I wanted to work in Intelligence and decode messages, but I was not accepted. I did very much want to go, though war and violence terrify me. Still I would not lie about my sexual proclivity. That would have been insulting, and why go off to war, perhaps to die, to fight for what one holds dear and true when one's person is unacceptable? That I could not and would not do.

> Isn't that great
> Isn't great great
> that isn't great

what's great
great isn't what it used to be
great isn't so great
what's great?

Tell the story. She told the story. It put a gun to her head. Can you tell the story is being told? No, she put the gun to its head and it blew her brains out. And can you tell the story is the end. The END. To Be Continued

This is followed by a list:

Do laundry
buy glue
meet S
phone W
toilet paper
tampax

That was all. There are a few blank pages, but I had come to her last entry. I turned the book over. I had read the diary through once and desired to read it again, even more slowly, now that I knew what was there and knew what to expect. Rereading allows one the opportunity to free oneself from one's initial anxieties and fears. I wanted to pore over and study each page as if each were a palimpsest; I was seeking something beneath Helen's words and the hastily thrown together captions and pictures.

Helen's artlessness can be deceptive. Her crudeness and vulnerability make an impression. She is often harsh; I knew her to be blunt. I was unaware of the fact that she hoped to be a filmmaker. Perhaps she once mentioned it. I am now assured that her sister did not kill herself; although I cannot be positive. But why would John have indicated that she probably did? Perhaps, like John, Helen's sister tried and failed. Still, I do not know.

I look about the room furtively, even despondently. I experience no immediate relief. I thought I would. Curiously, my guilt about having stolen Helen's diary returns. But I push worry aside to consider the meaning inherent in it, what is essential in it and to her. There is such a mixture here; she moves toward and then away from clarity. She is angrier than I supposed her to be. Her eclectic sources—many of which are cunning, others, merely silly—are launched and land as if all were the same; all are set and settled on the same plane. It is interesting, I think, as well as enervating and confusing. Obviously Helen is confused; she is a confused young person, young woman. She exhausts my resources. I feel frustrated. Helen seems to make few or no discriminations between things. To what end does she apply herself and her thoughts? I ask myself.

I am tired, tired even in my bones. Weariness has descended upon me as if it were a drug I had swallowed. It invades every part of me. I struggle out of the chair and walk to the door. Nectaria has left my dinner outside, in the hall, on a tray. Though covered, the food will be cold by now. I didn't hear her knock, and she must not have wanted to disturb me. I was hungry, but now I am too tired even to eat. I nibble at everything so as not to insult Nectaria.

I am also disheartened. Like Helen I kept a diary when I was young. It was nothing like Helen's. I tried faithfully to record the events of the day, to describe what I was reading and thinking, and to scrutinize and explicate my reactions and so on. She does little or none of this. But further I am disappointed. Certainly I did not find in the south the real Helen, certainly not her person, but having found her diary, perhaps I have found out too much and too little. For I have both more of a sense of her and less. I hoped, glimpsing her secret yearnings, I would encounter her true self. Yet she eludes me. Of course, I remind myself, Helen was not in any way attempting to create art, to invent, to make order out of the chaos of her young life. Still, and in any case, what I have discovered is not what I was looking for.

And Helen is not what I thought she would be. That is the short and the truth of it. Upon what basis can I judge her writing, these fragments that are not meant for other eyes? Read this and die, indeed!

I hold the purloined book in my hands. Sometimes I find her

person unappealing. In her diary she seems not at all like my Smitty, the Helen I conversed with and spent time with. Perhaps not time enough. But is there ever enough time? No, there is never enough time, and I have wasted time, chasing after her. I feel embarrassed and old. I despair of my foolishness. "I grow old, I grow old, I shall wear the bottoms of my trousers rolled. . . ."

I undress and change into a pair of freshly laundered flannel pajamas. This act in itself consoles me; the soft cotton material next to my skin reassures me. The smell of clean flannel is as sweet as the fragrance of the sweetest and ripest peach. Actually I prefer nectarines. Absentmindedly I realize that Yannis has not yet come in. But I am too distracted to bother much about his absence. He wouldn't have expected me in any case, since I had said in my note to him that I might be gone a week. He is probably with his mother.

I lie down on the bed and pull the covers up to my neck. Like a child I place my arms beneath the quilt. As if waiting for something, I lie still as a stone in the darkness. I will discuss this episode with Gwen tomorrow. I will figure a way to tell her I have the diary. She will offer a view different from my own, surely, and it will illuminate my position. How events turn one about and construe effects so different from what one expects from time to time! What did I wish to find? For surely if I truly wanted to, wouldn't I have been able to find it, once I had set my mind to it? I close my eyes and also, as best I can, shut my mind to these disorderly and disruptive questions. To sleep, "to sleep, perchance to dream." Alas, poor Horace!

PART · IV

THE INTERRUPTED

LIFE

CHAPTER

18

Some years have passed, long years and short ones too, since I began recording my impressions and experiences during this particularly intense and revelatory time in my life. It has taken me a while to return to this journal, but with the munificence of hindsight—which Gwen refers to as "thinking with the behind or through one's ass"—I decided to plunge into it once more. I have tinkered here and there with the material, but it is basically the story as I lived it. I did go south, I did meet some Gypsies, and Roman, it was Stephen I found, and so on. It is in most respects revealing, to me at the very least.

For less than a year, much energy and thought centered on Helen. Was it an obsession akin to Humbert Humbert's for his nymphet Lolita? Did Helen represent my last chance for freedom, my lost youth? Gwen humored me and humorously observed that my rabid voyeurism was much akin to her raging hormones. Then, from rabid voyeurism she pulled out of a hat the original concept of rabbit voyeurism. This, she contended, was the most difficult voyeurism to deal with, for every time one saw a rabbit one stood still, mouth agape, and because rabbits multiply so rapidly, there were so many, and soon the world would stand still, and so on. How she made me laugh! Especially at myself.

In the past and over the years, my voyeurism was something Gwen never failed to remark upon. But then we writers have generally acknowledged that in ourselves. She contested, rather too directly I thought at the time, for I myself had not thought of it, if you had wanted to see Helen, why didn't you casually ask Stephen if he knew where she was? She might have still been with him. It hadn't occurred to me at the time, on the beach, but I recognized instantly, and not without embarrassment, when Gwen confronted me with it, that my not asking it demonstrated some error in my approach. It struck me—though I dismissed it quickly and buried the thought—that I did not want to find Helen at all.

This discussion took place the afternoon of the day after I read Helen's diary. Gwen was as full as ever, full of news and noise, and wit and all the stuff of Gwen that made her so inimitably her. I was terribly happy to be in her presence once more. How important a true friend is! I provided her with an abbreviated account of my night with the Gypsies. Had I related too many details—I did not give the specifics of my fortune, for example— she would have known about my infatuation with Roman. I was rather humiliated, at my age, for having fallen in love like a schoolboy. It was my belief then that that ought not happen. I was in no mood for her teasing me about him.

Gwen was not as shocked as I thought she'd be by my theft of the diary. Rather she seemed to have expected it of me. Perhaps I ought to have been insulted but I was too surprised. I do not know how she knew me capable of this to this day. She contrived some linguistic play about criminal and critical that I thought clever.

Without much elaboration and in as cursory a manner as possible, I described the diary's contents. She didn't seem much interested—Gwen thought Helen typical—but I didn't want Gwen to be too interested. It was incumbent upon me not to show her the diary; I told myself that more eyes would only double the crime and doubly incriminate me. Inchoately I sensed that it would in some odd way expose me as well. While I sensed that, I didn't actually know it. It was not a coherent thought. In any case I knew I didn't want Gwen to see the diary.

I did not tell her that I was disappointed in it and in Helen. I could not admit that to her, then. Instead, I complained only of its lack of precision and that Helen was no precisian. Gwen laughed and renamed me Granddad the Grammarian.

What pleasure Gwen derived in annotating the torrid and tawdry details of her short-lived affair with John. They had had another night of pain and pleasure, as she put it, culminating in a shouting match. But things took a much more extreme turn the day after their ultimate and "second" last night together (a night which she had insisted she would never have again!). The change affected all—Alicia, John, Gwen, the town. Unbeknownst to anyone, John had met, when he first arrived, a young Greek woman, a widow, and had fallen in love with her; it had been a secret from all of us. Within a day of my departure, John had vanished. Soon it was determined that he had moved in with the young widow. It was of course a scandal in the town—Nectaria and Chrissoula were enflamed—one that heaped instant infamy upon the two lovers. This episode brought Gwen and Alicia together, somewhat, and they had, in my short absence, many drinks and some laughs over it or him. As is her wont, Gwen laughed about it more than Alicia, and to me had fun with the idea that Homo erectus, the one who stands, preceded Homo sapiens, the one who knows. Alicia rued the day she ever let John into her house. Gwen jettisoned the affair and him with, C'est la vie, l'amour toujours, c'est la guerre, all delivered in one great rush of breath.

For Gwen's sake, though she protested she didn't want one, unless she could cry at it, I held a party in her honor. Everyone attended. Yannis returned home, to me, a night or two before the grand event, but with a difference that I could not fathom. As I was any minute expecting Roman to appear, I took Yannis' alienation in stride. He helped me shop and cook, and just to spite Gwen I served more food than anyone could eat. I hasten to add, there were leftovers.

On the night of the party, at eight, the entire cast of characters began arriving, with the exception of Stephen the Hermit, whom

I had not invited, and knew to be, though the others didn't, on the other side of Crete. Alicia was resplendent in a pea-green sari. Wallace and his Dutch lover, Brechje, brought fruit and bread; I assumed they thought they would not be fed. Several uninvited but nonetheless welcome visitors—friends of Wallace's—were in tow. Roger entered wearing a tuxedo, which he might have rented. My banker Nicos and his wife, Sultana, came; Lefteris, the electrician, and his wife, whose name I cannot for the life of me recall; an intellectual German couple who had moved into the hotel, and Nectaria, Chrissoula and Christos. Later, even John and the young Greek widow, Ariadne, made an entry, shocking the Greeks in the room, annoying Alicia and amusing Gwen. There was Yannis, of course, as well as a few of the young boys who hung about town and turned up like stray dogs, decorating the walls against which they stood rather like ornaments. They spoke to no one but each other. There were assorted others. It was my estimate that, over the course of the evening, at least forty people stopped by.

They all wanted to meet Gwen if they hadn't already. I wanted it to be a marvelous night for her, as it was to be her send-off. Soon she would return to Manhattan, to what I did not know. The wine and ouzo were flowing freely, and the party, I believed, was immediately off to a great start. I knew it would be a hit, for it had to be—it had to be a howling success for Gwen. It was just what the doctor ordered, for me as well. I wished to forget the events of the last days, even months, and to forget especially my theft and reading of Helen's diary.

Fortunately Wallace was at his best; he even wore his pith helmet. His friends were most entertaining. Among them was a young woman named Annabelle, who had been in a Warhol movie, she said. Immediately she attached herself to one of the Greek boys and later spirited him away. They were an international contingent, Wallace and his pals—South African, French, Italian, American, and Dutch, of course. I could not speak with everyone and certainly not at length.

I was, though, a participant in one invigorating and vehement discussion. Gwen led the way, engaging Wallace and Brechje in the topics of art and expatriatism, which permitted Wallace to beat a favorite drum—Pound and Eliot. He regaled us with several short anecdotes, some of which I had already heard. There was the one about Édouard Roditi, a French, Sephardic-Jewish and homosexual poet, who was friends with T. S. Eliot. Wallace reported that after Eliot told Roditi he would allow Pound to edit *The Waste Land*, Roditi declared: "No, Tom, no. Tom, don't do it!" Wallace gossiped that Roditi claimed to have made love with Lorca in 1929, in Spain. Where Wallace got his information, I did not know.

To incite or defy Wallace, and perhaps me, Gwen argued that the expatriate and the avant-garde, birthed together, had expired together. *Fini*, she announced. The moment has passed. The avant-garde is dead! While I was used to Gwen and her comedies, her barbed ironies, Wallace was not; I thought he would have a fit. Gwen was thoroughly enjoying her provocative self. I poured everyone a stiff drink and muttered something about the vagaries of history, to soothe Wallace.

At this point, I think it was, we moved or traveled—there is a way in which talk is a journey—from history and death to Freud's concept of the unconscious. It was Gwen again who led us, or lured us, in that direction. But the moment the word "unconscious" rolled off Gwen's tongue, Roger bounded over. Hearing it, he leapt into the fray and went on about how it— psychoanalysis—was preposterous, wrong as theory and ridiculous in practice. He offered, as backup and defense, Gertrude Stein's rejection of the unconscious, or subconscious. I acknowledged that Stein had written "I never had a subconscious thought." To Gwen this was absurd, and I attempted to defend Stein, as did Roger, in his overheated way. But I did not like to find myself in agreement with Roger. He was usually wrong. Why had Gertrude rejected it so absolutely? I had never thought about it, but that is what Gwen's interrogation—what is at stake?—drove me to, later. I mentioned Stein's having also written, "I am I because my little dog knows me," which is so charming and wonderful a way of thinking about the self that all of us could appreciate it. I was also reminded, in a vague fashion, of

Helen's missing her dog. Wallace was more or less mute on the subject of the unconscious, still stung, no doubt, by Gwen's earlier remarks.

Everyone and everything flew off in a hundred directions. A good host, I went about being sociable, filling people's glasses and attending to their needs.

Later I overheard Gwen, Wallace and Roger. They were laughing. Wallace was roaring like a lion. Then Gwen proclaimed: All we need is two more people to make a Fifth Column. Roger, who is vehemently anticommunist, took exception and stormed off to another part of the room. He found Alicia and danced with her. At least I think that was the sequence. Were he a CIA agent, he would not have bounded off.

Wallace fell to his knees, at Gwen's feet, and recited a poem against apartheid—for her primarily and to anyone who was in earshot. He delivered it well, considering his condition, and I was impressed with the depth of his political passion. I liked him for it; perhaps Gwen did too, though she appeared more bemused than anything else. It was a better-than-passable poem. Minutes after, Wallace poured wine into his shoe and drank from it. It rather spoiled the poem for me, but Gwen didn't seem to mind. It is sometimes difficult for me to separate the person from the poem.

I strolled off to another part of the room. I observed that Alicia was merely tolerating Roger. She is capable of great tolerance. She can yawn in one's face and nearly suppress it; to appear that she is not yawning, she covers her mouth with a handkerchief and gazes at one, as if engrossed in what one is saying. Finally Alicia excused herself from Roger's grip, graciously, I was sure, and went to sit on the couch with John and Ariadne—the very one I had sat upon with John. I was unable to hear what transpired among them. I supposed that Alicia had decided to take the high road.

My attention was, in any case, suddenly directed to Roger, who ambled over, in that mincing way of his, to Yannis. Yannis was seated on a windowsill; he was scowling. Roger whispered in Yannis' ear. I watched, with aggravation more than jealousy. The two kissed—it was by then quite late in the night. With astonishment I watched Yannis grab his jacket. Roger glanced my way. The two summarily departed, together. I was momentarily stunned. I felt helpless, agitated and aggrieved. I had not wanted to be left by Yannis and certainly not for that snake-in-the-grass Roger. I did not want ever again in my life to be the one who was left.

Roger always takes my castoffs, I repeated to myself, and hoped that a miracle would happen: Roman would walk through the door. Instead, Alicia came to my side and said calmly, Oh well, Horace, dear, we can handle these things, can't we? She stated this as a matter of fact and with great delicacy. It hit just the right note. I thanked her for her kindness, and even though I was drunk, I curtsied as if before royalty, cognizant once again of our Queen Bee.

Dear Alicia, who had not sung in public in many years, the dear woman performed, I like to think, as a gift for me. She moved to the center of the room and rapped her wineglass with a fork, to call us to attention. She announced she would sing an aria from La Bohème. Everything and everyone halted. There was quiet, even from Wallace's boisterous quarter.

In Alicia's voice was such poetry, such beauty, that ancient spirits and memories overtook me, and constraint fled. The music of the gods! I closed my eyes. I dwelled on the heartbreak of Mimi's death, on the despair brought by sickness, on succumbing to tragedy, on loss, on love. I felt an unimaginable sadness for the world, for everyone who had ever been abandoned and who had been lost, for everyone who had loved and who had lost, and that gathered us all in, all. I opened my eyes and with them swept the room slowly, and I saw before me people I'd known for years. And even Wallace, who can be so annoying, even he and his pain, his foolish and profound anguish, touched me.

There were tears in my eyes. There were tears in Gwen's eyes. I had never before seen Gwen cry. For what or for whom did she cry? The sick musician who ate peanut-butter sandwiches at 4 A.M. and left her alone in her apartment? For her unwritten torments? For the problems of her race? Were we crying for the same things? Surely her flippant wish—to cry at her party—had come true, but how sorry I was. Still, sometimes it is healthy to cry. I believe that to be true. I had lost Yannis, I had lost Helen, and many more, and Alicia had lost John and others, and some had lost us. Gwen—ah Gwen—Gwen always expected to lose.

Alicia finished singing. We were ravished, rapt, silent. Then we applauded and cheered. Wallace threw kisses and he and his crowd clamored, Brava, brava! Gwen rushed to Alicia and kissed her hands. I will never forget that sight. It was so very unexpected. But in so many ways Gwen is and was unpredictable. In response, Alicia held Gwen's face in her hands and looked deeply into Gwen's eyes. From that moment on they were true friends. It happened like that. It does sometimes happen like that. And so what seemed to have been terribly sad at the time metamorphosed into something rather happy.

Two days later Gwen flew home. My life returned to normal, dominated by my usual routine. I finished my crime book—Stan Green does indeed crack the code in the young murderer's diary and simultaneously cracks the case. It was the easiest way to handle it; and it worked, I thought. I was conscious that I had not cracked Helen's diary, but then it was not in code. I held that it was poetic justice and artistic license that my protagonist would do so in my book. My publisher was satisfied, in any case, and that was what mattered.

Roman did not come to stay or even to visit me. I kept expecting him and then one day I no longer expected him. Who knows what happened to him after I left the encampment? Perhaps the old woman warned him against trailing after a gadjo like me. Yannis lived with Roger for a time. Their fights were monumental; sometimes both stayed home and out of sight because of the shiners they'd given each other. Yannis drifted away from him as well. Roger continued to work on his second novel, which still has not appeared. Wallace had another nervous breakdown. Stephen the Hermit returned but said not a word to me about our morning on the beach. I worried he would and fantasized that he'd accuse me of the theft. But he never did. John left the Greek widow Ariadne two years ago and disappeared; she abandoned Crete for Athens, seeking a better life, one not sullied by rumor and insinuation.

Alicia is still in her lovely home, surrounded by beauty, as nimble and unflappable as ever. She maintains it is the yoga. I continue to refuse to do it, though. Recently she met a Danish woman, a retired biologist, and they are now living together. I am happy for Alicia. As usual, Roger has nothing good to say on the subject.

Over the years, and with greater and greater infrequency, I remembered Helen. Once, carefully tracing the trajectory of my feelings, I discovered that my initial reaction to her diary was similar to my reaction to an attenuated affair of the heart in my sophomore year in college. I had had a crush on an upperclassman named Allan, who was to me rapture itself—he was the perfect man. In my eyes he was everything I wasn't. I joined his club, I signed up for his classes and then finally I conquered my fears and spoke to him, my hero. Boldly I proposed a date with him, for lunch at a lovely French restaurant, which he accepted. I dressed with such care and eagerness one would have thought I had an audience with the Pope. But the truth was, he was insipid—beautiful, but insipid. He had nothing to offer except his good looks, which taught me rather early that sometimes beauty is wasted on the beautiful. Yet I have never deserted the pursuit of, and fascination with, beauty.

I decided that Helen too was insipid and uninspired. That I had drawn inspiration from her became a disturbance to me, not unlike the occasional static on my shortwave radio. On Sundays it is my habit to listen to the BBC World Service.

CHAPTER

19

Not long ago, a letter arrived from Gwen. I awoke to see it sticking out from under the door, its airmail envelope beckoning to me. Nectaria had brought it upstairs and pushed it beneath my door, which she does from time to time when she thinks something's important. By now, she recognized Gwen's handwriting; and too, Nectaria liked Gwen. Gwen made her laugh. I hoped for one of Gwen's long, newsy, gossipy epistles.

25 November 1980

Dear Lulu,

Owing to a series of disasters, details of which I will not bore you with at this time, I have had to change my address and telephone number.

She then provided both. Next to the telephone number was the word UNLISTED.

I beseech you not to give these out to anybody—anybody at all—no matter how innocent-sounding the request (and this goes for the likes of . . .)

Here she enumerated the names of people we both knew and to whom I thought her very close and attached.

Everybody, in fact. I will tell you more when next we speak or see each other.

Love to you, G

The letter, its brevity, its absoluteness, the disasters she alluded to—all were greatly troubling. The letter was paranoid enough that I became thoroughly and irrevocably alarmed. I had been, for many years, expecting that Gwen would meet with doom—an accident or fatal trouble. Immediately I telephoned my travel agent, closed up my apartment, and gave instructions to Nectaria. The next day I was on a plane to Athens. From there I flew to New York City, where I stayed for two months.

Gwen was not at all surprised to see me and acted as if it was quite in keeping with me to show up unannounced on her doorstep, so to speak. This was of a piece with Gwen, not to be surprised. We caught up. We covered our lives and gossiped about everything that had happened since we had last seen each other, five years ago. For it had been that long—or short. I hadn't had Chinese food in many years and she invited me to dine at her favorite restaurant. This is where Gwen sagaciously announced, Sometimes history chooses for us and we are at its mercy.

In the course of that evening I explained to Gwen that I had reached the point in my life—I am nearly seventy—when I ask myself, How could I have done things differently? Could I have? I am not without regret though I am not filled with remorse either. It would be impossible to imagine a life that did not contain some regrets. My concern was: Was there a task with which I had been entrusted that I had not fulfilled? I felt relieved that Gwen was present to listen to me and to hear my plaints.

Ultimately—and I had determined never to bring it up—I expressed my disappointment in reading Helen's diary; I said I had not found what I was looking for. At some point in the years since I'd seen Gwen, I had been startled to recall the Gypsy's premonitory dictum, or curse: You only look for the right things.

I now related to Gwen the specifics of the Gypsy's reading of my palm. Gwen dismissed it, actually she went "Pooh-pooh, Lulu." With much droll humor, her conclusion was that it was just like me to suffer from a fate neurosis when that particular neurosis had largely been discredited in psychoanalytic circles. Even your psyche's out of date, she laughed. I laughed along with her.

Almost without thinking I returned to Helen and found these words issuing from myself: Isn't it strange that Helen never mentioned me in her diary? Isn't that very peculiar? There was a deliberate and mischievous air to Gwen that night. With a grin that was both insouciant and solemn, she answered, "I know what you were looking for, Lulu." "What?" I asked sharply. "Your name."

I was immediately and intensely annoyed. If that is true, I went on excitedly and with exasperation, then everything I thought about Helen was about me, and if that is so, it is the most typical kind of story—I was looking for myself—the most trite. How tiresome, how conventional. I excoriated myself over and again, on and on. I insisted that we drink to my stupidity. For when I believed myself to be most special, most inventive, most filled with imagination, experiencing life anew, and behaving most uncharacteristically, I was perhaps more than ever like everyone else and, what is more, most like myself, a self of which I was unaware. With sly glee, Gwen retorted: Quel unique.

To myself I said that I would rather believe I was under some kind of spell, an enchantment. My experience of Helen was, after all, mine. Yet experience itself—and this I had never thought before—is not pure and indifferent. I did not truly understand the Gypsies, nor did I understand Helen, I suppose, nor, more difficult to admit, even Gwen. Who was I to judge my own, let alone another's, experience? I thought this rather idiotically, for who else would want to stand in my shoes to judge my experience but me? Still, and after all, along with, part and parcel of, having an experience, one has many other things—the circumstances of one's birth, one's class, sex, race and so forth. Was I a Dickens? Could I see outside myself? Am I myself?

I gazed at Gwen's wry face. To her I asserted: One can never fully know oneself, and this is, perhaps, and in one sense of the word only, a fate one can never escape. Gwen followed with the idea that the only thing about someone else you can always be right about is that you're wrong. About yourself, too, I responded, returning to my predicament with a false merriment.

Having fortified myself with food and drink, I inquired of Gwen what her paranoid letter had meant. She asked which letter. The last letter, I answered. She groaned, "Oh, that pistol"—for epistle. "I had had it. Everyone was thinking and behaving so stupidly and no one was thrilling me, there were no thrills, no frills. I want to be thrilled to death, Lulu. I had had it. I was frazzled, not dazzled, by life. I was bored, and you know I despise being bored."

As if I didn't hear her, I pronounced gravely: Death is of course the one fate no one can escape. I reminded Gwen of our talk at the restaurant on the harbor that eerie night and how she had seemed to indicate that she was preparing to meet her Maker. I told her that for all this time I had worried that we may have invoked the fates, that very night. "Lulu, you'll make me die laughing" is how she responded. She was not dying, but it was the type of thing, the kind of tragic end that often occurs and that, I hesitate to mention, I was looking for.

Nevertheless, for whatever reason I had come, Gwen was very happy I was there. "You're here, Lulu, and I'm not even ready to give up the ghost. Do black people," she teased, "have white or black ghosts?" Then, more seriously, she said that she might leave New York, the States, and "give up the ghost of the music man—Lulu, you know the one."

What were or are the disasters you were alluding to? I asked. She enumerated several difficulties, big drags, but none had to do with drug dealers or the Mafia or cancer or whatever. Then Gwen paused. I could tell she was about to tell me a story. I ordered another bottle and poured the wine into her glass and mine.

Gwen had visited her family for the first time in years. When she was in college, she had detested going home for holidays and walking into their apartment. But finally, recently, she had gone home again. She carried on in this uncharacteristic vein and related a story from her past, which I had never heard, though I knew her then, or was just about to meet her. She was a sophomore in college—on scholarship, she reminded me—invited for a weekend at her best friend's house, a white girl from an old family, wealthy, of course. Everyone was wealthy. Gwen entered the friend's home, whose door was opened by a black maid. We were Negro then, Gwen said, unsmiling. The maid was in uniform; Gwen didn't know who was more surprised, mortified, she or the maid. The household was content, lulled, Gwen thought, by years of privilege and whiteness and money into a sleepy and unthinking acceptance of the good life. Gwen brushed past the maid, barely looking, barely able to look at her. That moment was indelible to her. She had never mentioned it to anyone. Then Gwen said, "After all these years, I can still remember it."

I was at a loss. What is it about that sentence, "After all these years I can still remember . . ." that can always bring me to tears. Whenever I hear it or come upon it, even in a newspaper article, I weep copiously. I didn't want to embarrass Gwen. Every one of us who has years more to live, if we do—and every one of us ought to be permitted three score and ten at the very least— every one of us will have a chance to look back and remember that and not that, this and not that . . . To recover, I muttered words, sentences, of this ilk to her.

Not only was this the first time in a long while, or ever, that Gwen had deliberately mentioned her family to me, it was the first time she had articulated so explicitly and plainly something of this nature, to me. With a start I realized again that Gwen was the one and only black person I was friends with and who was friends with me. That she had made such statements, with such emotion, about her history indicated a change in her, I believed, one that must have been painful to achieve, and perhaps indicated a change in me. A change in the times, too, I supposed. It was and is impossible to tell to what extent these things merged one into the other. This is the moment when, I believe, Gwen characterized us as the shrimp boats of history.

I was not certain what I should say. Gwen had not spoken in anger. She had not spoken to point a finger at me. I understood that much, I thought.

For a while we drank in silence, both of us musing and mulling over the many topics we had discussed. The restaurant had emptied and we were its last customers. We were closing the joint, as Gwen would put it. This was not at all unusual for us to do. In fact, over the years I have taken some pride in having helped toward that end many times. Gwen and I had tucked away several bottles of wine; I knew my morning would be ragged. But I didn't care. I was content.

Suddenly Gwen startled me out of my reverie. She was laughing aloud, to herself. What's so amusing? I asked. She could not yet speak, but she had stopped laughing, as abruptly as she had begun. She seemed to be laughing inwardly. "Lulu, Lulu," Gwen managed to whisper. "What is it?" I urged. "How do I know what she thought?" "Who, dear?" "Or if she was mortified?" "Who, dear?" I asked again. "The maid, my friend's maid," Gwen answered. "Oh, yes," I said, "I see." But I wasn't quite sure that I did, then.

Another surprise, though of a different order, was Gwen's announcement that she might leave New York, even the States. I complained that she had no right, having teased me mercilessly about being an expatriate. Gwen took my hand and said that she would run away to Altoona, Pennsylvania, or become a Buddhist in Colorado, just get off the Great White Way. Broadway anyway. I urged her to move to Crete.

Gwen couldn't bear it that Reagan had been elected President. I reported that Roger was over the moon about it. Not that Gwen had especially approved of the peanut farmer. She had been mildly puzzled, even somewhat disarmed, when Carter had spoken to the nation on TV, and, as she put it, had so hokily beamed himself to the American people to report on their malaise. "In French, Horace, he didn't mean mayonnaise." I repeated my hope that she'd move to Crete and live near me. She said she'd consider it. She has not yet decided. "You're quaint, Lulu," she said then. "Je t'adore."

Later that night, spurred on by the dialogue with Gwen, it dawned on me—dawn it was: a fulgent light streaked across the sky simultaneous with this idea, this is absolutely true!—that what Horace had written, which I, as his namesake, often quoted, was correct. That I may have figuratively lived it—even literalized it—was perhaps, I decided, not such a terrible matter. It depended upon how one thought about such things. "With the change of names, the story is told about you." A more modern translation of the Latin goes: "Change the name and you are the subject of the story." Undoubtedly I had absorbed Horace's words and allowed them to penetrate, to suffuse my mind and body, to subsume and consume me. I enjoyed that interpretation better than most of the others I dallied with. The break in my thinking, which I experienced and thought had occurred when I acknowledged, for one thing, that I was not always in control of the story, as I had imagined, probably flowed from this literary, this metaphorical, if not metaphysical, transformation. (At another dinner Gwen kidded me mercilessly about Roman, once I had surrendered that tale to her. Roman's nonappearance was all she needed for one of her transformations. She galloped on about roman, the novel, never returning, the novel's death, the end of authors, readers, reading, and so on.)

One might well ask: Did Helen truly exist? Was there a Helen? And were I asked, I might answer: She existed for me. Or, there was a Helen for me. And she was not insipid at all.

I returned to Crete, sanguine that Gwen was all right, or all right enough. Ultimately she admitted that she had wanted me to visit her, but she had not wanted to ask me. I was immensely moved by this, since Gwen is someone who cannot ever make emotional demands. Yet I was able to meet one, one that had been implicit and unspoken. I felt I was not a bad sort after all. Some could and might see me as a thief and a liar. Helen had called me a liar. And it is true, I have lied. I can admit it now. But I'd rather put it differently: I'd rather it be said of me that Horace embellished truths only to make them shine more brilliantly!

It was in the aftermath of my visit with Gwen, and in this spirit, that I was able to look again at this journal. Also I was able to reread Helen's diary. I did so last night, and it struck me differently. I have not looked at it, as I may have said, in years. This time I see more in it, or rather, different things in it, other meanings, which I will not bother to set out. I think I do see more because I am no longer, as Gwen explained, desperately looking for my name. I am taken particularly with Helen's inclusion of Aesop's fable about the jackdaw and the eagle. I recognize myself as one who thought he was an eagle. I ought to have known my limits. But how does one? Know thyself may be the question, not the answer. There may be a bit of truth in that.

It is curious. I am able to return to this journal, but I am no longer as certain of its meaning, to me, as I once might have been. I am not like Odysseus; this is not "the story of a man who was never at a loss." I have been. I am rather insecure about what I have written—I am not sure what I mean or, worse, if it means anything at all. This fills me with horror. But I borrow from and follow Jean Genet: "To escape horror, bury yourself in it."

Dear Reader, if I may call you that, if you and I are at all alike, if we share even a few traits, if you are even a little the way I was for the majority of my life, you may want to look back over this book, to exact from it a logic, to discern a plan. I am not saying there isn't one. By now you know I am somewhat cagey. Gwen sometimes calls me KGB. I myself have often finished a book and gone back over it, checking the news items, for instance, to assure myself of the time and order of the developments. I have been wary, dubious that the writer had tied up all the loose ends. You may want to do that. I encourage you to do so if you wish. But I can tell you that it will explain little. Perhaps nothing. In any case, you will not find yourself here.

And here is where I will leave you. As Stan Green would have it: This is it, the big nothing. I'm leaving you with the big nothing. (In the intervening years I have written two more crime books, one titled *The Big Nothing*.)

Someone once said of Gertrude Stein, "It was not what she

gave you, but what she didn't take away." One cannot give any-one anything. This is what I have learned. And while I do not leave you with anything, I do not take from you, either. If I have, I hope it is not an ordinary theft. This is what I have to offer. It is my gift, my only gift, to you. How I wish it were more!

In any case, I am working again on Household Gods, which now opens: After all these years I can still remember . . . I could not resist that temptation. At seventy, the only things one ought to resist are fat and salt. I have decided to cast Gwen in Household Gods; indeed, she will have a rather major role to play. I have also decided to return Helen's diary to her. I will think of a way to do it that will not incriminate me, and that will in some way please her. Someday I will find her and I will give it to her.

Now I will dress and walk to the market. It is a glorious day.